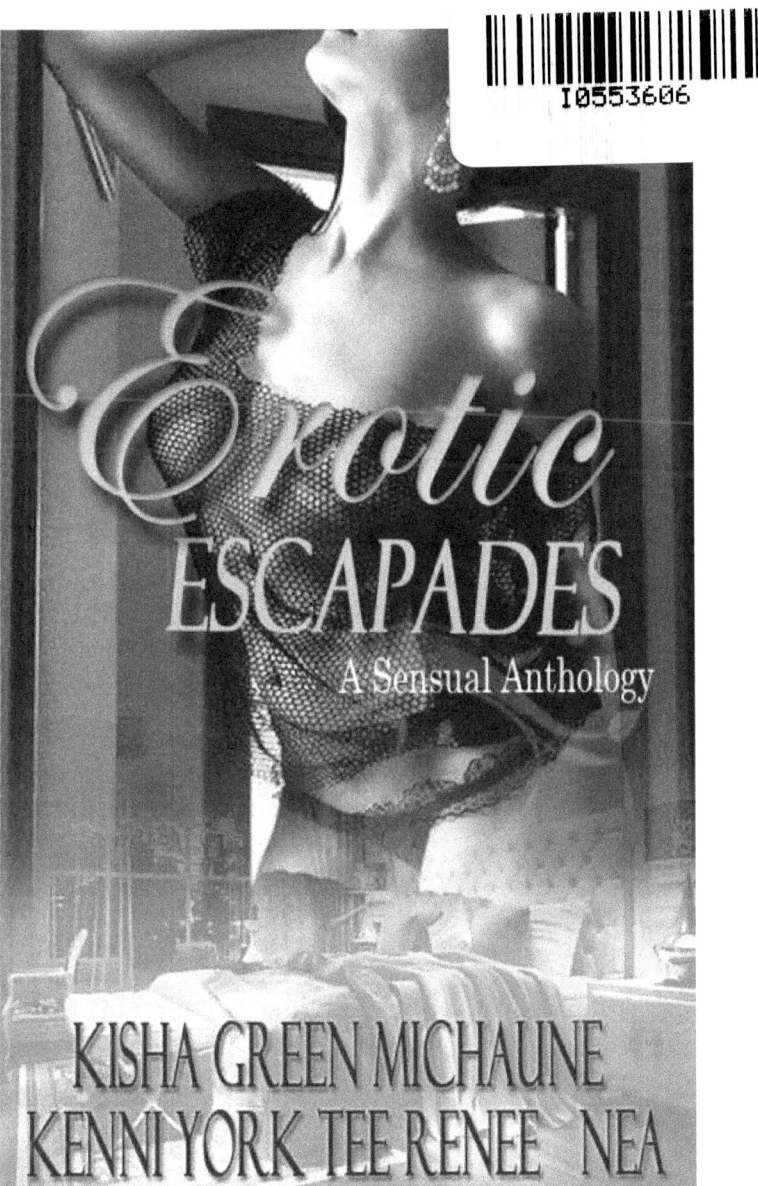

Erotic ESCAPADES
A Sensual Anthology

KISHA GREEN MICHAUNE
KENNI YORK TEE RENEE NEA

Library of Congress Control Number:

ISBN-13: 978-0692654927

Copyright © 2016 by Kisha Green, Kenni York, Tee Renee, MiChaune and Nea Stewart

Edited By: www.itsthewritestuff.com

Typeset/Format By: www.lmgconsultant.com

For information about special discounts for bulk purchases or to book an event, please contact the publisher at www.divabooksinconline.com

Dedication

Shawnn D. McPherson

1978-2015

Da'Von Levone Carter-Daniels

Get Well Soon

Rest In Peace ~ Gone But Not Forgotten

Keith "Keddie" Mosley

Anitra Miles

Acknowledgements

Kisha Green: I just want to say thank you to Jehovah for the gift of storytelling, the talented ladies on this anthology, my fiancé, Altorice & my family for all of their unconditional love and support, Tarra Daniels- Carter, Kyheem Davis, Kisha Shelton, Kiera Northington, Justin Young, Unique Penn, Diane Rembert and a BIG shout out to my readers/supporters.

MiChaune: First giving honor to God, I thank you Lord for the gift of writing. I love you Lord. Mom & Dad thank you for loving me, just for being me. You both are my heart's smile. To my two brothers and my sister, I love y'all. To all of my plus size divas and lovers thank you for riding with me. To my readers old and new, I thank God for each and every one of you, God bless!

Kenni York: Special thanks to the readers who support my literary endeavors and always encourage me to be a better writer with each project. My love is extended to The Literary Ladies of the ATL with a special shout out to Nika Michelle-Here's to midnight brainstorming sessions. Much love and thanks to my heartbeat, Terri Jones.

Tee Renee: I would like to thank God for continuing to bless me with more opportunities to share my gift with the world. To my love, children and family, thank you for loving and supporting me continuously. And lastly, to the awesome ladies that are a part of this body of work, thank you for being an inspiration to my life!

Nea: I would like to give thanks and gratitude to everyone that has ever supported my literary journey. Special thanks to Kisha Green for always believing in me. Another special thanks to my husband, Derek and my three daughters for keeping me grounded.

Intimate Reflections

Kenni York

"*O*h my God! Yes! Yes! You're the best! Mmmm." The petite woman's words trailed off into a mere mumble that turned into a sexy moan as Cal skillfully worked magic. Ginger, Cal's treat of the night, threw her head back against the plush pillows on the pillow-top, queen-sized bed, situated in the luxurious suite that Cal had rented for the night.

Sensual music played low in the background as they lay under dim lighting. Dinner had been expensive, yet unmemorable, as they'd gone through the motions of getting to know one another on the surface level by asking trite questions. All of the idle rigmarole led them to this very moment—this inevitable moment—they both had been yearning for, from the second Cal had winked in the beauty's direction from across the room at the bar.

"Yessss," Ginger hissed. "Don't stop. Don't ever, ever stop." She loved the feeling of Cal's firm touch against her smooth skin. Her body temperature was rising with each caress. She was in ecstasy like never before.

Cal was turned on, watching as Ginger gripped the sheets and squirmed about, crumpling the bed linen underneath her. She was still clad in her work attire—a black pencil skirt, which was pushed up, exposing her thong and inviting thighs, and a lavender collared shirt, of which the top three buttons were undone. She was like a dog in heat and Cal appeared more than ready to extinguish the fire and give her what she'd come for. Seated in the middle of the bed dead center between Ginger's legs, Cal pressed harder against the delicate flesh of Ginger's right foot, being sure to pay extra special attention to the arch. As Ginger moaned again, Cal smiled. It was only a matter of time now before all of the juices that were soaking up Ginger's panties would be dripping from Cal's lips. The anticipation was almost too much to bear.

Sensing that Ginger was almost at the point of begging for more, Cal raised her foot and slowly wrapped warm, soft lips around the woman's red-polished big toe. Cal hated red polish. There was something trashy and tawdry about a woman donning any type of red makeup. *It's only one night*, Cal reasoned mentally. Not even that long. Once the fireworks subsided, the tryst and the woman would be yet a mere memory.

"Oh my God," Ginger cried out again, her eyes popping open to stare at the vault ceiling. Never had she experienced this level of intimacy and she was dying to see what other tricks her new, forbidden lover had in store for her.

Cal sucked mightily on Ginger's toe, sending a rippling sensation up and down her body. With Ginger's toe prey to the wandering tongue and flexible jaw muscles that Cal took great pride in, Cal's right hand slid gently, yet determinedly up the inside of Ginger's right leg. There was no protest from Ginger, only a consenting gasp, as Cal's fingertips found the moist edges of Ginger's panties. Bending Ginger's leg at the knee and leaning forward, Cal slipped two fingers inside the leg of her Victoria's Secret lace bikini briefs. *Damn!* The mental exclaim came because of how moist Ginger was at first touch. *I knew she was aching for it, but I didn't know she was this into it*, Cal thought.

The toe sucking was over. Judging by the way Ginger was reaching down and caressing the smooth waves of Cal's well-kept temp fade, the sensual act had done its job. Removing Ginger's foot, Cal lowered to a laying position, using Ginger's inner thigh as a pillow. Easing the woman's panties to the side, Cal took a quick peek at her goodies. She was neatly groomed—not too hairy, but a far call from baby-smooth. Still, the scent of her pheromones and the desire to complete the lustful task propelled Cal forward. Ginger moaned in one long, loud hum as she felt the first flicker against her throbbing clit. Cal liked to tease at first; making them practically force the tongue action to escalate to a more starved, nearly manic level. A couple of more flickers and Ginger was no different from the others.

As if on cue, she grabbed Cal's head and intently bucked against the strokes Cal issued out. She couldn't take it anymore. With her left hand, she tore at the rest of the buttons on her shirt, working to free her B-cup breasts over the top of her low-cut, push-up bra. She ached all over for the orgasm that Cal was pushing her closer towards.

Regarding Ginger's gyrating hips and crazed fondling of her nipples as signs to move to the next phase, Cal ripped at the fabric of the woman's pretty panties to gain better access, before inserting two fingers into her drenched love zone all while taking her clit hostage.

"Oohh shit! You're gonna make me cum," Ginger warned, reeling from the assault her womanhood was enduring. She'd never known pleasure like this. Sure, she'd had oral sex before, but this was different. For her, this was wild. Cal honestly seemed to know exactly what to do to her body and exactly when to do it.

The finger thrusts got quicker and deeper. The sucking become more erratic and was accompanied by a slurping sound that practically drowned out the music that Spotify was whispering from Cal's Bluetooth speaker. A familiar tingle exploded inside of Cal's pants because of the unavoidable grinding that was occurring, and the erotic way that Ginger's body responded to every touch. Yes, they were both approaching their own waves of sensual bliss, but it was Cal's mission to make sure that Ginger climaxed hard and ferociously, so that she'd never forget the night a stud put it on her. Cal's tongue licked the entire circumference of Ginger's blazing core, even running across the opening where her fingers were steadily drilling in and out of her expertly. Cal's left hand expanded upward to grab a firm hold onto her right breast, giving it a squeeze with just enough pressure to make Ginger wince with desire.

Ginger spread her legs as wide as they would go as if inviting Cal to explore more of her. In fact, she needed it. She needed Cal to take over her body explicitly and make her repeatedly shudder in total ecstasy. Sex with Cal was a milestone. Cal knew that for years to come, Ginger would compare her lovers—male and female, should she choose to go that route again— to what she experienced on this night. However, Cal was certain that within a month, she'd probably forget the woman's name altogether. Still, she enjoyed the moment while it lasted and savored the rush of fluids that expelled from Ginger's body as she succumbed to the orgasm that dominated her body.

"Sweet Jesus! Yes! Yesss!" Ginger squealed as she climaxed in rapid convulsions.

That was a first. Cal had never heard anyone praising the Lord for her talents during the act. It was an ego booster to say the least and worked wonders for pushing her over the edge of her own sexual cliff into the land of a quiet orgasm. She could feel the sections inside of her boxers as her eyes fluttered from the temporary sensation that caused her body to relax. Sex was better than alcohol any day when it came to winding down after a long stressful day.

Ginger's body went limp and for a brief second, Cal collapsed on her leg, regulating her breathing and gathering her composure. Ginger began to caress Cal's head and purr as her legs twitched. Cal knew that signal. That was a sign that Ginger was revving up to go again, but unfortunately, that wasn't in Cal's plans. Quickly, she rose from the bed and began to remove the open work shirt she was still wearing.

"I've got an early day in the morning," Cal stated, looking over at the doe-eyed woman lying across her bed. "I'm glad we met. Maybe I'll call you when I come back in town." She walked over to the side of the bed, leaned down and kissed Ginger on the forehead. "You were great." She spoke these last words, before turning away and disappearing into the bathroom for a much-needed shower.

She'd wait there long enough for Ginger to realize that she'd been dismissed, collect herself, get dressed, and make her walk of shame right up out of Cal's hotel suite. It was nothing personal, but they always knew what it was. Cal never lied, never told them she was looking for anything more than the excitement of the moment. She was especially fond of the 'virgins'—the straight chicks who were secretly curious and couldn't wait to see what it was like to have a female between their legs. Sure, Cal was willing to be their entertainment for a few hours, sometimes even a whole night, but that was it. She sampling all that life had to offer, using her style and charm to romance the panties right off of her conquests. Cal was living the life that most men and studs alike dreamed of. Love didn't live within her and she carried around no strings with which to attach herself to anyone. Life was good. What could be better?

***

"Bruh, you killin' me," Boomer said, holding his stomach while doubled over with cramps caused by excessive laughing. "You ain't do her like that."

Prohibition, the gentleman's cigar club in Atlanta, was crowded for a mere Monday night. However, despite the droves of patrons, Cal had been determined to get up with the crew as soon as possible. Prohibition was their spot—they could eat, drink, smoke, and talk about anything without the scrutiny of their significant others, for those that had them, and without the fear of offending anyone within earshot. Boomer, Antwon, and Greg were the only friends that Cal could truly claim. Anyone else was just an associate. They'd all met through work at Builder Investment Group, where each held a different title. Boomer was the manager in the firm's mailroom, Antwon was the human resources manager, Greg was the executive assistant to the firm's president, and Cal was a junior level investment consultant. They all shared a common interest in admiring the beautiful female employee pool at B.I.G. Over a few lunches and mannish conversations; they had discovered that they also had common interests in basketball and fine cigars, hence the hangout spot being Prohibition.

Although Cal felt close to the others given their three-year long friendship, there was one thing that made Cal stand out from the group—Cal was the only female. It had taken a minute for the others to come to terms with the fact that Cal was a stud, who truly identified herself as a male. Nevertheless, once they got past the breasts they knew were hidden under her large size, finely tailored shirts and the vagina that rested within her expensive slacks, they were able to focus on her personality and accept her for who she was. The truth was, aside from the way she was anatomically built; Cal was very much like the rest of them and was probably an even bigger dog than either of them.

Cal Montgomery prided herself on her charisma, sex appeal, and impeccable good luck when it came to the ladies. Even the straight ones couldn't help but throw Cal a second look when she was in their presence. The way she presented herself screamed pure dude, one hundred percent stud. From the way she kept her hair neatly cut and groomed, to the flare of her wardrobe, consisting of only the highest quality articles that her handsome salary afford her the opportunity to splurge upon. The way that she spoke in a deep, raspy tone, right down to her swagger and the way she practically glided into the room with an air of confidence that even a blind woman could pick up on. Cal had no children, a great sense of humor, game for days, and a loft apartment in a gated community, drove a black 2016 Hummer H3, and made a decent living. She was every woman's dream and she knew it. Hell, it was a fact that she capitalized on when she entertained her flavors of the week. True, the chicks she messed with knew that she was a good catch, but by the time they were entering the bedroom, the women knew that Cal wasn't down for anything serious or even remotely resembling a commitment. They knew the deal and always consented to it, each thinking that she'd be the lucky one who would turn Cal Montgomery into a one-woman stud. Inevitably, they'd either fade away into the abyss once they figured out that it wasn't happening or they'd keep giving it a good ole' fashioned try, not wanting to forego the phenomenal sex that Cal never failed to make good on.

Yes, Cal was the epitome of a lesbian's dream lover, but that's all she ever planned to be to the many women she'd sexed in the city of Atlanta—a dream, a mere fantasy. Now, it appeared that she'd have to kiss the women of the city and the city itself goodbye as she prepared to make a career move. Cal had been offered a position as a senior investment advisor at Raymond James Incorporated in Tallahassee, Florida. When offered the position, the pay increase, the incentives, and the opportunity to advance more than made the decision a no-brainer for Cal. It helped that the company was open and that prejudices seemed scarce, compared to the adversity that Cal often was faced with while at B.I.G. One of the top grossing consultants at B.I.G. bringing in new clientele and showing impressive numbers at each review period, Cal was remiss to notice that she was frequently passed up for promotions. Her work ethic was unparalleled and clients never complained about her professionalism or knowledge regarding their financial needs, questions, and interests. The only reason that Cal could think of for the company to be so against moving her up as she so deserved, was their inability to want a black, male-identifying lesbian in a position of authority. It was bullshit and Cal had grown tired of it.

Cal took a slow, intent drag on the Cuban cigar she was sampling as the others settled down from their hearty laugh. She'd been relaying the story of her tryst with Ginger while in Florida, checking out rental properties the weekend before. "Man, I'm saying…I could tell that she was one of those that would clung to me for dear life. I didn't even wanna give her the opportunity to stick around and so much as think that there was more to come for her."

"Man, that's cold as hell," Antwon remarked. "I'm surprised you haven't had some chick pull a Jazmine Sullivan on yo' trifling ass."

The crew burst out into a fit of laughter once more at the thought of some crazed woman busting out the windows of Cal's precious H3.

"Shitttt. I wish a broad would," Cal commented, shaking her head. "That shit ain't cool. But I'm saying, it's not like they don't know what it is. I'm not like y'all no-game having brothas out here, telling these chicks you gon' wife 'em down and you want 'em to have your baby and shit."

"Facccccce!" Greg called out, cupping his mouth with both hands to aid the volume of the sound as he stared at Antwan.

Cal's comment had come as a low blow. It was no secret among the group; Antwon didn't hesitate to tell a woman exactly what she wanted to hear, in order to get the drawers. He'd gotten caught up at least two times at B.I.G. for messing with some of their co-workers and having the women think that he was all in, when in fact, he couldn't have been more disconnected from them. Antwon was like a kid in a candy store when it came to fine women—he just couldn't make up his mind about which one he really wanted, though he was certain that he had a sweet tooth.

"Aye, whatever, man," Antwon retorted, taking a swig of his apple beer. "A brotha can't help it if he fall outta love easily."

"You trying to tell us that you loved both Tasha and Gabrielle last year when you was seeing 'em both, and lying to 'em both 'bout how you were gonna introduce 'em to your mama, and move in with 'em and shit?" Boomer asked, not believing Antwon for a second.

"What? You don't think it's possible to love two women at the same time?" Antwon shot back. "Man, I'm telling you. That shit's rough. I was feeling both of 'em hard and I just couldn't bring myself to let either of 'em down. And then by the time I started feeling Gabrielle more than Tasha…I guess I felt obligated to keep kickin' it with Tasha, 'cause I didn't wanna hurt her. And you know…I still felt something for her."

"Yeah, that would be the rising of ya' dick, because you couldn't give up sexing ol' girl," Cal cut in. "Cut the bullshit, yo', and be honest. You didn't wanna give up the good-good."

Even Antwon had to laugh, because it was the honest to goodness truth. No man wanted to ever give up his good thing for some other dude to start hitting it, even if he himself was dipping out and sleeping with other women. It was an ego thing.

"True dat," Antwon said. "I can't even front."

Cal nodded and reached for her glass of Rémy Martin. "Yeah, and that's why I keep telling y'all to stop lying to these women, man. You ever heard that saying you can catch more flies with honey?"

"Okay," Greg said, raising an eyebrow. "But what that says to me is make sure the game you kicking is sweet enough for 'em to fall for it."

Cal shook her head. "And that's why ya' ass is single. No, in this case you gotta give 'em raw honey. Tell 'em the truth. Make that shit plain. Let 'em know what it is, but shoot it to 'em in just a way where their panties so drenched, that they can't help but to consent to ya' terms. I'm telling you, you'd be surprised by how many chicks are down for whatever just to be with you, so long as you give them the real and not place them in the middle of some bullshit later. Lies will only get you caught up and that's that shit that makes women bitter, angry, and scorned—when they find out you ain't nothing but a lying ass dog."

Cal was schooling the crew and they couldn't deny her wisdom. She had two things going for her that made the others pay attention and take notes. First, she was living proof that telling the brutal truth could get you mad play. The others saw it repeatedly with the way Cal always had a different beauty on her arm and in her bed. The truth was that often times; they lived vicariously through Cal and her accounts of her escapades. Second, at the end of the day, she was still a female. In a manner of speaking, there wasn't a better way to learn about the species, other than to get the knowledge, straight from one of their own.

"Yeah, yeah," Boomer blurted out, not wanting to hear Cal remind them of how their own love lives sucked. "Back to Ginger. Did she hit you the next day?"

Cal shrugged. "Never even gave her my number, even though she gave me her business card with her cell written on the back."

"You gonna get up with her when you get back?" Greg asked. "I mean right now she is the only person you really know in Tallahassee."

"Nah. I don't think I wanna do that."

"I bet," Boomer interjected. "After the way you just hopped outta bed and ran and hid in the bathroom like the sex was garbage, I'm sure ole' girl would be looking to give you the business if you tried to holler at her now."

Cal shook her head. "She knew what it was. If her feelings were hurt, she's got nobody to blame but herself." She winced as the cigar dangled from her full lips. "That damn red polish. Even if I was horny and just wanted some company, I wouldn't hit her, walking around looking like some street walker. with that bright ass stop sign red polish on."

"Man, what is it with you and red?" Antwon asked. "You acting like Eddie Murphy from Boomerang with his obsession with feet."

"Nah, it's not like that," Cal replied. "I just can't stand all that red war paint. It's like they're begging for attention…dying to be noticed when they put that mess on. You can't help but see it. Red is an eye-catching color."

"You tripping," Boomerang said. "It's really not that deep."

"For me it is," Cal retorted. "If you wanna catch my attention, do it a different way. You ain't gotta highlight ya' damn body."

The group fell silent for just a moment as they pondered over Cal's words. The others simply didn't get her disdain for the color and frankly, Cal wasn't up for going any deeper into her aversion. She subconsciously didn't feel like acknowledging or sharing that part of herself with her homeboys.

"It's hard to believe that you're actually leaving, bruh," Antwon said, finally breaking the awkward silence.

"Yeah, man. I'm happy for you though. You deserve it," Greg told Cal as he patted her on the shoulder. "You inspire me to want to do more and move on, man."

Cal smiled. It felt good to hear their encouragement. "Yeah, I'm excited. It's a new era."

"Shit ain't gon' be the same without you," Boomer stated. "I'm gonna miss you, man."

"We're gonna make sure to keep your chair empty in the break room," Antwon joked, "Unless some sexy secretary sashays her way over to the table."

"Awww man! Kicked to the curb for a skirt!" Cal said playfully. "You ain't shit."

"It wouldn't be just any skirt though. It's gotta be one bad ass sista. Otherwise, we'll preserve your memory."

"What the hell ever." Cal laughed and polished off her drink.

"So…" Boomer's words trailed off as he stared at Cal knowingly. "Have you said your goodbyes to the Mrs. yet?"

The others fell silent and looked over at Cal, waiting to see what her answer we be. They'd all been thinking about it, but no one had had the balls to bring it up until now. While the Mrs. wasn't a secret among their group, she also wasn't a topic they discussed often, due to the severity and complication of the situation surrounding her existence. Still, Cal threw her head back to signify that she had indeed been in touch with the infamous Mrs.

"How she taking this move?" Greg asked.

"I mean, what can she do?" Cal replied. "It is what it is and as usual, I never promised her anything. Considering the situation, she shouldn't have much to say, point blank period." That was all she cared to say about the matter. "So, who's picking up the tab since this is my farewell outing?"

Cal's abrupt change of subject let them know that she didn't care to discuss the matter further, which was alright with them. This was their last night hanging out and no one wanted to taint it with talking about a dead-end situation. Cal definitely had no interest in dampening the mood with details about the tiny speck of crazy that filled her life. It was guys' night and the shenanigans had only just begun.

***

"Make me cum, baby. Make me cum!" She was demanding gratification. It was just like her to try to force the moment, versus just letting it take its course.

Honestly, her straightforwardness and sexual openness was one of the things that Cal liked about her. She was truly down for anything, which pretty much explained why they connected in the first place. She wasn't one of Cal's typical conquests—she was more like a favorite snack versus being an appetizer as Cal so fondly viewed the plethora of women she spent time with. With this one, Cal could have her two, sometimes three times a week, and never tired of the heightened pleasure that came from each visit. However, they were always very brief, very quick encounters. No dinners, no small talk, no promises of there ever being more between them—just straight, forbidden, unadulterated, raw sex every time.

This time the Mrs. had sauntered through Cal's front door, dropping her fitted slacks and see-through blouse on the floor among the boxes that were packed full of Cal's belongings. She simply looked around at the rather empty apartment and raised an eyebrow as if to say she couldn't care less about the evidence of their liaison coming to an end. She was ready to receive what she'd come for and Cal was more than willing to give the well-endowed beauty exactly what she wanted.

The Mrs. had then taken a seat on top of a sturdy trunk and seductively slipped her satin panties downward, never taking her eyes off Cal, who was still positioned near the front door. The moment the undergarment hit the floor, the Mrs. spread her legs wide, giving Cal a bird's eye view of her perfectly trimmed snatch. Cal practically salivated where she stood as the Mrs. took her right index finger and began to toy with her clit, while smiling devilishly. Soon after, she inserted her finger into the plushness of her womanhood and Cal could hear the sloshing sound of her wetness. That was all it had taken.

Now, Cal was seated on the crate in front of the Mrs., thrusting three of her fingers into the woman and watching her legs tremble as she bucked her bare ass on the trunk, demanding that Cal give her the climax she craved. They never talked much, but during sex, the Mrs. was very vocal, a trait that Cal had come to appreciate.

"You love this pussy, don't you?" she asked. "You see how wet you get it, baby? Make it drip for you, daddy. Do it harder!" she urged as she lifted her legs, placing her feet flat on top of the trunk.

Cal fingered the Mrs. frantically with the fingers of her right hand; she used her left index and middle finger to create a circular motion against the Mrs.' clit. The double sensation drove her wild as she held on to the sides of the trunk to support her weight, while thrusting her pelvis to match the pressure being applied to the core of her sex.

"Oooh, that makes daddy's girl feel so dirty," she purred. "Daddy's dirty little bitch. I wanna cum for you. Make me cum, daddy. Come onnnnn!" she complained out loud in a seductive, yet crazed way that made Cal want to break out the vibrator, and send them both to orbit real quick.

Cal thought about replacing her fingers with her tongue and then remembered whom she was dealing with. They fucked in different places in different ways, but never once had Cal put her mouth on the Mrs. to kiss either set of lips that she possessed. It was a hard and fast rule that had been established the moment they began to fool around. Not that it mattered much, but Cal figured at least, she could honestly say she hadn't done that to the woman, should the discussion ever arise. It was bad enough that they were sleeping together; giving the woman the golden tongue would have only further complicated things.

Just as Cal was feeling the rise of her own release, she felt the Mrs.' walls tighten around her fingers and knew that the woman was about to explode. Her breathing changed, her moans became shrieks of pure pleasure as the dam broke; her orgasm unleashed a wave of euphoria throughout her body and a slippery trail from her throbbing pussy.

"Yesssss! Fuck yes! You're the best, baby! You're the absolute best!" she exclaimed, meaning every word of it.

Cal never grew tired of hearing accolades for the talented way she pleased a woman with her extremities. The positive feedback worked to boost her self-esteem. As the Mrs. composed herself, Cal withdrew her fingers from their moist hiding spot and rose from the crate to head into the small kitchen to wash her hands. She smiled to herself cockily, knowing that she'd given the Mrs. a powerful orgasm to remember her by. Grabbing a couple of paper towels and dampening them just a little, Cal returned to the cluttered living room and handed them to the Mrs. She took the paper towels and promptly began to clean herself before re-dressing.

"What? No round two?" Cal asked, shocked that she was satisfied with just one orgasm. Usually, she'd be down for back-to-back episodes and Cal wouldn't complain, because it never took long for her to cum and the scene was never boring when it came to the Mrs.

"Not today," she answered, buttoning up her blouse. "I have to meet him for lunch at La Grota in Buckhead."

Cal wasn't really interested in her plans, but found it intriguing how she could be sprawled out creaming all over the place for her and then half an hour later, be cozied up to her husband sharing a meal like nothing had happened. "Special occasion?"

The Mrs. shrugged as she adjusted the tail of her blouse inside of her slacks. "Lunch with a prospective, high-profile client." She zipped and clasped her pants before smoothing out the wrinkles in her attire. "It looks good when you bring your show piece to dangle from your arm, you know?"

Didn't she? Cal was well aware of how the Mrs.' husband regarded her as the typical trophy wife. It was the role that she seemed to not mind playing. She was a modern-day socialite, running around with the other wives of the true movers and shakers in Atlanta, pretending to give a damn about the many causes that she donated to. Lunching here and there while being seen by those who mattered, and of course, accompanying her husband on business trips and meal dates in order to help seal the deal whenever possible. It didn't hurt when there was a randy gentleman whose money her husband was trying to lure over to B.I.G. and the Mrs. would use her womanly charm and impressive figure to woo them on over. That hour-glass figure that she flaunted here and there was compliments of her husband—the breast implants, the tummy tuck, and even the minor procedure she'd had done to straighten the crook in her nose were all funded by the man, who had yet to suspect that his wife was getting down the way that she was.

"Sounds like a good time," Cal remarked sarcastically as she began to seal up an open, yet full box.

The Mrs. smiled and walked over to run her fingers over Cal's head. "Jealous are we?"

Cal chuckled. "Right."

"It would have been nice to have a little outing or something before you pull out this week. Maybe we can still make that happen."

Cal didn't even bother to give her eye contact. There was no sense in her trying to act brand new all of a sudden. Their relationship was what it was and it was ending on the same note that it had begun.

The Mrs. leaned forward and kissed Cal on her left cheek. "Let me get going. Try not to miss me too much, honey. And don't run down there and get caught up with the first set of boobs that catches your eye."

"Jealous?" Cal retorted jokingly.

The Mrs. gave a sinister laugh and smiled confidently. "Never that. You and I both know that you'll never find another woman like me. But I know you…I know you'll be starving for the feel of something wet and hot by week two."

Shows how much you know really know me, Cal thought. *By the end of week one I would have already hit something.* She looked over at the Mrs. whose hand was now lingering along her jaw line. Gently, Cal patted the Mrs.' hand before removing it from her face. "Thanks for stopping by. Glad we got to see one another before I head out."

"No worries, sexy," the Mrs. said, raising her right brow. "There was no way I was going to let you slip away without sending you off properly." She smiled and headed for the door. "Have a safe ride and I'll see you later."

You'll see me later? Cal didn't know if the woman had suddenly become delusional or what. *Didn't she realize that this was indefinitely the end of the road for them?*

"Shall I give Sidney your regards?" The Mrs. asked sarcastically as she reached the door.

Cal knew she didn't mean it. There was no way that she'd ever mention to her husband that she'd been with Cal. The conflict of interest was far too great and a feasible explanation, other than the truth, would be hard to formulate. Not that Cal cared much now that she was leaving, but still…it was preposterous that the Mrs. would feel inclined to confess her sins to her husband at this point.

"I'm pretty sure I'm the last person he wants to hear anything from," Cal commented.

"You're right. Though he's bounced back considerably by filling your position at record speed, I can tell that it's still a sore spot with him. I can see the wheels turning in that one-tracked mind of his. I'm no financial guru or anything, but I know that you made the firm quite a bit of money during your tenure. He's too proud to say it, Cal, but I know that B.I.G. is terribly sad to see you go."

It was the most they'd ever discussed their origins and the moment was kind of bittersweet for Cal. All the positive reinforcement she was getting from the Mrs.' statement would have been better coming from her husband, Cal's former boss, long before now. It would have been even better to be accommodated by the promotion that Cal could never seem to solidify. Nevertheless, it was too late now. The decision had been made and both Sidney Gardner and his beautiful, buxom wife were losing the best thing that had ever happened to them. *Tough shit*, Cal thought. She wasn't loyal to either one of them and the couple certainly didn't owe her anything at this point.

"Well, I'm sure the firm will continue to strive without me," Cal said dryly, more than ready for her fling for the last year to make her final exit.

Looking at her now, Cal wondered how they'd gone so long with their arrangement without getting caught. Thanks to a couple of glasses of wine too many on the Mrs.' part and a shot of Patrón on an empty stomach that Cal had eagerly downed, the two had connected at the firm's holiday gala in 2014. While standing in the mirror checking her appearance in the ladies' room, an uncomfortable feeling for Cal given her gender-identification, the Mrs. had strolled in wearing a dangerously low-cut cocktail dress. She'd stumbled through the door and looked up at Cal with lust in her eyes and a seductive smile resting upon her lips. Cal knew something was up the moment she saw the Mrs. turn the lock on the restroom door, preventing anyone else from coming in. She'd glided over to Cal, wrapped her arms around Cal's neck, and whispered in her ear, "I've always wanted to feel a woman's hand between my legs."

Cal considered unwrapping her boss's wife from around her person and guiding the woman back out to the party, resigned to simply forget what had just happened. After all, she was a stud and didn't exactly consider it a turn on that the sexy female viewed her as a mere woman. Cal had been all set to ignore the statement and hurriedly move past the awkward moment, but it was the Mrs.' next move that sparked the flame between the two of them and sent them coasting along their own private road of secret quickies. Determined to get what she'd followed Cal into the restroom for, the Mrs. then forced Cal's right hand between the velvety-smoothness of her legs.

"I'm not wearing any panties," the Mrs. cooed in Cal's ear, before licking the outline of it and sucking on the lobe that housed a mid-sized diamond stud.

Cal's heart rate had quickened and her eyes fluttered as her fingers touched the warm, inviting pussy that was being offered to her. The excitement of knowing that her coworkers, friends, and even her boss, Sidney Garner, were all on the other side of the door, not suspecting a thing had turned Cal on even more. She was too far gone to rely on her good senses. All she could see was ahead was her own satisfaction and the look of pleasure on the Mrs.' face as she jammed her hand between the woman's legs, massaging her pussy until she exploded. The entire escapade had taken little under fifteen minutes and for the remainder of the night, Cal couldn't help but feel horny thinking about how she'd fucked the boss's wife in the restroom. From then on, the Mrs. would pop up here and there and they'd experienced quick, hot sex in places that would have created a grand scandal had they been caught—from the Gardner's own bed, to Sidney's office. The Mrs.' car parked at the couple's country club, most company functions, and occasionally Cal's home, the two of them got it on as often as they could, never once giving much thought to the consequences of their actions.

The Mrs. smiled, assuming that Cal was contemplating another go at her finely sculpted body. "Ciao, baby," she said seductively. "Until we meet again." She turned and let herself out of the apartment.

We had a good run, Cal thought as she locked the door and returned to her packing. *But you can cancel it, because we'll never meet again.* As far as Cal was concerned, this entire chapter of her life, B.I.G. and the Mrs. included, were completely over. It was time to move on to bigger and better things.

***

The move was tedious and Cal was spinning on all cylinders as she hurriedly tried to create some sense of organization in her modest townhome that she was renting, as well as prepare herself for her first week at her new job. She packed the most essential stuff into her car and drove it to Tallahassee herself. A moving company hauled and dropped off the rest of her belongings, courtesy of her new employer, Raymond James Incorporated. *Too bad the movers weren't paid to also unpack the shit,* Cal thought, looking around at the clutter of her belongings. This wasn't the way she was used to spending her Saturday nights, but she knew that she had to get through the bulk of the stuff in order to be able to freely maneuver through her new home.

Chugging back a can of Heineken, Cal shook her head. The stress was minimal, but it was still there nonetheless. *A little stress reliever never hurt anybody,* she thought, as she leaned her elbows onto the countertop of her breakfast nook and stared at the boxes of cookware and dishes situated on the kitchen floor. She contemplated looking up what's her name, the chick that she'd had the one-night stand with during her last visit to her new city of residence. The thought was pointless for several reasons. She didn't intend to invite anyone over to her pigsty, and she certainly didn't want to hook up with the woman at her place, giving her the feeling that they were to become more than Cal had in mind. Getting a hotel room was out of the question. Sure, she was making big bucks now, but with what she was paying for her new home and trying to get settled, there was no way she was about to shit away even the smallest amount of money on a room for just a few hours. Let's face it, she wasn't going to spend the night with the girl.

Cal drained her beer and tossed the empty can into a black garbage bag lying in the middle of the kitchen floor. Taking a deep breath and dismissing the idea of getting into something, she opened a box and began to tackle the unpleasant task of setting up her kitchen. Her hands gripped the stainless steel pots and pans and she meticulously placed them in their new allocated spots in the cabinets closest to the stove. She wished more and more that she were palming firm skin and wet pussy versus cookware.

"Get ya' mind right," she chided herself aloud, trying to shake off the urges that were beginning to plague her.

As she worked, her mind drifted back to memories of her last tryst with the Mrs. She had to admit that the woman had some good pussy. The affair, if you could call it that, had been quite a turn out, although a major risk. While Cal enjoyed their quick romps in dangerous places, she often worried about the ramifications of her former employer finding out that she was turning out his wife. Then again, Cal wasn't even sure that she could take credit for the Mrs.' freakiness. After all, she had come on to Cal first, with no initial flirting or coaxing on Cal's part. Perhaps the Mrs. had always enjoyed a little pussy on the side of her dick entrée. Maybe Cal wasn't the first chick to sample the Mrs.' goodies, although she'd whispered to Cal that first night that she'd always desired to feel a woman between her legs. She could have just been talking shit. For all Cal knew, the Mrs. could have had a lineup of fems, doms, studs, and stems alike, ready and waiting to please her whenever and however she wanted. Cal wasn't jealous though; truthfully, she didn't give a shit. It just all went to show how their arrangement was purely physical; they were using one another for the same purpose—the thrill of getting their rocks off.

Still, Cal was glad that the situation was over and she no longer had to feel some type of way about the stability of her job in relation to her fucking the boss' wife. Although she was rather certain that Mr. Gardner had no idea what was going on, the possibility of him becoming hip to the truth had shaken her a few times. There were occasions when she'd wondered if that was the reason why she hadn't received the promotion that she deserved. The moment those thoughts hit her, Cal became even more indifferent, yearning for the next time she could make the Mrs.' scream out her name—she considered it her personalized benefits package, since B.I.G. was shitting on her.

"Fuck it," Cal said, her voice echoing throughout the stillness of the house. She couldn't take it anymore. Sitting in the house playing Martha Stewart, organizing cutlery and whatnot, wasn't getting it for her. She needed to go out and explore the city to see what kind of trouble the nightlife offered. More specifically, she wanted to scope out the females. Maybe she'd even get lucky and find someone with the same kind of gusto as the Mrs., who would be willing to give up the goods in the restroom of a bar with only the exchange of their first names.

Cal chuckled to herself at the thought of a fem dropping her panties at the sight of her charming smile and witty repartee. She bee lined for the bathroom in her master bedroom. She deserved a break and a treat if she could get one.

***

The bar was crowded, but Cal wasn't disappointed. The Sequoy Lounge was located midway between Cal's house and her new job. She figured it was a good place to start when trying to find a new hangout spot. If the action seemed to be popping, she might start the routine of dropping by for happy hour after work. During the first hour of sitting at the bar, she learned that the lounge offered a variety of entertainment options, from karaoke nights, comedy nights, to live band performances, and even spoken word. It was a grown and sexy type of place where the women came in a mixture of late twenties to mid-forties, collegiate to professional, single and horny, to taken but frisky, right down to the quiet ones being drug out for ladies' nights by their slightly rowdier friends.

The latter seemingly had Cal's attention as she noticed a group of four women at a nearby table snickering and looking in her direction. Cal looked at them over the rim of her cognac glass and then offered the group a quick, seductive, knowing smile. She turned away and ordered a third Henn and Coke before looking over her shoulder to ascertain that the women were still fixated on her. They were. Chuckling to herself, Cal slid from her bar stool and strolled over to the table as the acoustic sounds of the performing band filled her ears. She practically glided across the room in tune with the melody. From her seat at the bar, she'd already assessed the situation and knew exactly who to set her sights on—the quiet one whose eyes barely rose to meet hers as she stopped dead center of the ladies' table.

"Mind if I join you?" Cal asked.

A series of giggles and headshakes occurred.

"Not at all," the ebony beauty whom Cal calculated to be the most outgoing of the four spoke up.

"What brings you ladies out tonight?" Cal asked, being sure to give them all eye contact, yet letting her glance linger with the quiet one.

"It's our girl's birthday and her ass never goes anywhere," the ebony beauty replied. "So we drug her ass out so she could get some excitement in her life."

"Sounds like a good time to me," Cal commented, still looking at the shy woman, who was now blushing as she finally met Cal's glance. "How rude of me," Cal said. "I'm Cal."

"I'm Latoya," the ebony leader offered. She pointed to the fair-skinned blonde to her right. "This is Heather."

"And I'm Tonya," the woman to Cal's left replied, as she held out her hand.

Cal immediately noticed her long, red tips and felt repulsed. Still, she politely shook the woman's hand and then returned her attention to the shy one sitting right across from her. "And you are?"

"Jasmine," she said softly, pushing her glasses up on her the bridge of her nose.

Cal smiled, taking in her demure beauty. She was dressed in a shimmery tan dress, which hung over her left shoulder and had a gold chain resting upon her right. Her makeup was minimal and her hair was in beautiful golden locks that slightly rested upon the tops of her shoulders. Her body language was telling Cal that she was interested. *Was she a lesbian? Was she simply curious? Had she been with a woman before?* The questions were endless, but so were the possibilities. Sure, she was shy now, but Cal knew that within a matter of minutes, she could have the woman hitting Patti LaBelle notes from the pleasure she provided.

"That's a pretty name for a pretty lady," Cal complimented her.

Jasmine smiled and toyed with the stem of her wine glass. "You think so?" she asked coyly.

"I know so."

"Mmmm, mmm," Heather piped up. "It's getting a little hot in here."

"Let me find out you over here trying to pick up our friend," LaToya commented.

"Is that so bad?" Cal challenged.

"Not at all. Hell, she needs some excitement."

"'Toya!" Jasmine objected, feeling slightly embarrassed.

"What?" LaToya shot back. "I'm just saying, Girl, live a little." She looked over at Cal and smiled wickedly. "Truth moment?"

Cal wasn't really in the mood for idle chitchat with a chick she wasn't trying to give the business to, but she knew that in order to get Jasmine where she wanted her, she'd have to play nice with her homies. Ultimately, they would be the ones to egg on the escapade that Cal had in mind. "Sure," Cal replied.

"So, we were over here checking you out, which you obviously realized and we were wondering if you're a man or a woman."

"Oh my God," Jasmine gasped, lowering her head, completely humiliated by the way the course of the conversation was going.

LaToya clearly had no filter. She wanted to know just how risqué the situation was about to turn out to be, because the crew had honed in on Cal only after noticing Jasmine's eyes constantly wandering over in the sexy being's direction. "I'm just saying…inquiring minds wanna know."

"Mmm-hmm and throbbing pussies too," Toya mumbled, while putting her glass to her lips and snickering.

Jasmine wanted to disappear into the crowd. Cal could tell that she was a private person and there her friends were, putting her intimate business out on Front Street. *Throbbing pussy, huh*, Cal thought, wondering just how wet Jasmine was as she sat across the table, fidgeting in her seat. The fantasy of her wetness, soaking straight through her panties caused Cal to lick her lips seductively, before taking a sip of her own glass of spirits. *Yep, I can hit that*, she assured herself.

"Well," Cal said mysteriously. "I like to think that I'm whatever I need to be whenever I need to be it."

Jasmine's eyes shined brightly at the sound of that.

"I guarantee you that there's nothing a male can do that I can't do better," Cal went on. "And frankly, being a man, a gentleman, is all about your character, swag, and behavior. Just because a dude's anatomically masculine, it doesn't make him a man."

"So, basically you're a stud," LaToya cut in, getting to the point. She eyed Cal's physique as she sat confidently leaned back in her chair, clad in ash gray slacks, a mint and gray stripped button down, and a Cartier watch gleaming from her wrist. LaToya leaned in slightly and caught a whiff of Cal's DOLCE & GABBANA Light Blue cologne for men. She smiled approvingly. "Well alright then." She looked over at Jasmine and winked. "Handle your business, girl. I ain't mad at you."

Cal wondered if LaToya swung that way, given the way the thin, scantily dressed woman was eyeing her openly. She seemed like the type that would be down for whatever and that simply wasn't Cal's flavor. She wanted someone who didn't give off the air that she'd give it to any and everybody. No, Cal liked a challenge. She liked to target the ones who were curious and shy, the ones who were typically reserved, the ones that were supposedly off limits, and the ones who didn't even realize that they were actually gay. Something about Cal's aura, charm, and sex appeal just seemed to pull the freak right out of the most unsuspecting women. Once her prey got a little taste of her skills, they were usually hooked and left wondering where this kind of great sex had been hiding all of their lives.

"So, what is it that you need?" Cal openly asked Jasmine in front of her girls, making the woman's mouth drop open, though no sound escaped.

It was a clear come on, which wasn't lost upon any of them. Jasmine's friends fell silent, waiting to see how their girl would respond to the flirtatious question. Though they all knew that Jasmine was crushing on the stranger from the bar, they also knew that she was the least likely of the four of them to succumb to a mere random night of passion. No, Jasmine was the type that needed love and the moment you showed her a little bit of attention; she mistook it for the next step to the altar. Still, the girl had needs and the crew was all for her getting the cobwebs knocked out of her coochie since she hadn't been laid for nearly half a year, following her split from her husband.

"You looking for the sensitivity and gentility of a female's touch and familiarity with your every curve and desire?" Cal asked. "Or the domineering aggressiveness and back blowing dick down of a man?" Cal's eyes never left Jasmine's as she dared the quiet woman to deny that she wanted to get down and dirty then and there. "Either way, I've got you covered. To me, it's all about what you want and need. I'd like to talk to you about that…your wants and needs."

"Well damn," Heather gasped, feeling the heat at the table for sure. "I damn near came on myself from that shit."

Cal chuckled and reached across the table to grab Jasmine's hand. "Seriously, I'd like to get to know you better outside of this place."

Cal gave a little head nod to indicate that they should escape their current surroundings. "You know, in private. How do you feel about that?" She always wanted to make sure that the woman felt as if she was making a conscious choice to give herself over to Cal and not feel as if the occurrence was forced, although she was firmly planting the promise of a mind-blowing experience to come in their lustful little minds.

"Um…we can go to my place," Jasmine offered, shocking herself and her friends. "It's not too far from here."

That was right up Cal's alley, because she was adamant about not taking anyone back to her disorganized home. "Sounds good. Let me just go clear my tab and I'll meet you at the exit."

Jasmine nodded her consent and smiled nervously.

Cal kissed the backside of her left hand and sat back to give the others a final glance. "It was nice meeting you, ladies. Continue to enjoy your evening."

"Alright now," Tonya replied, shimmying in her seat, already ready to cheer her girl on for stepping out of her box and going for what she wanted.

"Look, you be careful with our friend, you hear me?" LaToya warned. "We don't wanna have to come looking for you with your suave ass."

Cal gave her a cocky, yet sexy smile. "Trust me' she's in good hands with me." Rising from the chair, Cal nodded her head. "Alright then, I'll meet you at the exit," she reiterated. Before walking away.

She was feeling herself. *Well, shit only twenty-four hours*, she thought, laughing to herself while remembering the Mrs.' prediction about how long it would take her to find herself horny and getting into something. Just as she hopped back onto her surprisingly empty stool at the bar, her elbow collided with that of another patron's.

"Shit," the full-figured, yet well-put together woman let out in a low southern drawl.

Cal was mystified as she noticed the red wine that had spilled from the woman's glass onto the front of her peach tube top jumpsuit. Quickly, Cal grabbed some napkins and tapped on the bar for the mixologist's attention. "Can I get a glass of club soda like now?" she ordered in her deep voice, handing the woman the handful of napkins. "I'm so sorry. I didn't even see you right here."

"No, no," the woman retorted, dapping at the stain that was setting into the satin fabric of her attire. "It's my fault. Too busy staring at my text messages, instead of paying attention to where I was going."

The bartender hand Cal the club soda.

"Thanks," Cal stated in a preoccupied manner. "Uhhh…can I get my check?"

"Sure thing," the bartender replied, turning away.

Cal focused her attention on the woman. She grabbed a couple of more napkins, dipped them into the club soda, and held them up to the beautiful stranger. "Uh? May I?" Cal asked, nodding towards the stain that rested at the swell of the woman's bosom.

The beauty smiled curtly. "I think not," she said, taking the damp napkins from Cal's embrace. She worked at the stain, noticing it lift slightly, yet not enough to deem the outfit suitable to remain out for the rest of the night. However, it would have to suffice for one drink and to get her home. "Hmmm. That'll have to do," she said, sighing.

Cal's tab was placed before her and she pulled out her wallet. "Listen, ummm…" She looked at the woman, awaiting an offer of her name.

The lady continued to dap at her top. "Sahara," she said pointedly. "Sahara James."

"Sahara," Cal repeated, loving the way the name rolled off her tongue. "Listen, take down my number in that cute little phone and call or text me on Monday to let me know how much it'll cost to get it dry cleaned."

The woman tossed the soiled napkins onto the counter and looked up at Cal. For the first time, Cal noticed how beautiful the woman's almond shaped, hazel eyes were. They were a perfect fit for her round face, plush lips, and amazingly flawless caramel skin tone, freckles across her nose and all. Cal's heart skipped a beat as she took in the woman's complete appearance, which screamed of class and elegance. Sahara's hair was pulled up in a messy curly bun; her edges coiled slightly, giving a glimpse of her natural, curly texture. Her neck was hugged by a thin silver chain, from which a hung a heart shaped charm with a solitaire diamond in the middle sparkling brightly. From her ears hung diamond encrusted mid-sized hoops. She was stunning and Cal's hormones were beginning to rage at the mere sight of her.

"It's not that big of a deal," she stated.

"I insist," Cal replied, unable to move her eyes away from Sahara's pretty, pink, glossy lips. "It's the least I can do for ruining your evening."

"My evening's not ruined," Sahara said. "My outfit maybe, but certainly not my evening. The truth of the matter is that I should be home going over some papers for work, but I haven't been outside of my house in ages so I decided to venture out." She chuckled. "I should have followed my first mind."

Cal felt bad and guilty for causing the beauty to have a pout upon those gorgeously kissable lips. She reached into her wallet and threw a couple of bills on the bar to cover her tab and the tip. Giving the matter a second thought, she pulled out three more twenties, giving two to Sahara and waving the third at the bartender. "Give her another glass of whatever she had," Cal ordered.

"Um, make that Patrón on ice with a splash of pineapple juice," Sahara called out. "I mean, since you're buying, I might as well get a real drink."

Cal smile. "By all means."

Sahara held up the forty dollars that Cal had placed in her hand. "Look…ummm…what did you say your name was?"

"I didn't, but its Cal. Cal Montgomery." Cal never gave any woman her last name at first meeting unless it was clearly a professional or platonic situation. However, since Sahara had offered her full name and since her presence made Cal want to offer her more than just her last name and forty dollars, Cal didn't mind one bit.

"Cal Montgomery," Sahara repeated the name and her tone nearly made Cal pull her into an embrace. "I don't need your money. Don't worry about the stain. They're just clothes."

"I would feel remiss if you didn't allow me to make this blunder up to you."

Sahara smiled, slightly intrigued by Cal's persistence, chivalry, and vocabulary. "That's very big of you. We need more men like you who know how to treat a lady."

Cal's ego was instantly boosted by Sahara's statement. "So, what's the likelihood of us exchanging numbers, so I can show you a little more genuine attentiveness?"

"Hey, I'm ready."

Cal caught herself from swearing aloud as Jasmine's sweet voice spoke filled her ear. She felt the meek, yet eager woman's tiny hand upon her shoulder as Jasmine cozied up to her seductively and possessively. Cal looked over her shoulder just enough to catch the glimpse of anticipation that flickered across Jasmine's face. She looked like she was ready to be fucked. There was no denying the relationship between the two of them at that moment. Cal turned back to face Sahara, whose eyebrow was raised slightly.

Sahara gave another one of her curt smiles just as her replacement drink was placed in front of her. "I'd say it's very unlikely," she finally answered, peeking over at Jasmine. She was unfazed and not surprised that the debonair brotha had a hot young thing waiting to fuck her brains out. "Thanks for the drink." She placed the extra forty dollars down into the safety and security of her strapless bra. "And for covering the dry cleaning bill. Enjoy your night."

Just like that, Cal had gotten shut down. There was a first time for everything, but Cal wasn't used to this. She had half the mind to renege on Jasmine and spend the rest of the evening trying to win Sahara over. However, ass kissing wasn't Cal's style. She simply rose from the table, smiled at Sahara politely, and walked away with Jasmine on her arm as if nothing had happened. If Sahara couldn't see that she had a gold mine in front of her, then that was too bad. Something told Cal it was best just to walk away anyway, because from the vibe she got from Sahara, the beauty wasn't a likely candidate for a causal relationship. Besides, Jasmine was a sure thing and all Cal wanted right now was some wet pussy to dive off into in order to take the edge off—nothing more, nothing less.

***

Jasmine's back was against the floor to ceiling window of her upper level, luxury apartment in the downtown area. Her dress was on the floor just a few feet away, along with her bra. Cal had been surprised to see that she wasn't wearing any panties, but during the fifteen-minute drive to her place, Jasmine had admitted that she'd chucked them in the ladies' room of Sequoy before rushing up to Cal at the bar. Jasmine peered down at Cal in action with a look of anguish blended with ecstasy on her face. She hadn't been touched in months and now she was nearly ready to explode for the second time in the last ten minutes. The first time, she'd climaxed quickly the moment that Cal had reached between her legs to see if she'd been lying about being panty-less. Now, she was gripping the frame of the window in the dimness of her living room as Cal gave her the business.

Jasmine's bare ass was pressed against the thick, cool glass of the window. Neither of them was worried about neighbors seeing them from the building across from them. In fact, the thought of some voyeur watching them gave Cal a hormonal surge. The thrill of it was almost as tantalizing as the actual act of making a woman cream for her. Cal lived for this.

"Fuck!" Jasmine's demure voice squealed out. "Fuck, fuck, fuck!"

That was exactly what Cal planned to do to her. She continued to hold Jasmine's clit hostage, sucking on it as if trying to suck the last corner of juice through a straw. She was relentless and could feel the tension building within Jasmine as she approached her next orgasm. Her legs were becoming wobbly as she stood on her tiptoes, trying to keep her legs spread eagle for Cal to have maximized access to her most sensitive area. Cal's hands ran up and down Jasmine's legs, feeling her extremities trembling. She smiled to herself, knowing that she was performing up to par.

Not wanting the girl to collapse on her, Cal rose from her knees and picked Jasmine up. She weighed little to nothing. Jasmine immediately wrapped her legs around Cal's waist and her arms around Cal's neck, clinging to her temporary lover for dear life. Cal nuzzled her neck and began to suck mightily on her neck as she took swaggered steps over to the sofa. Gently, she laid Jasmine down on the sofa and began removing her collared shirt, pants, and then boxers. It wasn't something that she typically did, but the core of her own sex organ was in need of some stimulation tonight. Ever since leaving the lounge, she'd been on hot, bothered, and on edge. Sure, she'd get some satisfaction out of finger fucking Jasmine and eating her pussy until she cried for her to stop, but Cal needed more. If Jasmine was hot for a little lesbian play action, she was about to get more than she bargained for tonight.

Cal lowered her body comfortably against Jasmine's, tilting her head downward so that she could take in the woman's large, right nipple. Cal closed her eyes as she ran circles around the hardened bits, nibbling as if she were starving. Her hand slid between

Jasmine's legs and found the moisture that continuously seeped. She was ready. If her body's natural reaction wasn't enough of a sign, her moans were an even clearer indication.

"I want you," Jasmine whispered. "I want you so bad."

"How bad?" Cal challenged, still devouring her nipple while sticking a single finger into Jasmine's pussy.

It was as if she'd inserted a nine-inch dick or something. Jasmine's breathing elevated to heavy pants, her hips began to gyrate erratically, and she grabbed Cal's head while arching her back, as if forcing her boob further into Cal's mouth.

"So…so bad," Jasmine stuttered. "S-s-so…soooo bad, baby."

Her canal grew even slipperier and Cal knew that the woman wasn't lying. She was in heat. Cal removed her finger and heard Jasmine as she huffed disappointedly. Cal released the woman's nipple and lifted her torso. Their eyes met and Jasmine gave her a questioning look.

"You want it, huh?" Cal asked, not giving her a chance to answer. "I want it too." She repositioned her body, lifting Jasmine's leg so that they could fit together like interlocking Lego pieces. Cal grabbed Jasmine's left breast, giving it a mighty squeeze as she began to work her hips, rubbing her clit sporadically against Jasmine's.

For a moment Jasmine laid still, unsure of what to do or how she felt, but within seconds, the friction she was experiencing began to make her blood rush to her core and she was once again in a fit of heated passion. She gyrated her hips once more, matching the thrusts and hip rolls that Cal was giving. The blending of their wetness as they sloshed against one another came in second place in volume to their moans. Cal's eyes were closed as she squeezed Jasmine's breast with one hand and the back of the sofa with the other in order to steady herself. She thrust her pelvis as hard as she could, hunching against the softness underneath her. Her body felt the pleasure of the sensations that she and Jasmine were creating, but her mind was in a totally different place. In her mind, she was strapped up and giving it to the pretty woman at the bar as hard as she could. The more she fantasized about the plushness of Sahara's breasts and how she could only imagine the woman's pussy would feel, the harder she bucked against Jasmine's soaked pussy.

Jasmine didn't mind the aggression of Cal's movements. It only intensified the feeling she was having as she herself replayed in her mind repeatedly the mere fact that she was fucking another chick. The thought alone was enough to send her teetering close to the edge. Her fingernails dug into the flesh of Cal's thigh, as she tried with all the energy she could muster up to gyrate just as hard against Cal and force her orgasm to release itself.

Cal bit her bottom lip with her eyes still sealed tightly. The feel of Jasmine clawing at her aided her fantasy as she envisioned Sahara scratching up her back, while she fucked her missionary style. She imagined the woman's legs bent as far back to her own shoulders as they could go, giving Cal optimal access to dive as deeply as possible into the oceans of her love, damn near touching the bottom of her stomach with her thick, long piece. The dream was so vivid, so intense that before Cal knew it, she was practically digging her own short, yet groomed nails into the delicate skin of Jasmine's breast as her orgasm began to peak.

"Oh fuck!" Cal called out, her body spasmed as she continued to whirl her core in circles against Jasmine's throbbing clit. "Fuck yeah!" She was cumming hard with her eyes still closed, wishing, dreaming, imagining that it was Sahara underneath her, screaming out her praises.

"Oooh, baby, I'm cumming!" Jasmine announced; her movements ceasing as her orgasm pushed her into a cationic state. "Fuckkkkk!" She rode the wave of pleasure and finally began to shudder up under the weight of Cal's body as her climax simmered down. "Yesss," she purred, her body going limp. "Mmmm."

Several jolts shot through Cal's body as she recovered from her own moment of pleasure. Coming to her senses, she opened her eyes and realized that she wasn't with Sahara and she wasn't at home. It was time to make her getaway. She didn't do sleepovers and she wasn't exactly in the mood for round two. She'd done exactly what she'd set out to do for the night—gotten a little action to take the edge off. Nevertheless, even beyond that, she'd walked away with something a little more. The thought of Sahara was already plaguing her. The whole time she'd been fucking Jasmine, Sahara's body was the one she'd been yearning to explore.

Remembering the way the exquisite woman had turned her down made Cal feel some kind of way. She had to admit to herself that as much as she wanted to play it cool, she really was fazed by the woman's aloofness and disinterest. That wasn't the kind of reception that Cal was used to. *If it hadn't been for Jasmine I would've pulled her,* Cal reasoned with herself as she untangled her body from Jasmine's and reached for her clothes. She couldn't blame Sahara for giving her the cold shoulder; after all she did have another woman dangling from her arm. That made for an awkward situation on everyone's behalf.

"You don't have to go," Jasmine said sheepishly as she turned over on her side and watched Cal get dressed.

"I'm afraid that I do, love," Cal told her in her same smooth, charismatic tone.

"Really...I don't mind. I'll even make you breakfast in the morning." Jasmine's voice was soft and low, but her desperation was loud and clear.

Cal appreciated the good time, but it was best that she let Jasmine know then and there that developing any kind of further expectations was not a good look. "I don't do breakfast," Cal said blankly, zipping up her pants and sliding her feet back into her Bed Stu oxfords. She gave Jasmine a smile of pity and kissed the woman on her forehead. "I enjoyed you."

Jasmine looked up into her eyes. "Call me tomorrow," she said weakly. "Maybe we can do dinner some night this week or something."

Call figured that the 'or something' was an invitation to fuck again. She wasn't opposed to the idea, but she also didn't want to make any promises. She could tell by the way Jasmine spoke that there was a possibility that the woman might become clingy and Cal didn't have time for those kind of issues so soon into moving to this new city. Reluctantly, she scribbled her number down on an envelope resting on Jasmine's coffee table and gave her the okay to give her a call within the next few days. Before Jasmine could make any other requests or get up the nerve to make an advance by way of initiating another round, Cal made a dash for the door.

During the drive home, all Cal could think about was Sahara. Cal wasn't big on kissing, but she desperately wanted to suck on the woman's sexy, full lips. Everything about her had exuded incredible sex appeal, even the cool manner in which she had denied Cal. Cal smiled. There was nothing more alluring, nothing more thrilling than a good ole' challenge. That's how she viewed her now and the one thing that Cal never did was back away from a challenge. She hadn't given her a phone number, but at least Cal had her full name to work with. Despite all of the unpacking, she had to do and jumping into her new position at Raymond James Incorporated, Cal knew she couldn't rest until she found the woman that had her hormones soaring, even after letting out a powerful nut. *I'm coming to get you, Sahara*, Cal thought, so sure that the woman would be yet another notch on her bedpost. *You have no idea what's in store for you.*

***

Persistence was one of Cal's strong suits. Whenever faced with a challenge, she never backed down, yet simply found creative ways around whatever hurdles were placed in front of her. In this instance the challenge was finding Sahara James; Cal had no idea where the woman worked or what she did for a living. She didn't even know what area of town she lived in. After working long tedious hours at the investment firm, trying to learn the ropes, Cal went straight home every day for a week, and toyed with various ideas and ploys to try to locate the stunning woman.

Never had she been pressed over some pussy like this, and as much as Cal hated to admit it, there was obviously something more to this chick then just bedding her. With the women that were already eyeing her openly and discreetly around corners at the job, as well as the women she knew she could pull over at Sequoy, Cal could have been in a pussy paradise. However, what fun was the conquest if no challenge was involved? By the following Saturday after their initial meeting, Cal was starting to grow just a little discouraged. She'd done internet searches yielding nothing and was beginning to wonder if perhaps the woman was only a figment of her imagination.

Deciding to go back to the roots of their encounter, Cal returned to Sequoy on Saturday evening, hoping that grabbing a drink on Jazz night was a routine for Sahara. Unfortunately, after an hour and a half of sitting idle and two Long Island iced teas later, Cal remembered Sahara stating that she hadn't been out in a while. Clearly, it wasn't her usual thing and Cal was almost certain that seeing her that night wasn't going to happen.

Cal's cell phone rang. She pulled it out and checked the number on the screen. Rolling her eyes, she sent the call to voicemail and signaled for the bartender. It wasn't anybody but Jasmine calling for the third time that day, and the twenty-third time that week. The first time Jasmine had called the Monday after their one-night stand, Cal politely explained to her that things were hectic at work, being that it was her first week and that she'd get up with her once things settled down. Apparently, Jasmine had grown impatient within the next twenty-four hours after that, because she constantly made it a point to call leaving messages inquiring about Cal's day, inviting her over for dinner, or attempting to make weekend plans to celebrate the end of Cal's first week at work. She was trying to play the girlfriend role, which only turned Cal off.

"Another?" the bartender asked.

Cal shook her head and studied the man's face. *It's the same dude*, she thought. "Say, you wouldn't happen to remember me, would you?"

The bartender smiled. "Sly guy from last weekend enthralled by a table full of honeys. Yeah, I remember."

Cal perked up. "You remember the chick I was talking to?"

The bartender looked up at the ceiling. "Uhhhh…the quiet, kinda clingy chick with the short dress? Yeah." The bartender gave Cal a sly smile. "How'd that go? That was almost a record for the quickest pick up and go I've seen since working here."

The macho part of Cal's ego took the statement as a compliment and she couldn't help but stroke her chin, lower her head a little, and chuckle. "Nah, nah. Not the one I left with. The woman that was sitting here at the bar with me. The one that spilled the drink…well, I knocked over her drink…"

"Oh yeah!" A light bulb finally clicked in the guy's mind. "Yeah, the snippy chick with the nice boobs."

Cal shot the bartender a dirty look.

The man threw his hands in the air. "Hey, I couldn't help but notice. Don't sweat it though, 'cause it's not my cup of tea."

Cal wasn't interested in hearing the man's opinion of Sahara. "She a regular here?"

The bartender chuckled as he quickly mixed drinks for a couple waiting at the other end of the bar. "Nah. Use to come through a while back, but last week was first time in a long time."

"What you know about her? She work or live near here?"

"Save yourself the trouble. I think you're barking up the wrong tree."

Cal was getting agitated. "Can you help me or not?"

The bartender shrugged. "Suit yourself. Gimme a sec." He hurried off to give the other patrons their drinks and to fill two more orders before disappearing from the bar for a moment. Seconds later, he returned and handed Cal a slip of paper. "The lounge's owner used to do business with your friend. I copied down this phone number from his Rolodex. Maybe it's still a working number."

Cal looked at the torn piece of paper as if it was a winning lottery ticket. This was a start. "Thanks, man," she said, tossing a twenty onto the counter and getting up to leave.

"You must be into all kinds of things," the bartender said, giving Cal the once over as if he was trying to figure her out.

"Excuse me?"

"I mean, what do you identify yourself as? Not to be all up in your business, but I thought y'all studs liked straight fems and that—"

Cal found it a little abrasive the way Floridians were questioning her sexuality so much during the short amount of time that she'd been living there. She knew that women and even men often looked at her with raised eyebrows, wondering what her story really was, but never had she encountered people that just blatantly grilled her about her sexuality.

"Not that I owe you an explanation," she started, cutting the overly comfortable bartender off. "But I'm a dom, not a stud."

"The fuck?"

Cal shook her head, not in the mood to school the brother on the ins and outs of lesbianism. "Yeah, you wouldn't get it."

"Well, whatever you call ya'self, I pegged you for a straight pussy chaser. Man, the way you pulled ole' girl the other night. But now, I mean…hey, whatever makes you happy. Get it how you live." The bartender snatched up the cash, threw his head back in a dismissive gesture, and scurried off to cozy up to the others huddled up at the bar.

Cal didn't know what the man was going on and on about but frankly, she didn't care. She looked at the paper in her hand and smiled on her way out of the door. She'd come in search of a lead for Sahara and now she had one. Let the games begin.

***

Cal sat back in her chair in the dimly lit restaurant, nursing a glass of Merlot. She'd taken a risk and if her intuition was right, it was about to pay off any minute now. Across from her, sat another glass of wine though untouched; her guest had yet to arrive. She'd taken the liberty of ordering ahead—a starter of fire-grilled flatbread with a roasted-red pepper sauce, and two entrees of caramelized scallops with gulf shrimp, over in-house made linguine and fire-grilled rack of lamb. It was the finest and damn near the most expensive cuisine that Sage Restaurant had to offer. Cal was pulling out all of the stops tonight. This wasn't her usual M.O., but she was dealing with a different type of woman and therefore, something different had to be done to get the ace in the hole.

Cal's phone rang. Nervously, she pulled it out, wondering if it was bad news or good news. Her brow knitted at the sight of the name displayed. I don't have time for this shit, she thought. Her eyes glanced up towards the entrance, but there was still no sight of her guest. Quickly, she answered the call, her tone laced with annoyance. "Hello?"

"Oh, hi. Finally, I got you," Jasmine gushed. "I've been trying to get a hold of you for over a week. You must've been very busy."

Busy not wanting to be bothered with you, Cal thought. "Yeah and I'm kind of in the middle of something now," she said, trying to keep her cool and not completely going off. She didn't know what the future held regarding her use for Jasmine. If the chick would just chill the hell out and play her position, then they'd all be better off.

"Do you think you'll be done soon?" Jasmine asked; hope lingering in her question. "I was hoping that we could recreate the night we spent together. I even cooked."

"You what?"

"I cooked. I made dinner, hoping you'd be free."

"Why would you do that?"

"Because I wanted to do something nice for you…maybe spend a little one on one time with you. Don't you miss me?"

Is she nuts? Cal thought. She opened her mouth to tell Jasmine that she'd lost it, but her eyes ventured upward and caught a glimpse of the firmest leg peeking out of the split of a black, body-hugging wrap dress that was screaming to be touched. She swallowed hard as the sleek body strutted over to her candlelit table.

"Look, you shouldn't have put yourself out like that," Cal said into the phone in a rushed manner. "I'm not gonna be able to make that. Call ya' girls over or something."

"But, do you think that you can make it when you're done? I really wanted to see you."

"Yeah, no. That's not gonna pan out either. Tell you what, I'll call you next week and we'll iron out the details." Cal quickly rose to her feet and pressed the END button on her cell before tossing it onto the table. "Glad you could make it," she said as her guest reached the table.

Sahara placed her hand on her right hip as she sat her silver clutch bag on the table. "You sure know how to make an impression, don't you?"

Cal smiled. "I aim to please."

"Do you?"

Cal's cell began to hum once more. She quickly snatched it up and sent the call to voicemail.

"Apparently, your aim is a little all over the place," Sahara commented, looking at the phone in Cal's hand.

Cal brushed it off and laid the phone face down on the table. "That's just business. Nothing that can't wait until later. I have something much more important going on here now. Please, have a seat," Cal urged, stepping around to pull Sahara's chair out.

She allowed Cal to seat her and watched intently as Cal re-occupied the seat across from her. "You're quite a charming fellow," Sahara stated. "But I suppose you know that already."

"Never hurts to hear it again."

"I bet it doesn't. Let's cut to the chase, shall we? Why am I here?"

"I presume it's because you were just as intrigued as I was by our first meeting, and you just had to indulge in a second round of clever repartee."

Sahara smirked, picked up her wine glass, and took a dainty sip. Her eyebrows rose approvingly. "Nice choice."

"Only the best for the most exquisite woman I've ever met."

"Is that your thing? Complimenting and charming girls right out of their panties?"

"It's in my nature to be kind and amiable. Now, if it lands me in a favorable situation, then so be it."

"That's the bottom line, isn't it? To land yourself in this infamous favorable situation?"

"It's a win-win for everyone."

"You're very sure of yourself, aren't you? So sure you're gonna end up in a favorable situation just because you shelled out a couple of hundreds for dinner?"

Cal didn't answer. Sahara's tone was indicative of an attitude that Cal hadn't anticipated.

"You planned this whole thing out to a T, huh? Probably going by the same playbook, you usually rely on with your harem. But you miscalculated some things."

"Did I?" Cal shot back, feeling a little defeated, but daring not to let Sahara get the better of her yet again.

"Mmmm-hmm, I'm not a 'girl' by any means."

Cal smiled, feeling that maybe she'd miscalculated her date's tone and brashness. "Of course not. I see nothing but a complete, stunning, mature woman in front of me. A woman I'd like to get to know better."

Sahara took another sip of her wine and shook her head. "You have no idea." She smiled. "And I don't wear panties either…I prefer thongs."

Cal licked her lips seductively and forced herself not to make a crude comment in return, although she was dying to slip her hand inside of the split of Sahara's dress.

The waiter brought out their appetizer and as Cal placed modest portions on the appetizer plates for each of them, Sahara surveyed her.

"You never answered me," she said.

Cal cocked her head to the side. "What's that?"

"Why am I here, Cal? Why did you go through the trouble of finding me and inviting me here? You've proven yourself to be quite the ladies' man. I'm sure you have plenty of women lining up at your door to share your bed. I'm no hussy; I'm no one-night stand… Judging by the harlot that was clinging to you pathetically when last we met; I'm certainly not your type."

Cal savored the flavor of the flatbread appetizer and considered the statement. It dawned on her that Sahara really thought she was a man. Sitting up just a tad straighter in her chair, Cal could almost feel the stroke to her ego. Not only that, but the woman viewed her as a 'ladies' man'. However, judging by the air of disgrace and the sour look upon her lips as she expelled her final words, Cal knew that this wasn't a good thing. *She's playing with me*, Cal thought. She's dangling the bait and putting a fuckin' wired fence around it.

"You're like a succulent entrée. A delicacy," Cal stated.

Sahara leaned forward with her elbows on the table and her hands wrapped around her wine glass, her rather large knuckles contrasting with her feminine French tips. "That's an interesting simile," she replied.

"Let me explain."

"Please do."

"You're rare and exclusive. Not everyone can afford you."

"Hmmm; I'm not for sale."

"I don't mean monetarily. I mean, not everyone has what it takes to measure up to your standards. I can see that you're a woman of great quality and morale. Not everyone can stimulate your mind and maybe even your body. It takes a special kind of man." Cal said the last word softly, testing the waters. She looked in Sahara's eyes, checking for any indication that the woman felt she was pushing it. Seeing nothing to defy her claim to masculinity, Cal simply took another bite of the flatbread and shook her head. "The others, the harem you mentioned…merely appetizers…something to try out until I find the main dish that suits my taste."

Sahara smiled flirtatiously. "And he's deep," she joked, taking a bite of the flatbread Cal had plated for her. "Here I thought this was just your clever way of saying you wanted to eat me."

You have no idea, Cal thought. It was true, she had gone through extreme measures to locate and woo Sahara, beginning with getting the phone number from the bartender. Returning home that evening, Cal had done a reverse search for Sahara online, using the number scribbled on the paper. The number turned out to be a residential landline registered to a S. Jones. Provided also was the home address for S. Jones, much to Cal's surprise. In this day and age, if anyone had a home phone, they certainly didn't have it publicly listed with their address attached. Thinking that it was purely fate, Cal tapped into her creative mindset and surfed the web, until she found a wine basket delivery company that provided a decadent Cristal and Godiva Chocolates arrangement. It was an expensive gesture and sent directly to Sahara's doorstep, with a note inviting her to dinner at Sage. Cal knew she was a woman of fine taste and would appreciate the effort and thought put into the invitation. She never doubted for a second that the curly-haired goddess would show up, either because she was impressed or intrigued.

"So what now?" Sahara asked.

The waiter approached, carrying a serving platter upon which rested their pre-ordered entrees. Sahara smiled approvingly as the plate of seafood and pasta was placed before her.

"Look at you," she commented; batting her thick lashes at Cal. "Your mother certainly raised a thoughtful gentleman."

"Indeed," Cal stated, failing to take yet another opportunity to set the record straight. "But to answer your question, now we enjoy the rest of our evening and get to know one another."

Cal's phone began to ring, interrupting her smooth response.

"You sure your little appetizers are going to let you do that?" Sahara jabbed, smirking at the phone as it continued to ring while lying face down.

"This," Cal said, picking up the phone and rejecting the call without looking at the screen. "This is unimportant. All that matters to me right now is you."

"Is that so?"

"Quite. In fact…" Cal placed her phone on silent and tucked it into her pocket. There would be no further interruptions of the night.

"All that matters is you," Cal repeated pointedly. "How's the shrimp?"

***

Dinner went well and Cal found herself more amazed with Sahara than she'd been at the bar. She'd come to find out that they actually had a lot in common, such as their degrees in business finance and their career paths. Although Sahara didn't want to speak much about work, she did mention that she was part owner of a modest financial advisory business. They pretty much had similar work histories, as far as Cal could tell. During the course of dinner and drinks after, they shared tidbits about general interests, memories from college, and aspirations for the future. It was the most intellectual and stimulating conversation that Cal had ever had with a woman. In the past, dinner was a no go and long meaningful talks were even more so out of the question. You did those kinds of things with someone you wanted to settle down with, not someone you just wanted to get up with for the night.

Sahara was different. Funny feelings stirred within Cal and she wasn't quite sure how to handle it. Physically, she wanted to undress Sahara and place those luscious pounds of hers into her mouth, but she didn't want to rush her and risk turning her off. No, she needed to see Sahara again, and then again. Cal was beginning to crave the woman, both sexually and mentally. She honestly enjoyed the mere presence of her. For that reason, Cal slyly invited Sahara back to her place. She'd busted her ass all week to get it presentable, just in case she was able to score enough points to get the beauty in her personal space. Much to Cal's surprise, Sahara agreed.

They took separate cars, with Sahara trailing Cal home. In her pocket, Cal's phone continued to ring, but she'd long since forgotten about even checking her messages. She was a ball of nerves. *I need to tell her,* she thought, wondering how the topic would blow over. It was clear that Sahara was convinced that Cal was a man. She'd had ample opportunity to lay her cards on the table and be upfront, but Cal liked the idea of Sahara viewing her as a real dude. She tried to use context clues from their conversations to see if the woman was actually heterosexual, or if she was a lesbian who simply believed in making a stud feel manly. However, by the time they'd hopped into their rides, Cal was still unsure. Nothing indicated that Sahara was a lesbian and she feared that telling her the truth at this point would not only send her into a whirlwind, but would also ruin any chances of a relationship sparking.

A relationship, Cal thought, shaking her head. Never once in her adult life had she ever truly considered having one of those. There must be something special about her. Cal slapped the steering wheel. "Fuck!" she hissed. Fate was cruel; why was it that the one time she was genuinely interested in a woman, there was a strong possibility that the woman wasn't even gay? She'd seen movies like this, where women posed as men and vice versa, falling in love with heterosexuals and ended up getting the shit beat out of them or worse. Cal wasn't afraid that Sahara would hurt her. Quite the contrary, she was more afraid that her confession would end up hurting Sahara.

"Nice house," Sahara commented, after parking on the street in front of Cal's house, and then walking up the driveway to meet her at the front door.

"It's a start," Cal replied, fumbling to unlock the door.

Sahara reached out and touched Cal's hand as it lingered at the doorknob. Cal's heart began to race and she wondered if Sahara could hear it practically trying to jump out of her chest. She turned slightly to look into Sahara's eyes under the glimmer of light coming from the porch lamp. She recognized the hint of lust and wondered if it was sincere or alcohol induced. Either way, it ignited the fire within her that she was already trying to keep contained.

"I want you to know that I don't make it a habit to go home with men I barcly know," Sahara said lowly, in her throaty drawl.

"I never assumed that for a second," Cal stated.

Sahara stepped closer, bridging the small gap between them and leaning forward with her full breasts pressed against Cal's side. Cal swallowed hard and fought the urge to fully turn to her and embrace her the way she'd dreamed of since their first meeting. She didn't want Sahara catching on to the truth before she was about to give it to her vocally.

Sahara reached up and cupped the side of Cal's face, moving hers in closer for a kiss that was inevitable. Cal savored the flavor of her hot and moist mouth, relishing in the plushness of her soft, full lips. Still not completely facing the beauty, Cal left the key sticking in the door and reached down to gently graze Sahara's round ass. Once she realized that there was no opposition, Cal then gave Sahara's left cheek a gentle squeeze. Her guttural moan drove Cal insane and it took everything within her, not to rip off her dress and begin exploring her body right there on the front porch.

Her breathing slightly irregular, Sahara withdrew from their kiss and once again looked into Cal's eyes. "We should go in," she said, smiling at Cal suggestively.

Cal simply nodded, tried to regain composure, and finally opened the door. Turning on a table lamp in the living room, Cal exhaled before turning to face Sahara. "Would you care for a glass of wine? We can sit in here and uh…have a little talk." *Yeah, I need to tell you the real and see if you're still down to let me cop a feel and then some*, she thought.

Sahara nodded, stepping close to Cal and toying with the collar of her shirt. "Wine sounds nice. And conversation…conversation's good. Maybe a little body language?" she asked, rather than stated.

"Uhhh, you know you're starting to flip a switch that may not easily turn itself off," Cal warned, reaching up to touch her fingertips against Sahara's lips as she lightly bit her own. "Damn you're sexy," she crooned, unable to stop the truthful compliment from leaving her lips.

"You're not so bad yourself, sir."

Damn it, Cal thought, remembering what needed to be done. "I'm gonna go get that wine. Make yourself at home."

"Can I use your restroom?"

"Sure, down the hall…second door on the right."

"Thank you." Sahara pressed a soft kiss along Cal's jawline and then turned to walk up the hall. "I won't be long."

Cal watched her alluring gait as she made her way to the bathroom. *There's no way I can fuck this up*, she told herself. Her hormones would get the best of her if she handled this situation incorrectly and managed to let Sahara slip through her fingers. Cal busied about in the kitchen, uncorking the wine and rinsing out wine glasses. She was oblivious to the multitude of calls coming to her phone. As she returned to the living room with a tray consisting of Riesling, two wine glasses, and a plate of Colby-Jack cheese with white grapes, the doorbell sounded.

"What the hell?" Cal muttered, looking at the time on the clock of the digital receiver.

It was nearly eleven o'clock. Since living there, Cal hadn't made any friends and certainly hadn't invited any appetizers over to please her. In fact, the only person she'd even messed around with or spoken to outside of work was Jasmine. *Damn it*, Cal thought, wondering if somehow the quiet vixen was a lot craftier than she'd given her credit for. *How the hell did she find out where I live?* She asked herself, hurrying over to the door. She had to get rid of her and quick. Cal threw a quick glance over her shoulder to ascertain that Sahara hadn't returned from the bathroom. She prayed that the woman was unable to hear the continued, yet low ringing of the doorbell from her location within the house. It wouldn't do her any good for Sahara to find another woman, especially the woman she'd expressed such disdain for, standing there at her door in the middle of the night.

Cal huffed and threw open the door in a panicked rage. She was done with Jasmine's stalkerish ass. It was bad enough that the thirsty chick was blowing her up and talking to her, as if they were in some relationship Cal certainly hadn't signed up for, but now the broad had the audacity to show up at her home uninvited and unannounced. "What the fuck is your problem?" Cal snapped, ready to hand Jasmine back her feelings before slamming the door shut in her face and carrying on with her evening.

"Well hello to you too."

"W-w-what the hell?" Cal was astonished. All she could process was the slender body of the well-put together woman standing before her with her black, double-breasted trench coat held open to reveal perfectly sculpted bare breasts and a welcoming pussy, whose covering was trimmed to a mere landing strip. Cal didn't know whether to salivate and demolish the treat before her or shut the door and pretend as if she hadn't seen a thing. However, she couldn't do either because the face of the person that this amazing body belonged to stunned her. Cal's mouth hung open and her eyes were wide with surprise.

"Looks like you're happy to see me," the Mrs. said, dropping the flaps of her coat and stepping past Cal to enter the foyer. "Surely you aren't going to leave me standing all exposed out in the crisp night air are you?" She turned and headed for the living room, stopping to see the refreshments on the table. "And here I thought that you hadn't gotten any of my messages, since you failed to answer or return any of my calls.

"Fuck!" Cal said, stepping away from the open door as she pulled her silenced cell phone out of her pocket; she discovered seven missed calls, six of which were all from the Mrs.' number. *Fuck my life! This can't be happening!* "H-h-how did you find me?"

The Mrs. dropped her Coach bag to the floor and slipped out of her coat, leaving it lying beside the purse, before walking up to Cal and throwing her arms around her lover's neck. "I have my ways. Did you think that I was going to leave you out here alone so that you could go get into trouble with some other chica? Not a chance." The Mrs. kissed Cal seductively on the neck, while pressing her body up against Cal's. "You know I can't go too long without having you, daddy."

Cal could feel the beads of nervous sweat forming along her temples as she grabbed the Mrs. by the waist and tried with all of her might to peel the woman off her. "We can't," she muttered as the Mrs.' mouth crushed against hers. "Elise," Cal called her by her given name, which she rarely ever did. "Elise, come on. P-p-put your coat…put your coat back on."

"Oh no, no, no," the Mrs. purred, grabbing Cal's hand and shoving it between her silky smooth thighs. "You feel that?"

Did she? Cal was about to die from the overflow of sexual tension that was building inside of her.

"I've been waiting all this time, took that long drive, just to feel these fingers deep inside of me…just to throw you down on your couch and ride your face." The Mrs. swiveled her hips a little, being sure to rub her juices all over Cal's palm. "You feel that hotness? That wetness?" She licked the ridges of Cal's left ear and spoke seductively. "You hear your heart thudding? That's the makings of undeniable lust." She pulled away and backed herself onto the couch, enticingly spreading her legs and welcoming Cal to the land of forbidden pleasure. "Now come take this pussy and claim what's yours."

All common sense scurried out the open door as Cal found herself crossing the floor, dropping to her knees, and devouring the tight, dripping wet pussy that awaited her. The unbridled passion and insane chemistry between the two of them had never been easy to ignore. One whiff of the Mrs.' sweetness and Cal was revved up and ready to go. Once the rush was over, they parted ways amicably until the next time. Cal had been certain that their unlikely liaison was over and done with the moment she'd crossed state lines, but the fact that the Mrs. traveled just to offer herself over to her made Cal go wild.

The Mrs. stroked the waves of Cal's head and moaned loudly, feeling the pleasure that only Cal's experienced tongue could bring her. She was craving more. She needed more. "Fuck me, daddy," she begged as she pushed Cal's face deeper into her pussy. "Eat it real good and then fuck me like the bad girl I am."

With her left hand, she squeezed her left breast and grinded her hips to meet every thrust of Cal's tongue. As she enjoyed the thrill of their reunion, the Mrs.' eyes set upon the figure of an unsuspected being whose arms were crossed, lips were pressed, and body was striking a pose, as if she was down to stand and watch until the couple was finished. Having an audience shocked the Mrs. at first but then, realizing that the woman wasn't going to announce her presence, she became oddly turned on. *Let her watch*, she thought. *Let her watch and kick herself knowing that tonight, she won't be receiving any of this dick down that's coming my way.*

"Oooh, shit," the Mrs. moaned loudly, putting on a show for Cal's guest. "You know just how I like it, daddy. That's it."

Cal's head bobbed up and down as she worked to suck every ounce of moisture and flavor from the Mrs.' womanhood. She slid two fingers inside of her, rough fucking her without abandon. The Mrs. loved every second of it as she spread her legs wider and humped her lover's face.

"That's it, that's it, baby. Eat your pussy, daddy. Mmmmm." Her eyes were closed now as she felt her orgasm slowly approaching.

Cal was into it; completely lost in the euphoric moment. Her own hips gyrated in her slacks as she felt the tension between her legs. Sex with the Mrs. was never dull or disappointing. Already on the edge of sexual explosion for the better part of the night, this was all that Cal needed to send her body crashing, right into the throes of a powerful orgasm. Her own groans grew louder though muffled as she felt the evidence of the Mrs. cumming hard around her fingers.

"Fuck! Ooohhhh. Suck it up, suck it up, baby," the Mrs. called out passionately. "Suck it all up."

Clap! Clap! Clap!

The round of applause resounding behind Cal brought her back to reality. She quickly pulled her head out of the Mrs.' lap and looked up into her eyes frightfully. The look she received in return let her know that the Mrs. had been well aware that they weren't alone. With a sense of impending doom coming over her, Cal rose from the floor and turned around to face the glare of repulsion from Sahara. No words she could say at this point would turn any of this around.

"I'll give him this," Sahara said, looking past Cal and speaking to the Mrs., who was smirking and still naked. "He's pretty convincing and cunning as hell, though trifling. Had me up here thinking that he was about something with the expensive gifts, dinner…wining and dining…And I was this close," she said, holding up her thumb and index finger slightly touching, "to giving him world class sex tonight." She focused her attention on Cal's dumbfounded expression. "What were you going to do, Cal? Have me in the bedroom, your tramp out here on the sofa, and then run back and forth between us all night?"

"I've got your tramp," the Mrs. piped up, sitting upright on the sofa.

"Elise, please," Cal begged her to shut up.

"Please what? This bougie bitch comes in interfering on my time, calling me out of my name and you want me to be quiet?" The Mrs. hopped up from the sofa, walked to the middle of the floor just before Sahara, and snatched her coat off the floor. She shot the woman a dirty look as she slipped into the overcoat. Then, she turned to glare at Cal. "Nice to see where your loyalties lie."

Was she kidding? Was she too under the impression that they were in some kind of tawdry relationship as well? Cal ran her hand over her face and let out a heavy sigh. The women in her life were starting to drive her nuts.

"Isn't it obvious?" Sahara retorted. "His loyalty obviously lies in his dick."

Cal's eyes met the Mrs.' and she could tell that her former boss's wife caught on to her little secret immediately. The shit was about to hit the fan. There was absolutely nothing one could do when a woman scorned was in action, and judging by the Mrs.' pissed off expression and the smirk forming upon her lips, Cal knew that she was about to be royally fucked and not in a good way.

"His dick huh?" the Mrs. teased.

"But I'm sure you know all about that with the way he obviously flings it everywhere." Sahara eyed the woman before her. Her nose turned up at the cheap way that the chick presented herself. Showing up at man's house stark naked was common, just like the tramp she was looking at. Sahara wasn't the least bit impressed with the woman's boob job, the diamonds she flaunted, or the hair sewn down to her ass. Hell, she had her own infusions and implants that were of higher quality, and presented in a much more lady-like fashion if you asked her. "You can have him, honey," Sahara advised. "Dogs deserve fleas." She shot Cal a look and turned to leave.

"Sahara, wait!" Cal finally managed to blurt out, moving to follow her to the open door.

"Save it," Sahara snapped.

"This *he* you keep referring to," the Mrs. said, bringing up the rear. "I'm puzzled as to what you're talking about."

Sahara didn't reply as she approached the threshold of Cal's front door.

Cal turned sharply and gave the Mrs. the evil eye, as she held her hand up warningly.

The Mrs. ignored her. "Because the only dick Cal knows anything about is the silicone kind," she said.

Sahara stopped dead in her tracks. A lull fell over the room as both Cal and the Mrs. stared at the woman's back, watching from behind as she processed the statement she'd just heard. Cal exhaled yet again, placed her hands on her hips, and hung her head while fighting the urge to turn around and choke the shit out of the Mrs. She'd always known that somehow the woman would cause her problems. She just didn't realize that the problems would occur in Tallahassee when she'd been so sure that it was a done deal.

Sahara slowly turned around and peered at the Mrs. with death in her eyes. She didn't dare make eye contact with Cal. "What did you say?" she asked pointedly in a determined and demanding tone.

The Mrs. crossed her arms and returned a nasty look of her own. "Bitch, you heard me. The he you're referring to is really a she."

Cal took a step forward. "I wanted to tell you," she struggled to get out. "I was going to tell you…tonight…when you came out of the bathroom. I…I thought…I thought you knew…that night…at the bar. I didn't realize that you truly thought otherwise until tonight…at dinner…And then I planned to tell you when we got here. I swear; I wasn't trying to deceive you." Cal was tripping over her own words, but it felt as if nothing she said was good enough to fix the shattered fragments of the connection they'd started to create.

"So it's true?" Sahara asked, taking a hard look at Cal's perfectly groomed body, wondering and amazed at how well she'd been fooled. Realization hit her like a waterfall methodically pouring down on her. She shuddered from the impact of the truth and the wheels inside of her brain began to turn as she connected the dots.

"It doesn't change how I feel about you or the connection we had," Cal answered, without giving a solid yes. "I mean, I didn't trick you into coming here. You came because you were feeling me. I'm the same me," she said. "Just without the natural dick you were looking for."

"Ain't that some shit," Sahara let out in a tone deeper than her normal octave.

Cal was afraid that she was about to cry. She opened her mouth to say something but she couldn't form any words that she felt wouldn't place her in an even more damning situation. Shit was bad; very bad.

"Surprise, bitch," the Mrs. spoke up, for she certainly wasn't as speechless as the other two. "You're diking now, boo."

Cal had just about had enough of her lover's snide remarks. If it weren't for her pop-up act, none of this would be happening in the first place. She wished that the Mrs. would just zip it and make her grand exit already so that she could try to salvage whatever chance she had left to get Sahara to give her a chance.

"Am I?" Sahara shot back.

The question stunned Cal, although she didn't quite catch the truth of her meaning. To her, she'd just shaken hands with defeat. Sahara was putting an end to them before they could even truly begin. "Come on," Cal pleaded. "Can we at least talk about this? I know I'm not exactly what you thought I was, but that's what the whole getting to know someone process is all about."

"Aside from the fact that you just screwed some random woman while still on a date with me, I'd say that you're pretty much screwed, because I'm not exactly what you must have thought I was either."

Cal was confused. "You know, you keep trying to convince me that you're not what I want, but I'm telling you, Sahara, tonight…for the first time ever…I thought about what it would be like to be in an actual relationship…with you."

"What the hell?" the Mrs. spat out. "Are you kidding me right now?"

Cal turned and pointed her finger in the woman's face. "Shut the fuck up! You've done enough. Whatever you thought you were going to accomplish by coming here, or even by telling my business, you can cancel it. We fuck from time to time…well, we used to. That shit is over and dead and frankly, you're not welcomed at my home. Go back to Sidney and play the good little plastic socialite wife that you always dreamed of being and leave me the fuck alone."

"You trifling son of a bitch!" the Mrs. screamed. "As much pussy as I've given you! I could have had your ass fired from B.I.G. ages ago. I could have told my husband everything, and then where would your tired ass be?"

"I'm sorry, what did you say your name was again?" Sahara asked the Mrs., her brain still working to put two and two together.

"Elise Gardner if you must know."

"Sidney," Sahara stated, the light bulb clicking on in her head. "Sidney Garner of Builder Investment Group in Atlanta?"

The Mrs.' brow rose. "What? Now you're going to tell me that *you* fucked my husband?"

"Sidney and I went to business school together. We uhhh…lobby for some of the same companies as clients. I'm with Raymond James, Inc. I'm part owner."

"I know of the owners. Raymond and Samuel James…a father-son team. So what? You're a wife?"

"No. Like I said, I'm one of the owners. The son of the team."

Cal's neck nearly snapped as she looked over at Sahara in awe. Understanding slapped her in the face and her mouth dropped open.

Sahara simply smiled victoriously. "See, we all have our little secrets. Looking at me is like looking at an intimate reflection of yourself…passing for one thing when you're really something else, without your suitor being none the wiser."

Cal's mind raced through a series of thoughts. All this time, she'd been attracted to a man. *How was that possible?* No one loved pussy more than Cal did, yet she was ready to give up her player mentality and turn in her little black book to lock down a woman who was really a man. The shit just didn't add up. Everything she'd ever been confident about suddenly became shaky. She questioned her sexuality and practically fell out as the notion of being with a man caused her to grow lightheaded.

"Well," Sahara said nonchalantly. "It's been a rather enlightening evening. Thanks for the drama. If you're ready to learn about something other than silicone dicks, Cal, clearly you know where to find me." She exited the house and made her way down the walk without turning back, a sly smile plastered across her face knowing that Cal was completely fucked up in the head.

The Mrs. stood still, wondering just how far Cal would have gone with the woman/man that had just left the premises. Tightening the belt of her coat, she walked around Cal and headed for the door herself, completely unfazed by Cal's manic breathing as she began to lose it. What did she care? Cal had made it painfully clear that she was nothing but a fuck that was no longer relevant in her life. With that, the Mrs. vanished into the night air, feeling betrayed and disgusted all at the same time.

Cal sunk to the floor staring out the door into oblivion as she clutched her chest. She had no idea who or what she was anymore. Just moments ago, she'd had two pussies at her disposal, or so she thought. Now, she didn't know what to think. The only thing that was clear was that her game had caught up to her and a change had to be made. Playing the field and feeling herself had landed her in this state of confusion, with no one there to help her figure out just what the hell was going on. It was over. Everything she'd ever prided herself in regarding her sexuality and ability to fuck 'em and leave 'em was over…dead…done. Not only had she lost the one opportunity she had to form a meaningful relationship, apparently she'd also lost herself.

Then it hit her. Sahara James was once Samuel James of Raymond and James Inc. Essentially, she was Cal's boss. Nausea took over Cal's stomach as she pounded the floor in anguish. This whole fiasco could cause her to lose her job. This time she'd been screwing around with wrong person yet again, only now it was much more likely that she'd be out on her ass. *Damn it,* Cal thought. There was no way around the truth—she was fucked.

World Wide Web of Deceit

Tee Renee

*D*amn, can the time move any slower? I have been at work damn near twelve hours and a bitch is hungry, horny and tired! I met this fine ass dude a couple of months ago on the online dating site, Plenty of Fish (POF) and tonight is the night that he makes me a woman! Dang, I crack myself up! Don't mind me, songs are always popping in my head and you know I love me some Betty Wright! Anyways, let me tell you about this piece of chocolate I got my hands on…Marcus, that's his name…Marcus Leroy Jackson. You know his parents are from the country, naming him that. He stands about six foot three, two-hundred fifty pounds of pure muscle, silky, dark chocolate skin and a smile that could raise the dead! My panties are getting wet just thinking about it! His lips are so damn juicy; you never want him to get to the center of your Tootsie Pop, if you know what I mean.

I normally don't indulge in the online dating thing, but my sister convinced me that it was a good idea, and so I decided to give it a shot. I remember the first time I saw his pic. OMG, I was like oooohhhhh he's cute! He had a baby face with the sexiest, seductive eyes I've ever seen on a man. I knew then that I had to have him and one thing's for sure; what I want, I get. We began flirting with each other, which led to texting, then phone calls, to eventually going out on a few dates. He makes me feel like a lovesick teenage girl back in high school. Never would I think a man could make me feel that way, especially a younger one. I'm only about five years his senior, but to me that feels like a lifetime.

I remember the first time we kissed, had to be on our second or third date, and man, I thought I was gonna pass out! His lips were soft like cotton and his tongue as smooth as silk. I had to tame my kitty because she was ready to devour him, but I made myself a promise that I would wait it out this time, before I gave up the goods. Now after about three months of dating, I'm finally ready to show Marcus why it was worth the wait.

I'm a little nervous about tonight…it's been so long for me, I hope this nigga don't wear me out…then again…

***

We walk inside his house and I excuse myself to the bathroom…need to do a once over on my kitty and make sure she's as fresh as can be. I can hear the music playing on the other side of the door, so I know he's anxiously waiting on me so we can get started with this long overdue love session. I decided to get undressed, and just come out in my ivory and gold matching bra and panties. As soon as I saw it at Victoria's Secret, I knew it would come in handy one day. The boy shorts cuffed my ass just right and the bra revealed the right amount of cleavage, enough to have him drooling on sight. I also made sure to coat my body with the sweet smell of Pink Sugar. I remember when he told me that just a whiff of it made his dick stand at attention; I went out and bought three bottles to make sure I wouldn't run out for a long time.

I walk into the bedroom and I didn't see him at all, so I ventured into the living room and there he was, sitting on the couch, massaging his magic stick to the beat of the smooth sounds of R. Kelly's "12 Play". I watched him closely, taking in every stroke, as my kitty started to purr. All I could think about was oiling him down with my sweet nectar. I began to move toward him slowly; eventually he looked up at me and smiled, but his hand kept moving. Without saying a word, I kneeled down in front of him and began lightly blowing on his balls. His nature started to rise and I knew that was my cue to talk into the mic and let my tongue serenade him.

"Ahhhhh," he screamed as my mouth connected the dots and took him all the way in; sucking, licking, and blowing, sending him into complete ecstasy. This game of suck and blow quickly turned into a man down situation. With a tight grip on my hair, he pushed his dick deeper into my mouth until I could feel his head knocking on my tonsils. The more I sucked, the deeper he went; pre cum started to drip and my pussy became wetter. He knew it too, because before I knew it, his hand navigated thru my secret garden like Tarzan in search of Jane. My legs started shaking as he slid his fingers deep inside of me, one at a time, filling my walls with pleasure.

"Damn, shit…"

"Yes daddy?"

"Girl what you doing to me?"

I opened my eyes and there he is, staring at me like a lion that's ready to devour his prey. I get up from the floor, slow and seductively, while he sits up so he can see what's about to happen next. I hadn't noticed the platter of fruit on the coffee table until now. He had it filled with strawberries, pineapple cubes, cherries and grapes. I grabbed a strawberry, licked it the same way I did him and then slid it over my right nipple, then the left…my nipples hardened instantaneously and my pussy began aching to feel him, but I wanted to take my time tonight. I've waited a long time for this and with all I have going on right now, my body needs this.

I take a bite from the strawberry and let the juice run down my chin onto my breast…he jumps to lick it off, but I push him back on the couch…tracing the dripping strawberry back around my nipples, down to my belly button, glide it across my inner thigh, and over to my treasure box. Mixing my juices with the berry's juices, he knows that he's in for a delectable treat. My pussy starts to tingle from the coolness of the berry, combined with the warmth of his tongue that is now licking and stroking my soft spot. Suddenly I feel his teeth on my fingers as he grabs the strawberry from my hand. He pauses and allows his hand to substitute for his tongue, while he eats what's left of our fruity helper.

I close my eyes and embrace the sensations that are taking control of my body. His hands are so strong, his tongue so soft. They are fighting for my attention and I'm so gone right now, I couldn't even begin to tell you who's winning. In and out, I feel his fingers, wait…no that time it was his tongue…back and forth he goes…in between each lick and stroke, he tells me how good I taste. Feeling a little left out of this dinner date, I take my right breast and begin to suck it, instantly increasing the fire that's burning between my thighs. I want him so bad right now!.He catches a glimpse of 'Act one: self-love' and a smile appears in the crease of his mouth. He knows I'm ready to fill my cup with his hot chocolate. Knowing him, however, he is not going to give in until after I've given him a sweet and sticky facial.

He puts himself in a chokehold with my thighs and goes in deeper with his fingers, while his tongue talks into my mic this time. He sang just the right notes that had my kitty screaming. As she showered him with her love, he buried his face deep inside, causing my body to climb the mountain of orgasmic thunder. Panting and trembling, I pull his face to mine and let my tongue tell him how much I need him. He accepts the invitation and slides right inside my Twinkie, causing me to cream even more.

He starts in slow, teasing my walls with the tip, making my pussy play Hide and Go Seek. One long deep stroke, repeatedly, as I close in tighter around him, squeezing him gently. Beyoncé purrs in the background, "Keep me humming, keep me moaning", and I arch my back in anticipation of him turning my cherry out. He cuffs my ass and lifts me off the couch carrying me over to the wall. Wrapping my legs tightly around his waist, he gets low and then enters me with all of him; careful not to let me fall, he drives down my love course until he successfully gets a hole in one. My body explodes and collapses in his muscular arms. The aftershocks from my earthquake awakens him…we make our way to the bed where he lays me down and turns me on my stomach. He pulls me up on my knees and prepares to take aim. Caressing my booty, he spreads open my cheeks, ready to enter me again. Dripping wet, he slid right in and went to work, never letting me up for air. His strokes got harder as our bodies connected, he grunts and I moan. I back up, he goes deeper and soon our bodies become one, creating the perfect cocktail…now we are intoxicated…drunk in love…floating…intertwined in each other's arms. He plants a soft kiss on the back of my neck and we pass out, anticipating the hangover the morning will bring.

Chapter One

Six months of dating Marcus and I'm starting to get a little bored. Don't get me wrong; the sex is still bananas, but he doesn't have much else to offer. It's crazy how having sex with someone can cause them to let their guard down, especially when they think they have you lost in emotion. Marcus is not as put together as I thought; turns out he is sub-leasing this apartment, is in between jobs and has three kids and three baby mamas! Now this is definitely not what I bargained for. I see now why the "dates" turned into "kickin' it sessions" at his house, or should I say, borrowed living quarters. I mean I understand the struggle, but I can't be settling, even if he can lay it down like no other. There are too many fish in the sea and I am still baiting my hook until I find the right one.

Ding! Firepipes69 sent you a message

Oh shoot, I know he ain't sending me a message via POF! Boy, I tell you these dudes think they slick! He's just trying to see if I'm still fishing! Ha-ha yessir, I am! Well, since he wants to play this game, let's go, because I have many years of practice behind me.

Let's see what this fool is talking about…

Firepipes69: Hey Ma wyd?

TooSassy4u: Nothing much, about to go to lunch with a friend

Firepipes69: A friend huh?

TooSassy4u: Yuup…wyd?

Firepipes69: I was trying to hook up with you but I see you got other plans □

TooSassy4u: Well it is the middle of the work day so of course I'd be busy…you know us working folks' schedules stay booked ;)

Firepipes69: I see. Well enjoy your lunch date and I'll holla at you lata Ma.

Hehe, he's mad now. Oh well. Watch this.

TooSassy4u: Ok Marcus I'll hit you when I get off work and see what you're doing then. Maybe we can go see that new Laurence Fishburne movie tonight?

Firepipes69: Idk yea maybe if I don't have my son tonight.

TooSassy4u: Hmm ok boo well just keep me posted. Ttyl :-*

Firepipes69: yea aite. Lata

I ain't a bit more got no lunch date, meeting, nothing; but what I do have is better things to do with my time, than waste it on a man that ain't going nowhere. I'll keep him in my back pocket for safekeeping, but for now, let me go check out these other notifications before my next client comes in.

***

Oops, forgive me! Where are my manners? I'm just telling y'all all my business and y'all don't even know who I am! Rude, I know, but believe me; I was raised better than that. My name is Keisha; I'm a thirty-year-old, real estate agent, and the youngest of eight kids. I grew up in a wonderful two-parent home and my parents are still together to this day; been married for sixty years now and they still act like two love sick teenagers. They were married at a very young age. My mom was fourteen and my dad was seventeen. My eldest brother was six months old on their wedding day. Back then, things were a little different. If you got pregnant, you immediately got married or soon after. They tell many stories about how hard life was back then, not only were they trying to learn about each other, but doing so while growing up and raising a family. I must say they did a rather good job with all of us in spite of.

All of my siblings either are married or are in committed relationships; I'm the only single one. However, since I'm the baby, they don't bother me too much about getting married, although my mom brings it up any chance she gets. I don't know that I want to get married to be honest, I am happy with my life just the way it is. If I could find one or maybe two good guys to spend time with every now and then, I'll be just fine. Call me crazy, but there's something about being free to love whomever I want with no strings attached. I guess I'm sort of like my great-grandmother; she divorced her husband because she said she didn't want a man telling her what to do anymore; however, she never got involved with anyone else. She was a devout Christian woman and lived the rest of her life serving the only man that mattered to her and that was God. I don't know if I'm going to go that far though. I need to feel the warmth of another body next to me.

Ding! TheChosenOne sent you a message

Awww snap let me see who this is. I think I'm starting to like this online stuff.

TheChosenOne: Hey lady! How are you?

TooSassy4u: I'm good. You?

TheChosenOne: Better now that I found you.

Oh lawd, here we go with these corny ass lines.

TooSassy4u: Is that so?

TheChosenOne: It is. What's your name, pretty lady?

TooSassy4u: Keisha. Yours?

TheChosenOne: Julian. Nice to meet you.

TooSassy4u: Nice to meet you too. So what brings you to POF? Have you had any luck yet?

TheChosenOne: My job keeps me pretty busy, so this became an easier way to meet women. No, not yet but hopefully that will change soon. What about you?

TooSassy4u: My sister suggested it and I've met a few cool dudes, been on a couple of dates but nothing too serious. What kind of work do you do?

TheChosenOne: I'm in law enforcement.

Hmmm, this might be good; my mind instantly thought about being put in handcuffs. Oh, yeah!

TooSassy4u: Interesting…are you a police officer, detective, what?

TheChosenOne: Detective, I've been on the force for 15 years. What do you do miss lady?

TooSassy4u: Wow that's great. I'm a real estate agent.

TheChosenOne: Nice. I will have to keep you in mind the next time I'm ready to purchase some property.

TooSassy4u: I'd be glad to help you. ☺

TheChosenOne: I don't mean to be too forward, but I'm not on here that much so would it be all right if I gave you my number? I'd love to get to know you better.

TooSassy4u: Well I normally don't give out my number this soon, but I guess you being a detective and all that means I could trust you right?

TheChosenOne: lol yeah you can trust me.

TooSassy4u: lol classic cop response…smh

TheChosenOne: no pressure love, if you feel like talking just hit me up…916.555.9790

TooSassy4u: will do. Have a good day.

TheChosenOne: you do the same. Talk to you later love.

TooSassy4u: bye ☺

I click out of this message thread and go into my inbox there are at least twenty messages in there. Time to weed through and see who's worth saving; I swear it be the ugliest guys that are the boldest. Most of the nice looking ones rarely send messages or respond when I reach out. Clowns! Probably got too many chicks hounding them anyways. I better get off this phone and get some work done; these houses ain't gon' sell themselves. Hopefully, I can hook up with my girls tonight for some food, dancing and libations.

Chapter Two:

It's Friday night and I am beat! However, I want to go out and hang with my girls for a little while, so we can catch up. I haven't seen them in about a month, being that I've been extremely busy at work lately. Today I showed six houses, had three meetings and managed to squeeze in a session with my personal trainer. She's awesome and I am loving the way my body is turning out. A girl has to keep her body tight! Don't get me wrong; I'm not hating on nobody and their chosen body type, because I know fellas that like women in all shapes and sizes; but for me, baby everything has to be smooth and firm.

I had to turn my notifications off from that damn POF, because my battery was dying quickly. I swear these dudes on there be extra thirsty. But hey, what else are they there for right? I don't know if I'm feeling this site too much. I mean some of the guys are real cool, but others not so much. Maybe I should try another site such as, Black People Meet, Match.com, and EHarmony; hell, one of them has to have a better quality of men. Hopefully, the girls can give me some insight on this.

I know one thing; I need to get some new dick quick, or else I'm going to go bat shit crazy! You know the kind I want? The kind that will have you creaming in your panties all day while you're at work. The kind that when you close your eyes and think about him, an orgasmic sensation flows from your breast to your honey pot. The kind that will have you caressing your leg while you're driving home from work; slowly easing your way up your thigh into the crease that separates it from the wet spot forming in your panties, that is, if you wear panties. I bet you're wondering if I do, huh? Well, to answer the burning question in your mind; no I don't, and I haven't for about five years now. It's the most liberating feeling I've ever experienced. And no, I don't have to worry about no period panties either, because I don't get one of those anymore, thanks to my handy-dandy Mirena. Another great invention mankind created.

Anyways, back to the subject at hand. When you get it that good, it gives you goosebumps all over your body. You can't even eat thinking about that mess. Lawd, I haven't had any that good since my ex-boyfriend, Kevin. He could look at me and my legs would fly open. It was as if they had a mind of their own whenever he was around. I've known him since I was in kindergarten and we've had an on again, off again relationship since the eighth grade. He was the first boy I ever kissed, the first boy I gave my cookies too, as well as the first boy I've ever loved. For whatever reason though, none of that mattered to him. He was a hoe back then and he still is now.

Every time I see him, he makes all these promises about how we're going to get married and have children one day, and blasé, blasé; but never makes good on any of it. My girls think I'm crazy for not believing him, but they don't know that we've been doing this song and dance for way too many years and I'm smart enough to know that it just ain't gon' happen. The problem is I'm clearly not smart enough to stop letting him get the goodies. I promise I be trying to stay far, far away from him; sadly anytime his dick calls, I answer.

Ring! Ring! Ring!

Now will you look at this…speak of the devil. Kevin's name appeared on my cell phone. Should I answer? I know I shouldn't, but…ummm…well, let's just see what he has to say.

"Hello?"

"What are you doing?"

"About to take a shower. Why, what are you doing?"

"About to come join you."

I knew it; I knew it. This fool got issues. Ones I don't have time for.

"Ha! No, you're not. I'm getting ready to go meet Ayanna and them for dinner. I'm not fooling with you tonight. Where's your girlfriend at anyways?"

"What girlfriend? Man Keisha gon' with all that bullshit, okay? I told you I don't have a girlfriend. Now quit tripping and let me come through."

"Yeah okay, whatever you say. Tell that to the chick that keeps playing on my phone. Apparently, she didn't get the message that y'all weren't together anymore. And no, you cannot come over here; I just told you I have plans. Is that all you called for?"

Silence. He's probably trying to think of a good lie to tell, but I already know the truth. I should have followed my first mind and let him go to voicemail.

"No, that's not all I called for. I called to tell you that my mom is having her sixtieth birthday party next Saturday. I'm sure she would love it if you came. Me coming over there was just a plus."

"Dang, I forgot her birthday was coming up. Sure, just text me the info on the party and I will definitely be there."

"Cool, I'll let her know. Back to you, though; wassup, you trying to do something or not? I can make it quick."

"Kevin, please don't do this right now alright? I have to go."

"Wait, wait, don't hang up. Keisha, I know things have been rough between us lately, but no matter what we go through, you know I love you more than any other woman I have ever been with. I can't get you outta my system no matter how hard I try, and I know you feel the same about me. I'm not ready to let you go."

I let out a deep sigh. As much as I believe his words, his actions are a whole other story. Why is it that men can't seem to make them match? Do you know how many times I have heard this same ole rigmarole? Too darn long. It's time he either put up or shut up. I can't deal with this anymore.

"Listen, you know how I feel about you and I would be lying if I said I didn't want things between us to go back to how they used to be. The problem is, you don't know how to be with just one woman. Now if what you want is an open relationship, then say that, but you don't. You can't fathom the idea of me being with another man, yet I'm supposed to sit around here and be happy with just you, while you wander around town with every woman in sight. That is not my idea of love. What I need from you, you are unable to give. I am starting to become okay with that. I need for you to do the same."

"I hear you. It's cool. Can we at least have some phone sex then?"

"Ha-ha! Bye Kevin! I will see you next week. Have a good night."

"A'ite. Tell the girls I said wassup. Be safe."

"Thank you, I will. Talk to you later."

We hang up the phone after sitting in silence for another minute. My body yearned for his touch; my mind screamed for me to walk away. They say all is fair in love and war, but this doesn't seem fair at all. I look over at the clock and time is ticking away. I head to the bathroom, undress and climb into my see through shower. I turn and look at myself in the mirror adjacent the shower door. Why wouldn't any man want to have this all to himself? Hmmm. Well I guess for now the only man that is going to get my body or at least enjoy my sugar walls is Mr. Dependable, my shower toy. I'm sure they call him that, because he's always there to satisfy your needs.

I adjust his position on the bench in the shower and grab my waterproof bullet from beside the soap dish. I turn the water on, the heat welcoming my body into its trance. Taking the showerhead from the hook it rested on and allowing the stream to moisten me, I shared the downpour with Mr. Dependable. Now that we're both ready, I place the showerhead back on the hook, aiming the water flow directly at my breasts. I ease down onto him, slowly and steadily. Immediately my G-spot tingled. Once I settled into a comfortable rhythm, I allowed my bullet to join in the fun. One hand on the wall to keep my balance, I made love to myself with the help of my trusty partners.

Up and down, I went; the coolness from the bench teased my butt while the warmth stirring between my thighs increased. I could feel my knot of pleasure coming undone. It was only a matter of time before she exploded. As my walls tightened and the vibrating sensation sent waves up my spine, I knew the end was near. The mixture of movements caused my head to spin. The sound of the water sloshing beneath me combined with the buzzing cords my bullet played. Suddenly the nectar that was building up squirted from my water hose and onto the shower floor.

Damn that felt good.

I climbed off of my boo, put the bullet down, grabbed my loofah and shower gel and began to clean my body. Aftershocks were still plaguing my body. I dried off with my plush Egyptian cotton towel and headed into my room to get dressed. As I was putting my coconut lime lotion, my doorbell rings. I throw on my robe and go see who it is. I look through the peephole and to my surprise, there was Kevin; standing there looking delicious in a black hat, gray pea coat, black slacks and shoes. Peeking from behind his coat, I see a gray dress shirt and tie. I swear this is why I can't get over him. He defies me on every hand and like a fool, I keep allowing it. I turn my back to the door and have a mini argument with my downstairs neighbor. She wants to let him in and I'm trying to convince her why this is a bad idea. Back and forth we go, until finally I turn and unlock the door one lock at a time.

He doesn't say a word upon entering. He steps in, unbuttons his jacket and lays it on the arm of the sofa. After closing and relocking the door, I just stand there watching him, trying to figure out what his next move is going to be. God, he looks so good. My neighbor is jumping out of her skin. I whisper to this hoe to calm down and curse her for being so thirsty. I mean we did just finish a wonderful session with Mr. Dependable and his trusty friend, so why she feels the need to get some more, and from Kevin at that, is beyond me. This tramp gets on my nerves.

He walks over to me, his breath fogging up my glasses, and starts disrobing me. My words are caught in my throat. He senses that and places his finger over my mouth. "Shhh. Just let me love you," he said. I just stood there in a trance. His fingers found their way to my neighbor's house. My uterus clenched. I was rooted to the middle of my living room floor. While his fingers wandered around downstairs, his mouth engulfed mine, infiltrating me with his tongue. My body melted into his arms. He laid me down gently on the living room floor and imparted his love all over my body. There was no fight in me whatsoever. I allowed him to have his way with me; I have to admit, I enjoyed it. Kevin had his way with me for at least an hour; leaving me breathless, dazed and confused. He kissed my frontal lobe as he gathered himself and exited my front door.

Mustering up as much strength as I could, I make it back to the bathroom to erase the remnants of our lovemaking he left behind. Thirty minutes later, I'm in my car dressed in my Forever 21 black skinny jeans, gray sweater, and black Chinese Laundry stilettos. When I made it to the restaurant the girls were already there, sitting at the table waiting for me. Here comes the interrogation. Renee goes first.

"Ummm, what took you so long? We've been here almost an hour waiting for you."

"Please don't start, Renee. All that matters is I'm here. Did y'all order already?"

Mishaya chimes in, "Just appetizers and a cocktail. What's wrong with you? You look stressed."

"She needs some dick, that's what," Portia exclaims.

"Naw, I don't think I need any more of that," I state, shaking my head.

They all look at me in shock. In unison, they holler out, "Whaaattttttt!"

I take a huge gulp from the water glass sitting in front of me. I really don't want to tell them about Kevin, because this fun filled night is going to turn in to an all-out brawl. They hate him because of everything we've been through. I don't blame them, though. It's my fault for telling them all my business in the first place. My mother always told me you can't tell your friends and family everything, because they will still be mad at him, while you've forgiven him and moved on. Portia is the only one of my friends who knows about my online dating, and about Kevin still coming around from time to time. She's the least judgmental of our crew, and she knows how to keep a secret too. She'll play along with Renee and Mishaya as if she knows nothing, then call me afterward and fall out laughing about all they had to say.

"Here y'all go. Pick your mouths up off the table and chill out. It ain't that serious. I've been dating here and there, and let's just say I'm not in a drought zone anymore. Where's the waiter? I'm hungry."

Mishaya looks at Renee and they both frown up their faces. Portia picks up her glass of Pinot Grigio and grins at me from underneath the rim. I shot her a wink and stuck my fork into Renee's salad, taking a bite of its contents. The waiter finally comes over to take our orders. While waiting for our food, I decide to change the subject from me and onto something else.

"Have either of you tried online dating?" I inquired.

"Girl naw, it's too many crazy fools out here for that," Mishaya declared.

"I did a long time ago, back in the days of Black Planet," Renee admitted.

We fell out laughing. Jesus, she's so old school. I was just coming out of high school at the end of that site's reputation. I heard it used to be popping, though.

"Renee, what a way to tell your age," Portia laughed. "I've tried it before. It can have its good side. You just have to know which sites are good and which ones aren't. Usually, the paid ones are the best, because let's face it, if a man is going to pay to find a woman online and vice versa, they have to be serious about it. Don't you think so?" asked Portia.

"I guess you have a point there," I said. "Well, what about POF? Have any of you heard of that one before?"

"Girl, please; that is just a hookup site! Ain't nobody serious on that mess. All they want to do is get some booty. The girls and the guys," said Renee.

"And how do you know Miss Thang?" I asked.

"Because my brother is on there. He said all he and his boys use that site for is some easy pussy. He said all you have to do is give out a few compliments, schedule a meeting time and place, and it's on and popping. It's disgusting if you ask me," she continued.

I swallowed the huge lump that formed in my throat. Hearing her say that does make it sound kinda gross. Is that all I am to these guys? Is that all they are to me?

Portia jumped in, "Renee, why are you always so judgmental? This is 2016 and if I want to have a random sexcapade with someone, that's my business and it doesn't make me a hoe. Maybe if you got down off your high horse sometimes and lived a little you, wouldn't be single and uptight. Jeeeeez, you drive me crazy sometimes."

"Well, who said I was talking to you? Keisha asked a question and I answered her to the best of my knowledge. You feeling guilty about something?"

"Bitch please, ain't no guilt here. I'm just stating the obvious." Portia rolled her eyes and excused herself from the table.

Mishaya asked, "What's gotten into her?"

"The hell if I know, but she needs to quit tripping," Renee said, while taking another bite of her shrimp scampi.

"Ain't nothing wrong with Portia, and you know it? She may have gotten a little upset, but she ain't lying about what she said. Both of y'all be acting like you're angels sent down from Heaven without a sin in sight. And we all know that is far from the truth," I admitted, taking up for Portia while she was in the restroom.

The table fell silent. The only sounds came from our silverware hitting our plates. I waited until Portia returned to her seat before speaking out to the group again.

"Look, I was just asking a question. I didn't mean for it to get everybody all worked up. My sister had suggested the site to me and I just wanted a different set of opinions. So thank you for your input but I didn't come here to be arguing all night. I came to have some fun with my girls and that's what I intend to do. Either you all are joining me in that or I can just go out and look for some new friends. This mess is for the birds." I looked around at all of their beautiful faces. These women have been in my life since college and I in no way want to stop being their friend over a stupid discussion. The truth was Renee and Mishaya did act like "goodie two shoes". However, we were supposed to be bigger than our minor flaws, and love each other no matter what.

Portia raised her glass in the air. "Keisha is right, we shouldn't be fighting over something so stupid. Let's make a toast." Everyone else raises their glasses to meet hers. "To the most beautiful women to ever grace the face of this earth. May we love one another despite our flaws, and never let anything come between us." We all shout out, "Here, here," and clink our glasses together.

We finished eating and making small talk. Then we headed out to a local nightclub, where Mishaya's boyfriend was the DJ. It was packed in here. The music was bumping and the people were grooving. I made my way to the bar, while the girls went over to say hi to Lonnie. He and I aren't on speaking terms anymore. We kicked for a minute, but it all ended when showed up at a party he was DJ'ing at one day and caused a huge scene. Lonnie asked me to choose and when I couldn't, he left me alone. Of course, that just added to Mishaya and Renee's hate for him.

I ordered myself a lavender lemon drop and found my way to the VIP area where the girls were. Thankfully, Lonnie still allowed my name to reside on the list with them. We stayed at the club dancing our lives away for about three hours, before retreating to our separate homes. I sent an email out to my morning clients rescheduling for next week. I am too tired to be showing houses all day, especially after the night I've had. Before turning off the lamp next to my bed, I glance at the notifications on my phone. I had seventeen from POF and five from Kevin: two missed calls and three text messages. I hit clear, put my phone on silent and placed it face down on the nightstand. Grabbing my night mask from the bedpost it was hanging on, I slide it on my face and nestle myself into my bed. Everyone and everything will have to wait until a later day. I'm tired and in desperate need of some beauty sleep. It didn't take long to find my comfort zone and before I knew it, I was knocked out, fast asleep.

Chapter Three

Monday morning came sooner than I expected. My weekend was pretty chill. I mostly lounged around the house in my pajamas, watching old Blaxploitation movies and looking up new listings for my clients. I scanned through my messages on POF and even responded to a few. I hit up that detective Julian and we have a date scheduled for later this week. I decided against responding to Kevin. I don't feel like one moment of great sex warrants a newfound relationship. Besides, I don't want to send him the wrong message, especially to his mom's birthday party. I know he's not ready to settle down and neither am I for that matter. When I was ready for all of that, he wasn't. Now I'm enjoying my life as a single woman. It's going to take a whole lot more than what he's offering to take me off my current course.

I decided to work from home today, because I don't feel like dealing with the crazy people I work with. Besides, I get more work done without my boss running in my office every five minutes. I swear, he acts as if he can't do anything without my help. How he got that job, I will never understand. After a few hours of scrolling through different properties, I opened another tab in my browser and typed in the URL of Blackpeoplemeet.com, and proceeded to set up a free profile to see if I would get any good hits. I chose a new name, SexyandSearching, and a new profile pic, hoping nobody from POF would recognize me. I see a few guys from POF on here, but not very many. I guess this is a different kind of crowd.

I scrolled through about five pages of eligible bachelors, before stumbling upon one that really caught my eye. His screen name was. Ready4luvnow. I couldn't tell his skin color, because his profile pic was a black and white photo, but he still was handsome nonetheless. I am partial to dark-skinned brothas; however from what I'm seeing on this screen, if he is a light bright, I'll have to make an exception this one time. Let me send him a message right quick. Shoot. You can't unless you pay for a paid membership: 2.99 a week for six months, 3.49 a week for three months, 4.19 a week for one month; all billed in one-time payments. Well damn, I'm not about to give them all my money and have only seen one good prospect so far, I will get this one month subscription for 16.75 and see what happens. I pull out my credit card from my wallet and upgrade my account. I can now send and receive messages and a whole bunch of other stuff.

I went back to the search engine and typed in his name, Ready4luvnow, and decided to send just a flirt first. Let's see if he responds. I click back on the other tab and finish scrolling through houses. Five minutes later, my computer makes a sound. I look around and notice that the BPM tab is flashing. I click on the tab and see an instant message from Ready4luvnow, plus a few other flirts and inbox messages.

Ready4luvnow: Good Afternoon Miss Lady. Thanks for the flirt.

SexyandSearching: Good Afternoon. You're welcome. What's your name?

Ready4luvnow: Chaz. Yours?

SexyandSearching: Nice to meet you, Chaz. I'm Keisha.

Ready4luvnow: Well Miss Keisha, what brings you to BPM?

SexyandSearching: Just trying something new. I don't have a lot of time to go out and meet guys because of work, so I'm giving this a try. What about you?

Ready4luvnow: Pretty much the same. Any luck so far?

SexyandSearching: Not really. Been on a few dates. You?

Ready4luvnow: Same here.

We talked for another hour and got to know each other a little better. He owns his own business, distributing sex toys to some of the larger adult store chains across the U.S. He's thirty-six years old, never been married, and has a teenage son that lives with him. He grew up in Puerto Rico, until his parents moved to the states when he was about ten years old. So far so good. He stated that he would be going home for the next couple of weeks to visit his grandmother, but would love to go out when he got back. We exchanged phone numbers and agreed to keep in touch while he was out of town.

The rest of my week was pretty much the same: more clients, more houses, more meetings, and more notifications from my online dating profiles. Finally, Friday is here again and I'm preparing for my date with Julian. We decided to meet at Buffalo Wild Wings for dinner and to watch the game. The Cowboys were playing the Chargers that night, so this will definitely give us more to talk about since those are both of our teams. I was running late, so I sent him a text giving him a heads up. He asked if he should order for me and I said yes.

I got to the restaurant halfway through the first quarter. The Cowboys were up by fourteen. I texted him when I got inside to see where he was. He said he was sitting at a table across from the bar. I had the hostess walk me back to find him. He was decked out in his Charger's jersey, blue jeans, white Air Force Ones and a Charger snapback. He smiled when he saw me approaching the table. He stood to greet me with a hug and kiss on the cheek.

"I see you representing tonight," I said.

"Why of course. You look mighty fine yourself," he replied.

"Thank you. I hope I didn't keep you waiting too long."

"Naw, you're good. I ordered the spinach artichoke dip to start, the appetizer sampler, and honey BBQ wings. I hope that's cool with you."

"Sounds good to me. So how was your day?"

"Crazy as usual; I swear, the weekends are the worse. These fools are out here acting up. I feel sorry for the guys that are actually working day to day in these neighborhoods."

"I can only imagine."

"How about you?"

"My day was pretty good. I closed on two houses today and have a few more waiting to be approved. So I guess you can say today was a good day."

Julian laughed, "Yeah okay, Ice Cube."

A few wings and a couple of touchdowns later and I was feeling real good. I really enjoyed his company tonight. He was very easy to talk to and I wasn't quite ready for the night to end yet. However, I didn't want to seem too anxious. I mean, it is our first date. Whom am I kidding, that don't mean much to me. He walked me to my car and we stood their talking for a few more minutes. Finally, he asked if I wanted to come back to his house for a nightcap. I agreed and followed him in my car to where he lived.

Now you know the saying don't judge a book by its cover? Well that rang true tonight, because when we pulled up in front of his residence, I was not too sure about going inside. He explained that the owner was doing some remodeling to the front and landscaping the yard. I was still a bit skeptical. Once we got inside though, I was thoroughly impressed. The condo was humongous. Hardwood floors all over, the kitchen had a classic, yet modern feel to it, and the dining area housed a high dining table with square barstool type chairs surrounding it. On the opposite wall, adjacent to the table hung a 60-inch flat screen TV. There was a sunken living room, complete with the typical bachelor pad, black leather sofa and love seat. There was another flat screen in there too, but a little smaller than the one in the dining room.

The bathroom was exceptionally clean and everything was in its proper place. I have to say Julian was winning me over, one granite tile at a time. We sat at the dining table and played a few games of Dominoes, talking trash to each other the entire time. He was trying to get me back for my boys beating his earlier in the football game. What he didn't know was that my grandfather was the Domino king! I learned from the best and just because I was a girl, didn't mean I couldn't kick his butt in what was considered a man's game. Not wanting to kill his pride, I let him win the last two games. I had already beaten him in three.

We moved into the living room after the last game and settled into a conversation about our childhood. I shared with him about my parents and all my siblings; he told me about him growing up without his dad, and losing his only brother to a gang war when he was twelve years old. His brother's death was one of the reasons he decided to join the police force, but little did he know, his desire for wanting to change the mindset of the youth would be a lot harder than he thought. He shared more stories about his work as a detective and inquired a lot about my life and my real estate career.

Before I knew it, my head was resting on his chest and we eventually wrapped ourselves in each other's arms on the couch. I must've dozed off for a minute, because the next thing I knew, he was kissing me. I welcomed him into my mouth and pulled his hand down to caress my bottom. He lifted my shirt from my pants and slid his free hand up to my breasts. Gently massaging them, it wasn't long before my nipples reacted to his touch. I wanted to reach down and see what he was working with but decided to wait until we got into this a little more. We kept kissing for a while and then he lifted me off his body and ushered me into his bedroom.

Suddenly my nerves started to kick in. I sat on the edge of the bed while he went to the bathroom. I looked around his oversized master suite and noticed a large picture of Dorothy Dandridge, lying on a couch, looking stunning. I looked deep into her eyes for direction. She looked back at me and said, "You let the wind blow you this way, and ain't no use arguing with the wind". She's right. I'm a grown woman and whatever I choose to do is on me; and tonight, I'm choosing to let all my inhibitions go and let nature take its course. Julian came back into the room in just his gray boxer briefs and white tank top. He was a little skinny for my taste, but looked good nonetheless. He comes over to the bed where I'm sitting and grabs my hand.

"We don't have to do this if you're not ready. I'm just fine lying here with you in my arms all night," he admitted, sincerity plaguing his eyes.

"Julian, I will admit, I am a little apprehensive. Let's not put too much stress on it and just see how the night goes."

"I'm cool with that. How about we watch a movie, your choice."

"You got any action films?"

"I sure do. Be right back."

He walks out the bedroom and comes back with The Contract, Pixels, and Hitman: Agent 47 and Standoff. I chose Pixels of course. I love Pac-Man. He places the movie in the DVD player and climbs in the bed next to me. I get comfortable, removing my shoes and tucking my feet underneath the blanket he had laid across the bottom of the bed. He then went into the kitchen and made us some popcorn, and brought back two glasses of lemonade to wash it down. Throughout the movie and in between handfuls of popcorn, we fondled each other seductively. I respect him for giving me an option; however, I am leaning towards exploring him tonight.

By the end of the movie, we resumed our lip locking session from earlier and allowed the fire between us to grow. One by one, the pieces of clothing I wore came off, followed by his boxers and tank. He released my lips and made his way to my neck, breasts, belly button, and inner thigh before devouring my honey pot. The smell of my sweet nectar filled the room. I locked my legs around his neck in anticipation. The power he'd used to control my upper lips was now taking my clit into bondage. Locking her down in a position known all too well to police officers when apprehending a criminal, she collapsed in his embrace and confessed all her crimes quicker than a suspect on The First 48.

He grabbed a condom from the nightstand drawer and slid it on with ease. Making his way back to my cove, he didn't have a hard time getting in, becoming immersed in my juices. His revolver was average-sized, but packed a lot of punch. A few strokes in and I thought I was in for a treat. Then all of a sudden, he lost his composure. Before I knew it, he was screaming from the mountaintop and I was left lying there, wondering what happened. Feeling like a fool, I got up and made my way to the bathroom. I washed off and put my clothes back on. When I came back to his room, he was lying back on the bed smiling. I made up an excuse about having to show a house very early in the morning and told him it would be better if I just went home. He tried to talk me out of it, but in the end, he agreed with me. He walked me to my car and kissed me goodbye. I told him I would call him later in the week. We said our final farewells and I drove home in silence. As much as I enjoyed his company tonight, after that episode, I'm not sure if I'll ever speak to Julian again. Only time will tell.

Chapter Four

I woke up this morning feeling refreshed. The last three months have been super crazy. My workload has tripled, which financially is a good thing, but physically daunting. Kevin finally got the hint and agreed to leave me alone to live my life. The night of his mom's birthday party was very eye opening, especially when his girlfriend, the one he kept denying, showed up there with a baby bump and a positive pregnancy test. The whole family went crazy, Kevin cussed her out, and I sat my gift on the table, kissed his mom goodbye and left. I sent him an email explaining my position on things and I haven't heard from him since. Instead of worrying about his drama, I have been giving my energy to better things. Besides work, I've continued to go out on dates and hang out with my girls. Portia was diagnosed with ovarian cancer, so that has taken up a lot of my time as well. I hate seeing her in pain. We are all taking turns going to her doctor's appointments and spending nights at her house. I'm praying that she gets better soon.

I have yet to hang out with Chaz, although we do talk on the phone as often as we can. Between video chatting, emailing, and texting, one would think we were in a long distance relationship. He wound up staying in Puerto Rico longer than expected, due to his grandmother taking ill. Thankfully, she got better though, and this time apart made room for us to get to closer before we took it to a physical level. We seem to have a lot in common and so far, everything between us is good. I am nervous though, because the last few times I've thought things between me and a guy was good, they turned out bad. I remain hopeful though, because I believe that everyone deserves a fair chance, to either blow it or prove me wrong.

I cleared my schedule for the weekend so I could spend some long overdue time with Chaz. We arranged to meet at his house for dinner Saturday evening. He is cooking for me, instead of taking me out. At first, I thought he was acting like another Marcus, using the excuse of his son being home with him that night and by him being in and out of town so much the last couple of months, he wanted to just chill at home. If it hadn't been for him keeping me interested all this time, I would have declined. I'm all for chilling, but not when it takes the place of a man taking me out, thinking that I'm not worth spending a few dollars on. Hell, I can chill at my own house. I don't need a man for that.

Being that he lived in Baldwin Hills near my aunt's house, I parked my car there and had him pick me up. That way if the night didn't go so well, I wouldn't have to drive all the way back to North Hollywood in the middle of the night. He picked me up about six thirty that evening. The intoxicating vapors of Curve cologne tickled my nose hairs. I was excited and you could tell he was too. We arrived at his house ten minutes later. He came around to my door and opened it for me, and guided me into his humble abode. When we got inside, I could smell the aroma of seafood floating through the air. I told him that was one of my favorite things to eat. He introduced me to his son, Xavier, and his little friend, Jasmine.

Now the story is that the son's mother died when he was a baby and this little girl is the daughter of the mother's boyfriend, who's in jail for her murder. Supposedly, the little girl is in foster care and he found her when they moved to this area. Apparently, they go to the same school and the foster mother recognized him from the court proceedings of the murder trial. He felt compassion for the little girl and allowed her to come over on the weekends to get a break from her crazy life. None of this makes any sense to me, but okay, I'll roll with it for now.

Anyways, after exchanging a few pleasantries, the kids retreated to Xavier's room to play video games. Chaz escorted me to his bedroom, to a seat he has set up for me with a TV tray in front of it. He brought my plate with garlic crab legs, fried prawns, French fries, and a salad in and sat it on the tray in front of me. I say my grace and commence to filling my mouth with this wonderful feast. He sits on the edge of his bed and watches me.

"You're not eating?" I ask him, feeling nervous, wondering if this fool slipped something in my food.

"Naw, I don't really eat seafood that much. I have some chicken in the oven for me and the kids. It should be ready soon."

Whew. Okay that makes sense. I was about to get an instantaneous stomachache for a minute. We continued to talk and when his food was ready, he called the kids to the kitchen then joined me in the bedroom. The food was delicious. I stuffed my mouth as if it was the last meal on earth. Yeah, yeah, yeah, I know, not really ladylike but guess what; I was hungry and being that we have been talking all this time, he was warned about my appetite. After eating all of that, I wasn't sure I could handle anything else; that was until he mentioned banana splits for dessert. My trainer is going to kill me come Monday.

We ate our dessert on the bed and watched TV while sharing more about our lives. I inquired more about how he got into distributing sex toys, and he about my getting into real estate. He says he sort of just fell into the business. He did a ten-year bid in prison, for what he wouldn't say, and when he came home, he wanted to do something that would allow him the freedom to travel and take care of his son. He met a white guy who had a small distribution company and they formed a partnership. After about three years, he bought the guy out and the rest is history.

His mom now handles most of the business, while he spends his time traveling to different cities and states, trying to gain more customers. He has a full team of drivers and customer service reps; not bad for an ex-felon. His parents are divorced now, but remain pretty good friends. He has one sister, who also helps with the business, and one brother who is in the Navy. Although they're not together anymore, his parents still live in San Diego in the same house. He says they felt their love had run its course and found more pleasure in just being friends. They are about the same age as my parents are, so I imagine they really don't want to die alone, which is why they still live under the same roof. I don't blame them one bit. More couples should take on that attitude, especially nowadays.

I shared with him how my family has been in real estate my whole life, so it was natural that I would get into it too. We've always owned our own house and a few businesses too. I explained how the joy I get from seeing new homeowners get their keys totally makes up for the ups and downs this business has. I'm pretty good at saving my money, so I never have to worry when things are slow. I bought my first house when I was twenty-five with my own money, no help at all from my parents, a moment I'll forever be proud of.

The conversation took a ride through various subjects and eventually led to talking about sex and some of our experiences. Nothing too out of the ordinary for either of us, at least we hadn't disclosed those things at this point. He asked me was I open to toys and of course I didn't deny the pleasure that they bring me. I'm sure that made him happy, him being the sex toy king and all. Getting more into my business, he then wanted to know what my first experience with one was. Oh Lord, I really don't want to live that moment, but since we're having a good time, I won't ruin the mood.

"Are you sure you wanna hear that story?"

"Yeah, what's so bad about it that you don't want to share?"

"It's not bad; it's just embarrassing as hell, that's all."

"Hmmm…now, you really have me curious," he laughed.

I rolled my eyes at him and began to tell the details of my most embarrassing moment.

"My first bullet I got when I was seventeen. My best friend, who was a year older than me, worked at an adult novelty store, called Naughty but Nice, so she bought me a bullet to try out. We had been talking about getting one for a while, but weren't old enough to go into the store. Once she turned eighteen and started working there, we were anxious to try the product. Anywho, I used this bullet for years. I had it hidden at the bottom of my drawer before I went off to college, and I would use it whenever I came home for a visit. So one day I went home to use the bullet and it was dead. I bought new batteries, put them in it and it still wouldn't work, so I said forget it and threw it away. My mother and my aunt were at my house that day, chilling and watching they stories on TV. My mom comes in my room to empty the trash and takes my garbage can with her to the garage where we kept the big cans. All of a sudden, the bullet decides it wants to work, so as my mother is on her way to dump the garbage out, the can starts vibrating! Now she and my aunt are like, 'OMG, what the hell'? They pull the garbage bag out, cut it open, and out falls my bullet, bouncing and buzzing all over the kitchen floor. They hollered! I stayed in my room for the rest of the day, extremely embarrassed. For two years they called me 'Lil Buzz'."

Chaz's face is red and he guffaws, managing to get out, "I can only imagine your face when that happened." He doubled over on the bed in hysterical laughter. I elbowed him in his side.

"It's not that funny, dang." I pouted.

"Aww, baby girl, don't get all bent out of shape. You have to admit it was funny, but I won't make fun of your feelings."

"Yeah whatever." I folded my arms like a little kid and lay back against the headboard. He grabbed my face and kissed me softly on the lips.

"You gon' stay mad all night?"

I just sat there looking at him. He kissed me again. Nope I'm not budging; keep trying, homie. He kept kissing me repeatedly until finally my arms fell to my side. He pulled me on top of him, and immediately, I felt the rising bulge in his pants. Oh my. He cupped my backside with his enormous hands and helped me grind on his erection. Even with our clothes on, he felt like he was inside of me. The pressure mounting in my sex was invigorating. I couldn't even begin to understand what he was doing to my body; I have never felt an emotion such as this, not even with Kevin. Feeling my elixir flood my jeans as my body shook uncontrollably, I reached down and unzipped his pants. It was as if I was being taking over by an alien force. I was in an orgasmic trance. I didn't want to let this feeing go. I was overwhelmed with desire and needed to discover what more he could give.

I pulled his pants down to his ankles and was welcomed by a very enticing package. I wrapped my fingers around him, feeling the pulsation from his loins in the palm of my hand. He stared at me intently, savoring every moment. Immersed in my own thoughts, I invaded his private parts with my mouth. I think I moved too swiftly, because I almost choked on him. Easing back a bit, I let my tongue serve as Nancy Drew, uncovering all his secret spots. I devoured him more than I did my dinner and once again, he served me dessert the flavor of banana faintly present in his jizz. I normally don't swallow on the first date, but whatever this was that had control over my mind, body, and soul, made room for a lot of first time don'ts.

He lifted me up to his mouth and kissed me deeply, stealing the exhales of my breath. I longed to feel him inside of me. While still on top of him, he flipped me over on my back and unbuttoned my shirt with his teeth. Reaching his hand behind me, he unhooked my bra, in one swift move. Damn he's good, I thought. Freeing my voluptuous breasts, he grabbed them both and placed his mouth around both of my nipples. Inhaling deeply, he played tennis with them, using his tongue as a racket. I lost myself in his licks and sucks. The lake forming in my sea of lust soaked the bed beneath me. I squirmed. He let go of my breast and headed downtown. Once he got to a comfortable spot in the lake, his tongue went deep sea diving, making his way down to the bottom, before coming back up to shore for air.

Before I released again, he stopped. He got up and went into his closet. What he came back with shocked the heck out of me. He undressed completely and did the same to me. He grabbed my ankles and turned my body sideways on the bed, causing my legs to hang over the side. He stood in between the bed were my legs were and the wall just a few feet behind him. He picked up this huge white and lavender "massager" and plugged into the wall behind him. What in the world is he about to do with that? No way is that going inside of me! Sensing my tension, he started kissing my thighs, turned the massager on and laid it gently on my clit. Awwww, now I see. Feeling me relax again, he rose up from my legs and turned the handle towards me. "Keep it right there, okay?" he said, not really waiting for a response.

He changed the channel on the TV to the R&B love song station and came back over to the bed. He spread my legs apart and entered me, causing my body to jolt backward. I closed my eyes, giving in to the pleasure consuming my body. Once he settled into a comfortable stride, he lifted my legs up to his shoulders, pulled my socks off, and began sucking my toes. There were sparks flying from every part of my body. The sensation from the massager, the electrifying pressure from his girth, combined with the tingling in my toes, proved to be the most luxurious, erotic escapade I'd ever been on.

We went on like that for hours; we gave new meaning to the Kama Sutra. I don't even remember when we stopped. I woke up about eight the next morning, lying in his bed. He served me breakfast and we spent the next two days, repeating our love fest. I had no idea one man could bring you so much pleasure. I should send BlackPeopleMeet.com a bonus check! I wound up spending the entire next week with him, only going home to grab my laptop and changes of clothes. I took advantage of the vacation time I had saved up, and cancelled all the showings I had scheduled that week. Nothing else mattered at this moment, because he gave me all I needed and by the end of the week, I became his inamorata…

***

Two months later, I was still in sexual bliss, even though some of Chaz's stories were beginning to seem real suspect. That little girl, Jasmine, seemed to never go home. I finally asked about it and he first said that her foster mother was in the hospital, so he offered to keep her until she got better. Around the third week of her being there every day, his story changed to that was really his son's half-sister. The real story, or so he says, is that the mom died not when his son was a baby, but when the little girl was around two years old, his son was four at the time. Jasmine's father was still the cause of her death, according to him. He claims that while he was in prison, his mother kept his son, but didn't want to keep Jasmine. So when he got out of jail, he went looking for her, because his son kept asking for her. He found out from a family friend that she was in the same foster home that the mother had lived in when she was little; being taken care of by the same lady. Thus, explains her age. He apologized for lying and said that it wouldn't happen again. He wasn't sure of how I would accept it all, so he said he waited until he felt we were in a position of trust, before he would give me the whole truth.

He also admitted to me that he was a sex addict and once upon a time, he lived in the house with two women, kinda like sister wives, except they all slept in the same bed together every night. I couldn't believe my ears when he told me that. Since I don't judge people by their past, I let it go. I was truly blinded by the penis and it was starting to show. One night Portia invited us over for dinner. The chemo had really helped her and she was getting back to her normal self. I had to go to my office to turn in some files, so I told Chaz I would meet him there around seven. I got there a little early and helped Portia finish cooking. Some of our other friends joined us and it seemed as if we were going to have a good time. Around 7:30, Chaz finally shows up. I answered the door and introduced him to everybody. We were all in the living room watching Fruitvale Station and enjoying our meal. I went into the kitchen and fixed his plate, and rejoined the festivities. After everyone finished eating, we sat around talking and laughing. Chaz started to act rather standoffish. Portia looked me and nodded towards the kitchen. I grabbed a few of the plates, and followed her. Once in the kitchen, she asked what his problem was. I told her I had no clue, but I was going to find out. While we were in there talking, I heard Portia's boyfriend ask Chaz what he did for a living, and he responded in a very rude manner. That was my cue to step in.

"Hey baby, can I see you outside for a minute?" I called over to Chaz, while walking towards the front door. He got up without a reply and followed suit. He left the main door open, so unfortunately, everyone inside could hear our conversation.

"What's wrong with you? Why you acting all stank?" I asked him.

"Cause man, this shit is boring. I could've just gone out with my friends tonight," he declared.

"What friends are these and where were y'all planning on going?" Now I'm pissed, not because he has friends all of a sudden, but he didn't think to mention it to me when I asked him to come with me over here to Portia's.

He replies, "Some of my buddies from my old neighborhood are in town and are all at the Hollywood Improv for a comedy show tonight. I told them I would meet up with them, but then I forgot I promised you I would come here. But now that I'm here, I'm mad 'cause this ain't my type of kicking it."

Confused as all get out, I simply stare at him trying to find the right words. "Well, I'm sorry my friends and I are boring you. Gon' head and go meet your homeboys. I'll catch up with you later."

He tries to smooth things over, "Man, Kesh look, I'm not trying to upset you. I apologize if I did. I'll stay if you really want me to."

"Naw, it's cool. You better get there before the show ends. Just text me and let me know you made it home. Okay?"

"Are you sure?" I nod my head yes. He kisses me on the cheek. "Alright, thanks, babe and tell Portia the food was delicious."

I watched him walk down the steps onto the sidewalk and to his car. He climbed in and took off as if the police were after him. Portia came outside, scaring me half to death.

"I don't like him, Kesh; something about him doesn't sit well with me."

"He's cool, Portia, really he is. I don't know why he's acting like that. I have never seen him that way."

She touches my shoulder. "Hmmm…well, if you say so, but if I were you, I'd keep my eyes wide open where he is concerned. Come on back inside, I was just about to cut the red velvet cake Mishaya made."

I followed her back into the house and apologized to my friends for Chaz's rude behavior. I left Portia's house around midnight. Not one single text from Chaz appeared on my phone. I had a missed call from Julian and Marcus though. No way I'm entertaining those fools tonight. I fell asleep shortly after climbing in bed. Two days went past before I heard from Chaz again; he finally sent me a text.

Chaz: Hey lil mama, sorry I've been out of touch. The fellas and I decided to drive down to Tijuana that night and my phone wasn't getting any reception over there. I thought about calling you from the hotel but the international charges were a bitch. I'll be home later this evening. Call you when I touch down. Love you. Talk to you soon.

What a crock of BS! Little does he know; I hacked into his voicemail last night, and heard some woman telling him that she'd had a great time. I also checked his BPM page and saw that he had logged on less than six hours ago. I may be a fool in love, but stupid is what I'm not. Wait until I see him tomorrow, it's on! But for now, I'm going to act like nothing is wrong, and I reply to his message.

Keisha: Hey, baby! I miss you! I'm glad you and your boys had a great time! Get home safe! See you soon! Love you 2! TTYL.

Later that night, he called around ten o'clock; I let him go to voicemail to let him get a whiff of his own medicine. I'll deal with him later. I checked my messages to see what he said; nothing major, just that he was home, tired, and would call me in the morning. Cool with me. I turned my phone off and went back to bed. The next morning I got up, got dressed, cooked myself a nice breakfast and prepared myself for the day. The rainy season had hit, so not many people were scheduling showings. I had a few houses that were nearing their closing date, so I decided to work on those files once I got to the office. I decided to send Chaz a message.

Keisha: Hey, love! I'm headed to the office for a few hours. How about we meet for lunch at Roscoe's on Manchester? Let's say around one o'clock.

Chaz: Sounds like a plan. See you then.

Perfect. I went to my office and completed what I needed to do and then let my secretary know I was gone for the rest of the day. Chaz and I had some unfinished business to tend to. So that I won't make a scene at Roscoe's, I got there early and ordered my food, the Obama Special and a Lisa's Delight. One tends not to act crazy with a full stomach. Chaz came in, right on time and joined me at the table. The waitress took his order and left us alone to talk. I remained cool, asking him about his impromptu trip to Mexico and he filled me in on the fun-filled details. I told him about work and made small talk about the kids and other stuff for the next hour.

It's crazy how a man can mess up and know they wrong, so they start putting it on extra thick. I let him think he had me and agreed to go back to his house for an afternoon romp in the hay. The kids were still at school, so that meant we could be as loud as we wanted. I started to go right in on him about his BPM profile, but my girl had a different agenda. She wanted to get fed first before I broke up our happy home with my findings. She was right, though; if this was going to be the end, we might as well go out with a bang.

We finished our love session a few hours later. I got up to take a shower, not knowing how his reaction was going to be once I questioned him about still having his profile. After my shower, I laid across the bed and lotioned up. He was on his laptop, checking inventory. I bet he was. Tired of beating around the bush, I came right out with it.

"Chaz, how come you still have your BPM profile? I thought we agreed that we were going to shut our profiles down?"

"Well, how do you know if I still have mine if yours was closed?"

Ha! He thinks he's slick. "I reactivated it to check and see if you had done the same and to my surprise, not only was yours still active, you had been on there within hours of me checking."

He sat there looking stuck on stupid, then quickly retorted, "So now you checking on me? Dang, what happened to put your trust in me? If you must know, sometimes it takes them a minute to close your profile and because I originally paid for the six-month special they had before I met you, I didn't have time to cancel it before they ran my card again. So I'm stuck with it until the year is up. I already sent them an email about it too. They said since they already charged my card, there's nothing I can do. That day you saw me on there I was checking to if there was a way I could cancel it from the app on my phone, but I couldn't."

"Well damn, you got the app on your phone too? I didn't even know they had an app. Look, I hear what you saying about your card and all; I'm just trying to see if you're still looking, 'cause I thought we had something special. And if we agree on something and things don't work out as planned, then you should let me know, instead of hiding it."

"Yeah, you right. My bad. Is there anything else you want to know?"

"Nope, I'm good. I'm going to the living room to watch some TV. You joining me or not?"

"Yeah in a minute. Let me finish sending out these emails and I'll be there."

I went in the living room and plopped down on the couch. That fool is lying out his behind and he really thinks I'm that stupid to believe him. I know I should leave him alone but I don't have enough proof yet to prove my case. Portia's words started to haunt me. I flip through the channels until finally landing on the Jefferson's. I need some of George's antics to lift my spirits right now. A few minutes later Chaz joined me on the couch. He fixed us some ice cream and lit a fire in the fireplace. Yea he's guilty. That's the only time he puts a log in here.

About an hour after eating the ice cream, he claims his stomach was hurting and said he was going to the bathroom. He was in there for about thirty minutes, so I started to get worried. I walked down the hallway and stood outside the bathroom door across from his son's room. I could hear him talking on the phone. I wonder who that is. I leaned my ear against the door to see if I could make out his words. All I could hear was him kee-keeing and responding as if a woman was on the other end. Ain't no man doing that kind of laughing with another man, unless he's a fun boy. Something said to twist the knob on the door to see if it was locked, so I did and to my surprise, it wasn't. You should have seen his face when the door flew open and I was standing in the doorway. He paused for a second, allowing me to hear the woman still talking. She was going on and on about God knows what. I stood there; hand on my hip, waiting for him to acknowledge me. He told his caller to hold on a second and pushed the mute button on his phone.

"What's wrong, you okay?" he nervously asked.

"Oh, I'm good. I was coming in here to check on you to see if you were all right. Who is that on the phone?"

"It's my aunt, babe. Don't worry, babe, I'm cool. I'll be out in a minute." He forced a smile on his face, though his eyes showed nothing but fear. I closed the door and went back in the living room.

Twenty minutes later, he was still in there. This time when I got up to go check, I heard his voice, so I sat back down. I thought he was coming back in here with me, but no, he went into his room. This Negro is tripping for real this time. I waited and I waited until finally, I couldn't take it any longer. I marched my butt back down the hallway and into his room. There he was, laptop in hand, still laughing on the phone with this woman. I know this wasn't his auntie, because he was asking her about her family. I swear men are stupid sometimes, can't even get their lies straight. I stood there listening for a good two minutes, before he felt my presence near him. He jumped and dropped the phone. You could hear her saying, "Hello? Hello? Chaz, are you there?" He picked up the phone and disconnected the call. He sat the phone on the bed and looked up at me.

"Chaz, I don't know what is going on, but I know good and well that wasn't your aunt. I don't have time for this foolishness. I'm going home. When you get your shit together, give me a call." I didn't even wait to hear his response. I snatched up my belongings and basically, ran out the door. I ignored his calls for the next three days. In the meantime, I went back on BPM to check his page again, only to find out that he had blocked me! Aha! This man is ill. To make sure I wasn't losing it or that they really had finally deleted his profile, I created a new one without a picture and went to search for him. Sure enough, there he was; and do you know he had the audacity to put up the pictures I took of him that time we drove up to San Francisco and went to the beach? Unbelievable. I'm beginning to feel like Portia was right about him.

While I was sitting there reeling from this newfound information, I decided to do a little more digging. I started typing in various dating sites and found this fool on almost all of them. Even some I never heard of like singlefathers.com. When did they create that site? Lord have mercy, this fool is not only addicted to sex, he's addicted to online dating too! Maybe this is how he cures his habit. Oh Lord, what have I gotten myself into? I don't want to call him, because I know he's going to find a way to dispel everything I have to say. I don't know what to do. Thankfully, I'm going up to Sacramento to visit my parents for Christmas. Being there will help keep my mind off him.

Chapter Five

It's Christmas Eve and my parents' house is full of people. All my siblings are here with their children and grandchildren for some of them. Everybody was camped out in every corner of this house. My mom had it decorated to a tee. We cooked a bunch of food and desserts. Kids were running all around. My dad and brothers were in his man cave watching ESPN, while my sisters and I sat in the family room, catching up. It felt good to be around my family. They always made the hustle and bustle of my life seem like a walk in the park. In our usual tradition, we stayed up 'til midnight and let the kids open their gifts. There was wrapping paper all over the floor. My mom went and grabbed a few garbage bags from the pantry, and handed them to us to help pick up the trash the kids were throwing about. By that time, I went and laid down in my old room; my body was aching. I checked my phone to see if I had missed anything of importance, even though I had my calls and emails on vacation mode. There were a few Merry Christmas messages from my boss, a bunch of random dudes from POF and

BPM. One was disturbing message from Chaz that said, "Call me when you get this, it's urgent!"

I pushed the phone icon at the top of the message screen. A few seconds later, I heard ringing in my ear. He answered frantically, "Keisha, hey, I've been trying to reach you for a week now. Are you okay?"

"Yes, Chaz, I'm fine. What's up? Are you okay?"

"Well, I am now. I didn't know what had happened after you left my house that night. I know you were upset and when you didn't respond to my calls, I got worried."

"No need to worry, Chaz. Like I said, I'm fine."

"Dang, why you sound so cold?"

"No reason," was all I could say. I know he doesn't think I'm just going to act as if nothing happened. Those days are over. He'd better come correct or not at all. Besides, I don't know if I even feel like being bothered anymore. He has too much going on for me. My vagina was questioning my reasoning, stating the obvious fact that I said I didn't want to settle down right now, so why not enjoy the great sex? Even if her point may be valid, I have to be honest with myself and acknowledge that I have caught real feelings for Chaz, and the way he's handling things can only lead to heartache for me. Shoot, I could've stayed with Kevin if I was gonna deal with this. At least, with him, I knew what I was getting. All Chaz does is lie on top of lies.

"Look Keisha, I know I've been messing up, but I told you I had an issue. I'm trying to deal with it, it's just hard, ya know? I promise, if you give me one more chance; I'll make it up to you. Please?"

"I don't know, Chaz. I need some time to figure all this out. How about for now, we say that we're done. I'll be home in a few days. I'll let you know if my feelings have changed then. Merry Christmas, Chaz. Good night."

"Wait, Keisha, please don't hang up. I love you, I really do. I can't lose you. You are mine and I'm not letting you go. Take all the time you need. I'll be here waiting for you when you get back. Merry Christmas."

We hung up the phone and I cried myself to sleep. What a Merry Christmas this turned out to be. Not wanting to put a damper on our family celebration, I woke up Christmas morning with a new attitude. We went to church, followed by ice-skating at the makeshift rink in Old Sac. We all had a ball. Tired and hungry, we went back to my parent's house and filled our bellies with leftovers. We spent the rest of the night playing Dominoes, Scattergories, and Monopoly.

***

I decided to go home early and surprise Chaz. Talking to my mom and sisters, I learned that men make a lot of mistakes and sometimes that means we as women have to overlook them if we feel that their good outweighs the bad. He has so many other great qualities, and maybe if I suggest counseling for his sexual addiction that might change things between us. I headed straight to his house from LAX; I didn't even bother to see if he was home. I paid the cab driver and headed to his front door. All the lights were on, so that was a good sign. I knocked on the door and Xavier answered and let me in. I sat my suitcase down near the front door and walk down the hall to Chaz's room. I heard voices as I approached, but I assumed that was just the television. I opened the door and there was a woman sprawled out across his bed in nothing but a pair of black Louboutin's with the spikes on the toes. I didn't see Chaz anywhere, so I waited by the door. Shortly after, he came out the master bathroom, naked as well. The woman sat up on the bed smirking, staring me down the whole time. He looked at her puzzled, then turned and saw me standing at his bedroom door.

"Shit. Keisha, let me explain." He grabbed his robe, put it on and walked towards me.

"No explanation needed, Chaz. I just came by to let you know I was back in town earlier than planned. I guess I should've called first. I'll let you get back to your company."

I shut the door and headed back down the hall towards the front door. I grabbed my bag and walked out. I took my phone from my jacket pocket and texted my secretary:

Keisha: Hey Danielle, thanks for helping me set him up. It's up to you if you wanna stay and get yo back blown out. If not I'll see you Monday at the office.

Danielle: You're welcome, Keisha. I thought about staying, but he just asked me to leave. Get home safe. I'll text you when I make it home.

Keisha: Alright boo thanks again. I'm going over to my aunt's for the night. TTYL.

Danielle: Cool. Good night.

Keisha: Nite.

Can't Let Go

Kisha Green

*T*he fourteenth day of the second month of the year is a day to be wined and dined, or be reminded that you do not have anyone special in your life. Valentine's Day is what many call a man-made holiday couples use to show how much they love one another. Kelly Newman had it all; being married to millionaire, Alex Newman ensured that. The chemistry between the two was undeniable. Alex always surprised her with luxury gifts or sexy rendezvous. Valentine's Day the year before was definitely unforgettable.

Kelly recalled coming home and being met in the garage by Alex, who took her hand and asked her to follow him, which she did without hesitation. As soon as they walked inside their home, Alex turned around and asked softly, "Do you trust me?"

Kelly let out a giggle and blushed. "Of course I do, sweetheart, why do you ask?"

Alex continued to lead his wife through the house and made his way to their master bedroom, with Kelly ready to act out his plan.

"Lay down," Alex ordered. Kelly obeyed as she removed her Tory Burch flats and lay on the bed, propping two pillows underneath her head.

"What are you doing?" she asked as Alex covered her eyes. "Babe, I can't see anything," Kelly said.

"That is the whole point," Alex replied as he tied the knot in the satin blindfold.

Alex carefully rolled her body onto her stomach and started to fondle her. He first removed her pants, while unbuttoning her shirt, making sure not to move the blindfold. Kelly laid there in a purple bra and matching underwear. Thinking to herself how glad she was that she'd decided to wear a matching set that day.

Alex removed her undergarments and began placing soft kisses all over her body.

Kelly cooed in delight as goosebumps appeared all over her body.

Alex removed his clothes, rolled her body back over on her back, placed himself between her thighs, and continued to caress and arouse Kelly's erect nipples. His hands roamed over her body and massaged her left nipple with his tongue, which drove Kelly wild. His curious tongue made its way to her abdominal area, where he circled her belly button, until he placed soft kisses right above her pubic hairline. This drove Kelly wild and her legs spread wider, anticipating what would happen next. Alex wasted no time kissing her clit, ravishing her love canal with his thirsty tongue as he sucked and slurped on every part. Giving it the most devotion he could muster, he paid careful attention to her clit, as it stood erect and appreciative of the dedication it was getting. The feeling of utopia surging through Kelly was like nothing she had ever felt, as she moaned and her hips gyrated in pleasure. The feeling did something indescribable to her and Alex knew this; it was his power he had over his wife, the one moment where she was a slave to his rhythm. Kelly's body began to tremble and shake as her legs twitched, and her body began to jerk from side to side. Alex took delight in watching his wife climax right before his eyes, the movement caused him to stop and watch her body respond to his work. Kelly bit her bottom lip as moans escaped her mouth.

Her clit was pounding with need, and as much as Alex wanted to resume licking and playing, he could not deny feeling her legs spreading. Kelly was eagerly inviting him to continue to lick his way down through her engorged lips. His tongue was warmer than the creamy substance and it felt incredible on Kelly's skin. Alex wasted no time and meticulously cleaned her pussy as the orgasm built up again for another explosive release.

Alex was rock hard, but he refused to let Kelly come; she began begging him to enter her and after minutes of heavy breathing and panting, Alex bent his wife over. A soft breeze passed her ass and immediately his hard wand was eagerly waiting to enter her opening. Kelly quickly lifted her ass to assist in getting to feel what she impatiently yearned for. Kelly was already soaking wet and having his dick inside of her was exactly what she needed at this particular moment, to take her to another world of exhilarated bliss. Alex wasted no time; he slid into Kelly easily and her pussy welcomed him without a fight. Alex took his first stroke and went deep into her canal; he felt the walls wrap around his dick as she tightened her grip on his member. Kelly reached down with her perfectly manicured hands to play with her clit. Alex's dick was hard and rigid as he aimed with pure accuracy, hitting his wife's walls from every angle. Kelly was in a zone, working feverishly on her clit with her fingers, which in turn made her pussy more wet and excited. He began to moan loudly, indicating he was ready and without a word, Kelly could feel him shake as he released inside of her. Hot sticky cum filled her insides quickly, and Kelly's orgasm shot through her body, meeting his electricity. There were sparks of light flashing behind her covered eyes as she smiled. Kelly loved these moments.

Her life had been a good one, but lately, Alex seemed more consumed with work and business trips. The couple's lovemaking actually had been too far in between. After many months of being dissatisfied with the distance between her and Alex, she was very pleased that after several months of asking, she finally got him to agree to come to bed early, so that they could reconnect. A couple that once made love several times a day reduced that quota to once every so often, and when it did occur, it was quick and usually uneventful. When Alex arrived home last night, Kelly greeted him at the door, wearing nothing but a pink negligée and a smile. She welcomed him with a long, wet, and soft kiss. She then took him by the hand and led him into the living room, where she proceeded to kiss her husband again. Kelly wasted no time as she unbuckled his belt, slid his pants down and kissed him again. Shortly thereafter, Kelly grabbed ahold of his swelling member; her grip revealed the veins visible and pulsating, as she looked into Alex's eyes with lust and said, "Mmmm," seductively. She then instructed him to have a seat and he obeyed. Once seated, he watched as his wife sexily removed her lingerie slowly. Kelly had been watching a few YouTube videos of strippers, so she was attempting to imitate them. Although the dancing wasn't exactly a combination of her Zumba and Hip Hop Abs class, she did have some moves. Alex had to admit it was a nice show and she knew that he was enjoying it, because he hadn't taken his eyes off her. Kelly then turned around with her backside facing him, and bent over in front of him while spreading her ass cheeks, making sure he saw her freshly waxed pink kitty. Kelly knew Alex was slightly disappointed that she did not proceed to take him in her mouth and let his dick make love to her mouth. Nor, did she bless him with foreplay; her pussy was throbbing and she wanted to feel him inside of her as quickly as possible. Kelly then quickly straddled him and her wet pussy immediately greeted him. She was able to consume him with one deep thrust and started with a slow bounce that progressively sped up. He enjoyed the way her perky vanilla breasts jiggled up and down in unison with her love box. Kelly could sense that he was ready to release as his breathing intensified, and then he suddenly let out a loud groan and filled her with his milky release. Kelly slowly climbed off, kissed her lover on the lips and as she made her way to the bathroom, she noticed her own liquids running down her thighs and legs. While in the master bathroom, she heard Alex in the bedroom and the television blaring some sports information. Kelly decided on a quick shower and figured they could pick up where they left off in the living room and begin part two.

Kelly finished her shower and exited the bathroom to see her handsome spouse lying across the bed, wearing nothing but a smile when they made eye contact. Kelly smiled and thought about how much she loved her man, because he always made sure she was happy and had a smile on her face. Alex was a true provider in every sense of the world.

"I want to feel you inside of me so bad," Kelly breathed.

"I knew it." Alex's eyes glinted naughtily, and then his mouth covered her nipple and his tongue swirls its center, sending shocks of pleasure all the way to her groin. Moments like this made Kelly feel so good.

Kelly started to groan and purr because she could not contain herself. She threw off Ralph Lauren plush bathrobe as she straddles her man. His hands grasp around her bare ass exciting her, and then he spanked her bottom harder. Kelly gives into a scream of enjoyment and brings herself down on his erection. Alex then flips his wife over so that now she is on the bottom and he is on top of her. He looks directly into her big blue eyes and whispers that he loves her. He then begins to enter her body, which fills Kelly up, because the two connect perfectly like a hand and a glove. The rhythmic unison almost causes Kelly to release her juices all over Alex's manhood; her body tremors as she moves up and down with each thrust he pumps inside of her. Alex's hips are moving in a circular, slow motion, giving Kelly sheer delight and a feeling she cannot explain or control, so she lets out faint screams.

"Oh yes! Baby!" Kelly shouted at him. It hasn't even been more than ten minutes, but she was ready to explode because of the electricity between the two.

Alex takes one long and deep thrust inside of her and it felt like he had tapped the back of Kelly's tight vaginal wall. She started to shake and tighten up on him as a release came from within; if she didn't know any better, she might have thought she had urinated on herself. Kelly is screaming in pure bliss, but she doesn't know what she's saying; her words are incomprehensible. For that moment, she was not of this world, but a place of ecstasy where only the couple only existed. Kelly could feel the orgasm all the way to the tip of her pretty, pedicured toes. She moves and thrust against him, never wanting the feeling to ever end.

"Come for me again, baby!" Alex ordered and pushed himself deeper inside again, until Kelly felt completely full. Kelly was in a state of shock, unaware that this much liquid could be expelled from a human body.

The air leaves Kelly's lungs as she inhales and exhales, and then viciously comes again, falling and flowing with the waves in my ocean of pleasure. Alex is so close that Kelly can feel him throbbing inside of her as he moves in and out, setting his rhythm to the beat of her heart. His hands grasp the headboard and he moves Kelly against himself and explodes in orgasm again, her moisture in a pool around him as he finds release inside his wife with a loud groan.

Alex then collapsed on top of Kelly and the only sound was the beating of their hearts as they both laid in post orgasmic bliss. There is no word to describe how powerful of a connection the two felt and that particular moment. The Newman's connected on so many levels at this exact moment in time; they would never forget this Valentine's Day.

ONE YEAR LATER

On this Valentine's Day, Kelly should have been on a tropical island, a fruity drink in hand with the cute umbrella, while her hunk of a husband applied suntan lotion over her body. Instead, she was walking the corridors of an upscale mall, overdosing on retail therapy.

Alex was away on business yet again, but before leaving for his flight that morning, he left a credit card with no limit on their granite kitchen countertop. This had become the norm for the couple. Alex traveled for business and Kelly shopped. Even as recent as a year ago, there was more chemistry, but lately that was no longer the case. She had recently remodeled their entire home and was working on doing the same for their summer home in Boca Raton, Florida. When Kelly wasn't spending money, she was a fashion blogger, which was easy since she was a fashionista. Kelly was gorgeous; some natural and some enhanced with the help of top-notch physicians. Kelly stood tall and she had the best legs and showed them off every chance that she got.

"Welcome back, Mrs. Newman," the cheerful Victoria's Secret greeter spoke happily.

"Hi, Shanna."

Kelly thought maybe her sex life needed spice and perhaps some nice lingerie at her husband's expense would liven things up once he returned from Minnesota.

"I am looking for something sexy," she spoke softly.

"Well, come right this way, we just got some new goodies that you might like."

Kelly wasn't interested in buying something new, but she felt she needed to do something different, because it had been almost six months since the last time they were intimate. She had needs and desires and had grown accustomed to Alex fulfilling her insatiable appetite. However, his working constantly took first place in the marriage. She often asked about their relationship, and he quickly reminded her that if she wanted the lifestyle they currently had; then she had to accept the fact that it would mean spending nights alone. At the time, Kelly just didn't know that those nights were going to be quite frequent when he'd initially said it. Nevertheless, she was not about to become another bored and lonely housewife, lusting over the pool guy or landscaper because she was sexually frustrated. Nor would she be getting drunk off wine with other lonely ladies, having Pure Romance Parties to pass the time.

Kelly ran her fingers over the satin lingerie placed before her and closing her eyes, thought about a better time in her marriage.

"Excuse me, are these yours?" an unfamiliar male said.

Kelly opened her eyes and, she was startled when she saw a tall, dark, and very attractive black male staring at her.

"Huh, what?" she asked annoyed.

"Those satin sets you have been holding; I wanted to know if you were…"

"Oh, these." Kelly blushed as she dropped the set back into the pile.

"Yeah, those; you seemed deep in thought about them, so I wanted to know the magic they created."

"They are a good investment, trust me on that." Kelly winked.

What am I doing? She thought as she stood there in the middle of the store. She'd just flirted with a strange man, a strange black man nonetheless. She wasn't racist, but she'd never had much interaction with black men, other than in passing while out. She'd never an actual conversation and definitely never flirted as she was currently doing. Alex would be livid, since he wasn't exactly fond of black people in general. There was something about this guy that was mysterious, but also very attractive. Kelly looked at him again out of her peripheral view and noticed a tall man in a nice, gray wool pea coat; he was dressed in black slacks that accentuated his tall, thin, yet muscular frame. Overall, an attractive man, but something about him made Kelly a bit uncomfortable.

"How can I be sure of your recommendation?" he asked flirtingly.

"Excuse me?" she asked perplexed.

"You said it is a good investment, and I want to know how I can be sure. Are you going to show me how they look on you?"

Kelly could not believe his boldness and looked around the store to see if anyone was listening or paying attention. It appeared the other shoppers were so engrossed in their own worlds that they did not take notice. She knew she should not even be engaging in any type of conversation with this strange man, but he was attractive. Besides, this was the only attention she was getting and she was curious.

"Don't worry, you don't have to answer now," he said as he handed her his business card and exited the store.

Kelly stood there, holding the card in her perfectly manicured hand. She read the card and smiled before placing it in her purse. She inhaled, slowly exhaled, and then proceeded to walk out the store. This was unreal and she quickly walked to her car. Once she retrieved her keys and pressed the button, the doors unlocked on her luxury sedan; she entered her car and sat there staring ahead. As she looked at the cars in the parking lot, she couldn't help but think of the handsome stranger. She started the engine of her car and began to drive. The entire car ride home was in silence, because she could not get him out of her head. Once home, she took her purchases, putting them in their appropriate places, and changed into a tee shirt and leggings. She walked to the kitchen and was initially going to grab a bottled water, but quickly changed her mind. Kelly grabbed a glass and poured herself some Dornfeld red wine that had been chilling in her refrigerator and walked back to her room. She retrieved the business card and her cell phone from her purse and sat on her chaise lounge just staring at the card. Part of her wanted to call, but the shy and timid girl did not, because she knew better. In the last year, the relationship she once shared with her spouse had gone from good to bad in a short period of time. The more she expressed her dissatisfaction to Alex, the more gifts and money he gave. Regardless of how she felt, it still did not excuse the fact that she was sitting there, currently deciding whether to call a stranger or not. Alex was gone for a week, so it wasn't as if she was worried about being caught on the phone, but she felt it was morally wrong. Kelly took a big gulp of her wine and quickly placed the glass on the nightstand. She looked at the business card and her phone, and kept looking back and forth contemplating, while still unsure of her next action. Kelly took her vows seriously, but the last year had gotten so bad, anything looked well than what she was currently dealing with.

Without any more hesitation, she looked at the screensaver picture of her and Alex and pressed her thumbprint to unlock her phone. She dialed the ten numbers slowly and softly, as if she was waiting for there to be a reason to place her phone down. No such luck; the phone was ringing and by the third ring, she was ready to hang up.

"I knew you would call."

"Excuse me?" Kelly replied uncertainly.

"I said, I knew you would call," he repeated himself.

"Ummm. How did you know?"

"Because I know me."

"Oh, so you are so sure of yourself?" Kelly asked.

"Yep! As a matter of fact, I am."

So are you going to tell me your name? It is only fair since you know mine," he said.

Kelly smiled and took a sip of her wine, while looking at the professional business card that read Wesley Phillips. It stated that he worked in investments and listed his phone number and email, along with his website.

"I am waiting," Wesley said, taking Kelly out of her temporary daydream. Kelly was shocked that she had been so bold and now that she was on the phone, she had to do something. Just as a deer caught in the street in the headlights, she was frozen with fear.

"Hello Wesley, my name is Kelly," she spoke almost in a whisper.

"Kelly, huh?" he asked sarcastically.

"Yes, Kelly is my name." Kelly got off her chaise lounge and proceeded to walk to her gourmet kitchen and pour more wine.

The red substance was giving her courage that she normally did not have since having him on the phone.

What are you wearing, Kelly?" he asked.

"Excuse me?"

"Don't be coy with me, Kelly; I met you while you were shopping for lingerie."

Kelly let out a small laugh, not because what he'd said was funny, but more so that she was in shock at what he was requesting to know. Lastly, she didn't know if she should answer honestly or lie.

"I am wearing clothes."

"Oh, okay, smarty pants. Well, I am wearing boxers and socks, wanna see?"

Kelly could not believe how bold he was, but at the same time, it was that much more exciting that he seemed to be carefree and unpredictable.

"No thanks, but thanks for the offer."

"What kind of phone do you have, Miss Kelly?"

"I have an iPhone 6."

"Oh, word? A'ight bet."

Wesley ended the phone call and Kelly sat there in disbelief that he had hung up the phone. She was beginning to like his witty personality. She sat in silence drinking when her phone rang; she looked at the screen and she could see his face, and she was shocked as to how he did that. She could not help but see a handsome face and a bare chest. At first, she didn't know how to answer the call, but then she saw she had the option to accept or decline. By the time that she figured out what to do, the phone was no longer ringing. Subconsciously, she hoped that he would call her back. The phone was silent and she sat there, instantly saddened. She finished yet another glass of wine and headed to open another bottle. She did not want to take the chance that Wesley would call back and she miss it, so she placed the smartphone in her bra as she retrieved more wine from her Allevino wine refrigerator. She grabbed the electronic corkscrew and opened her second bottle of wine, refilling her glass. So many thoughts were running through her mind, but she had to admit; even though the conversation was quick, she liked the attention that Wesley was giving her. It felt good to have the spotlight on her. At that instance, her phone began to ring; she quickly put the glass down, and retrieved her phone from her bosom. She saw Wesley's handsome face again and this time, she pressed accept.

Wesley was a hunk of a man and even though Kelly could only see a small glimpse, the view she was getting, made her mind wonder. Not sure if the boxer view was on purpose or not, she did not shy away.

"Oh, my bad, Kelly," Wesley said as he moved the cellular device to show his washboard abdomen and his chiseled chest, all the way until his face was in full view. Kelly enjoyed what she was seeing; she felt guilty, but only for a minute, because the view she saw made her curious as to what else was Wesley going to show her.

"You have beautiful eyes; they are as blue as the sea."

"Thank you, Wesley."

"Call me Wes."

I like your hair color; dirty blonde, I see."

Thank you."

Take your hair down," Wesley commanded.

Kelly removed the hair tie, shook her head, and her tresses cascaded to her shoulders.

"You have beautiful hair."

"Thank you."

"Do you always do what you are told?" Wesley asked.

"What do you mean?"

Nothing, beautiful."

The two continued flirting for the rest of the night, until they both fell asleep. Kelly awakened on her bed still dressed and feeling groggy. *Too much wine*, she immediately thought and started to reminisce about her late night conversation with Wesley the night before. The two had spoken about everything under the sun, from their upbringing, scholastic abilities and saving the best for last, romance. Kelly got off the bed, plugged her phone into the charger on her marble nightstand and walked to her dresser to retrieve a lavender Vickie's Secret pants suit. She grabbed her matching undergarments, headed to the bathroom and showered in silence. As she washed her body, all she could do was think of Wesley and his sexy voice. Not once did she think of her husband, except for when she applied body wash to her washcloth, and glanced at her 8-karat wedding ring sitting beautifully on her left hand. Even covered in suds, it was a gorgeous sight.

Kelly sprayed Burberry body spray all over her pulse points after bathing, as she admired her naked body in the mirror. *How could someone not desire me? Alex has to be a fool not to want this.* She finished getting dressed and when she went back into her room, she could hear the notification from her cell phone, letting her know she had an unread text message.

What turns you on?

Kelly read the message seven times and each time, the smile on her face widened. Something about Wesley definitely turned her on.

Under normal circumstances, she would have ignored that message and kept it moving, but the curiosity in her would not let her ignore him. She was a married woman, but her husband was out of town and all she had was time and opportunity on her hands.

Hello, are you there?

Kelly did not know what to do. She wanted to respond, but she was scared.

Wesley wasted no time as the next message came in.

I know you see my question and by you not responding, I already know the answer.

Kelly smiled and immediately responded, *Oh yeah? What?*

I knew that would get your attention beautiful.

You want to know what turns me on? Well…it is YOU!

I knew that, Wesley responded back.

Oh ok, Kelly replied quickly.

Can you do me a favor, beautiful?

What's that?

For you to meet me at the Borgata. Don't worry about a thing. I'll make all of the arrangements.

Borgata?

Yes.

As in Atlantic City, Borgata?

What other Borgata do you know?

Shut up, smartass!

No thanks, I have a husband.

I know you do, but I wasn't inviting him, I was inviting you.

Kelly did not want to continue texting any longer; she wanted to hear his voice. She walked to the kitchen, poured some lemonade into a glass and took a long sip, before placing the call. Her heart raced as the phone rang in her ear.

"Hello, beautiful."

"Hello."

"So did you want me to pick you up?"

ONE YEAR LATER

Kelly looked at her reflection in the five-star hotel room's bathroom mirror she was staying in for the weekend. She examined every part of her face, turned the faucet on and began to wash her face. She was almost unrecognizable, because for the last year she had successfully been having an affair with a man none of her friends or family would ever approve of. When Kelly was with Wesley, she did not see a black man nor did she even see herself as a white woman. All she saw was an incredibly attentive man, who didn't want to do anything but keep a smile on her face. It was never her intention to have an affair with any man for that matter, but Wesley was persistent and very attentive. That was partially the attraction, because it reminded her of how things used to be with

Alex. They had taken trips together, and went on many dates. She had never really been a fan of urban music; Kelly now found herself enjoying R&B music and began to take a particular liking to Raheem DeVaughn. Wesley had taken her to several of his concerts of his and they often made love to his music in the background. *So many good memories*, she thought, as she smirked in the mirror; she thought about the sexual chemistry the two shared and exited the bathroom.

Once in the bedroom, she walked over to Wesley, who was sitting on the bed looking through emails on his phone. He sat there with no shirt and just a pair of slacks on. Kelly could not resist, because he was incredibly handsome; she began to trace down the line of his zipper with her perfectly manicured fingers. Once her fingers made it all the way to the end, she waited for him to stop her, but he didn't; he took his eyes away from the smartphone and winked. He began to flex his hips and watched but more so eagerly anticipated what was going to happen next. Kelly unzipped his zipper and the room was completely silent, except for the breathing of the two. To her surprise, he wasn't wearing his boxer briefs; it was just flesh against rayon.

"Ooh daddy, no underwear, easy access right?"

"Nope, I like to feeling of my dick against the fabric."

Kelly took Wesley's manhood into her soft hands and just looked in total awe.

Something in the way he said dick that turned Kelly on more and she felt her pussy begin to throb. She positioned herself and started to tease the head of his dick with her attentive tongue. Kelly danced on the head with her tongue for several minutes before completely deep throating his member. She had him entirely engulfed in her mouth and down her throat and this turned Wesley on, because he loved watching his manhood disappear into Kelly's mouth. Kelly's eyes were closed as she made love to Wesley's dick with her mouth; she took patient care with it, using her tongue. After many minutes, she broke out of her trance and looked in her chocolate lover's eyes, with her lips looking pouty and wet. "Do you like when I taste you?"

Wesley couldn't even concentrate because of the euphoric feeling taking over him. He was disappointed that she had stopped and so desperately wanted her to resume. He took her head and placed it face-to-face with his wet hardness.

"Suck it, beautiful. Take me as far as you can again, please baby. Take all of me into that sweet, hot throat of yours and have your way with me. I so desperately want to fuck your mouth and control you by your hair; will you do that for me?" As the words exited his mouth, he looked into Kelly's eyes; his intense eye contact said it all as his spine relaxed and he prepared for ecstasy.

Suddenly, a heavy knock on the door quickly interrupted the lovers' moods. The two stopped and curiously gazed in each other's eyes. Wesley said nothing, while Kelly liked the idea of someone possibly eavesdropping on the other side of the door. She returned to licking the shaft of his manhood when a familiar voice killed her mood.

"Kelly, I know your whore ass is in there, so open the fucking door!"

Back At One

MiChaune

CHAPTER ONE

"*D*amn!" She was highly stressed and her vibrator friend wasn't doing its job. Allysia needed some release and she needed it fast. She wasn't dating anyone so, Allysia did what she had to do. She picked up the phone and called her estranged husband, Fred. His country ass seemed surprised to hear her voice, but when she told him to come over, he came running.

Allysia knew when she married him, she was just settling, but she didn't have time to look for real love. She certainly did not have the time to search and hunt or even worse, wait to be hunted. Her company was just getting off the ground, so she had no problem letting love take a backseat to her career.

***

"Oh shit!" Fred was opening up Pandora's Box with his powerful tongue. He licked away all of Allysia's juicy secrets as he stroked her clit with his tongue, and wrapped his lips around the plump lips, below her hips. Who knew a little pink flap could bring such pleasure?

Her body tingled all over as his tongue tangoed with her clit. She'd never had a seizure but the way her body was shaking and saliva was pouring out of her mouth, she just knew she was on the verge of having one.

I probably would have bit my damn tongue off! Allysia thought, that was just how intense her orgasm was. She unloaded all of her liquid ecstasy into her ex's open, eager mouth.

That was just the beginning though. Fred flipped her over, smacked her thick ass, and rammed his eight-inch dick inside Allysia's wet pussy. She wanted to wrap her lips around it, but it was obvious that he wanted the hotness that only her love tunnel could deliver.

The man pumped hard and fast, his thrusts were quick and short. Allysia tried to speak, but every word got caught in her throat as Fred's nuts slapped her behind. Then he slowed down; the slower, longer thrusts felt so damn good that she started speaking in tongues. Allysia didn't know what the hell she was saying, and he didn't give a shit. He just kept on pumping, picking up the pace, until the thrusts were short, quick, and hard again. She felt his dick pulsate just before he screamed, releasing his white chocolate inside of her.

"Damn!" he said, almost out of breath.

Damn was right, Allysia thought. Her soon to be ex-husband knew how to make him some serious love. She once thanked God for that man each and every day, because he had brought it each and every day. No man had ever eaten her pussy or fucked her as well as Fred had. He had always left Allysia completely satisfied.

Allysia's elevator of bliss was rising towards cloud nine, but just before she got to cloud six, Fred's ass had the nerve to ask, "So, have you thought anymore about having a threesome?"

"Now I remember why I left your country apple ass!" Allysia screamed. *Why did he always have to go and ruin the moment?* Her elevator quickly descended and before she knew it, she was at ground zero again. He had been bugging her about the threesome bullshit for over a month. The more she said no, the more his dumb ass asked the question.

The only thing Allysia felt she could praise her soon to be ex-husband for, was his sex. Were it not for his tongue and his dick, she wouldn't have shit good to say about the bastard.

The rest of their marriage sucked. Other than their sex life, there wasn't a relationship. Allysia was always busy working and Fred was busy being Fred. He changed jobs as frequently as she changed panties. Outside the bedroom, she couldn't stand Fred's country behind.

Allysia jumped out of her beautiful, deep Cherrywood bed that sat on a high pedestal.

"Get yo' country butt up and go home. I mean it!" Allysia was so fed up with her entire situation; she thought smoke was coming out of her ears.

Fred looked at her in pure disbelief.

"Did you not hear what I said?" Angrily, she reached down, grabbed his clothes and shoes and threw them at him. "Get out I said! I don't wanna see you anymore, and don't worry, I won't be calling you again. I'm also going to see the lawyer. It's time to make this divorce final." Allysia turned and walked away, feeling more liberated than she'd ever felt.

Allysia stepped into her massive bathroom with the jet Jacuzzi and shower and turned everything on, before walking into her expanded closet that she'd had custom designed. This fabulous closet was even bigger and better than Kimora Lee Simmons' closet from her reality show, *Fabulous Life.*

She peeked over at Fred as he was leaving and she wondered where the man she fell in decent like with, went. *His dang knees are all ashy and crusty. He used to be built. He was never that fine, but his body was the shiznit. Now, it just looks like shit, even though he can still work it.* It made her wonder why he wanted the other woman so bad. *I'm a badass woman all by myself. Full-figured, yeah, I am, but I'm sexy as sin.* Allysia shook her head as she looked at her naked reflection in the mirror, before stepping into a steaming hot bubble bath to relax.

After her bath, and morning massage from her personal masseuse, she ate the fabulous breakfast prepared by Juan Frisco, her personal chef, and delicious eye candy. Shortly after her meal, she couldn't help but rub her thighs and nipples, fantasizing about Juan Frisco, until the ringing of her phone's alarm jarred her back to reality, reminding her to be sure and stop by her lawyer's office before work. As always, she had to make sure that she was looking fresh in one of her custom-designed, two-piece pantsuits. Allysia headed out her front door, satisfied with her appearance, and ready to start her day.

***

"I want a divorce! Everything is mine, because he hasn't worked for shit. He will walk out of this marriage the same way he walked into it—ashy and broke!" Allyisa skipped the cordial bull and got straight to the point. She and Fred and were only married for six months. Her thirtieth birthday was six months away, and she wanted to celebrate a milestone and her long, overdue divorce to Fred!

Allysia's patient lawyer finally smiled, spoke up and said, "That's fine, Allysia. If you are certain that's what you want then I'll file the papers right away."

"Thank you, Osbourne." She slid on her Chanel shades and turned to walk away. Glancing over her shoulder, she caught Osbourne looking at her juicy, round ass. *God knew what he was doing when he made full-figured women like me! That's why He blessed me to make my multi-million-dollar company, Ample Delights.*

Leaving, she got back into her platinum-colored Lexus and headed off to her office in downtown Manhattan. Her personal life was a failure, but her company was a success. She wished it could wrap its arms around her on those nights when her bed was cold and lonely.

CHAPTER TWO

At 4:45 a.m., La Donna awoke to the sound of her rooster alarm clock. You could take the girl out the country, but you couldn't take the country out of the girl! Shoot, LaDonna wished she could have brought her rooster, Walter, with her to New York City. She had an interview that morning for the secretarial position at Ample Delights. *I'ma straighten my hair this mo'ning*, LaDonna thought as she was frying bacon and scrambling eggs. She leaned forward, almost burning herself on the grease.

"Lord, I'm so nervous about gettin' this job that I almost burned myself!" she said aloud to the surrounding walls.

Having come from a big family, she wasn't used to being in a house alone. LaDonna was one of twelve children born to her parents.

After having breakfast, LaDonna laid out her best dress. It was navy blue, with a white sailor collar. She had white stockings and matching navy blue shoes. LaDonna smiled to herself. She knew the outfit just might do the trick, and land her the job she so desperately needed.

LaDonna Jenkins moved to New York, without much more than a suitcase full of dreams and eyes that still sparkled with innocence. At age twenty-five, she was still fairly young and tender with thick thighs and a seductive smile. The youngest of her siblings, LaDonna was born and raised in Willacoochee, Georgia. She was the first one in her family to ever venture outside of the Peach State.

Even though she loved her family dearly, LaDonna wanted to see what life outside of Georgia was like. It was almost as if something was calling or even pulling her to New York City. She didn't know what it was, but she packed up her bags, kissed her family goodbye, and set out to discover the Big Apple. However, she's been in New York for two weeks with no job, and her money was running out, fast. If LaDonna didn't get the job at Ample Delights, she'd be on that midnight train to Georgia, on the first thing smoking.

After straightening her long, thick hair, LaDonna took a quick bath and slipped into her Sunday best. She stared at herself in the mirror and smiled, revealing deep dimples in each cheek. She had turned her long hair under with a curling iron. It looked pretty, resting on her shoulders. Her size fourteen dress fit nicely; it was one of her favorites.

LaDonna closed her eyes and prayed. "Lord, please, let your will be done. If I'm to stay here in New York City, I've got to have a job. Otherwise, I can't 'ford to stay up here. So, if it's your will, Lordy, I pray for this job in your name. Amen."

LaDonna took a cab to her destination. She tipped the driver four quarters that he didn't seem to appreciate. He grumbled something in a foreign language as LaDonna exited the cab. She said a quick prayer for him. She didn't understand why people had to be so rude and unhappy all the time.

LaDonna stared at the tall building in front of her before entering. She had never seen a building so tall in person. It had to have twenty or more floors, and according to LaDonna's directions, Ample Delights was on the top floor.

LaDonna wasn't used to riding in elevators. Twenty flights of stairs was a long way up, but it was safer than the elevator. LaDonna took a deep breath as she followed the sign that read, *STAIRS*.

"'Scuse me," a deep voice said.

LaDonna turned around to see a tall, dark man staring at her. He was wearing a uniform with the name, Ronald, stitched on the brown shirt.

"How far up you going?"

"I gotta interview at Ample Delights," LaDonna told the stranger. She felt nervous as she noticed him staring at her. She read the approval in his eyes when he smiled.

"That's all the way up top. You'll be out of breath by the time you make it that far. Why you don't just take the elevator?" He pointed toward the stainless steel doors. "It's a lot quicker."

LaDonna shrugged her shoulders. "Ain't too comfortable in no elevator." She was enjoying her conversation with Ronald. He didn't sound like all the other city folk. Ronald spoke LaDonna's southern dialect.

"I tell you what; I'll join you and keep you entertained. Before you know it, the ride will be over and you'll be having your interview. What's your name?"

LaDonna extended her right hand to him. "LaDonna Jenkins." The simple touch of his warm hand against hers sent chills up and down her spine. She couldn't deny that she was attracted to Ronald.

"I'm Ronald West." Ronald had already fallen in love with LaDonna's smile. Her eyes twinkled every time she smiled, and those dimples were as deep as the ocean. She was beautiful; LaDonna was curvaceous, and Ronald loved a full-figured woman.

"Come on. I don't want you to be late."

LaDonna allowed Ronald to lead her to the elevator. He talked to her and told her jokes the entire ride up, and as promised, before she knew it, they had arrived at the top floor. LaDonna closed her eyes and thanked God. The elevator ride wasn't half as bad as she had thought it would be.

"Good luck," Ronald said, as LaDonna stepped off the elevator. "I sure hope you get this job. I would love to see your pretty face every mornin'."

LaDonna blushed. "Thank you. I hope so, too."

The doors closed and Ronald disappeared.

LaDonna was twenty minutes early, so she got a magazine and took a seat. No sooner than she sat down, the elevator doors opened again. A beautiful, full-figured woman, fashionably dressed, and carrying a briefcase stepped off. She smelled like fresh Georgia peaches.

"Hello. May I help you?" the woman asked LaDonna.

"I got an interview with a Mrs. Donaldson in 'bout fifteen minutes," LaDonna answered as she held tightly to her resume and purse. She didn't know the woman. For all LaDonna knew, the woman was there for the same job and might try to sabotage her.

"Ms. Donaldson," the stranger corrected her. "Mrs. Donaldson is my mother."

LaDonna looked at the woman strangely.

The woman laughed. "I'm Allysia Donaldson. I'm the founder and owner of Ample Delights. And you are?"

LaDonna laughed nervously. "LaDonna Jenkins. I'm here for the secretary job."

She handed Ms. Donaldson the resume the woman at the library had helped to prepare for her. LaDonna didn't know much about computers.

"Well, if you would like, we can get started. Follow me," Allysia said.

"But…but don't you need me to get you some coffee or something?" LaDonna asked. "It's really no bother. I'll be glad to fetch you a cup."

"Thank you, Ms. Jenkins. That's very nice of you." Allysia sensed that LaDonna was a good person. She didn't have the type of experience Allysia was looking for, but something about her was endearing. According to the resume, LaDonna hadn't done much outside of farming and some manual bookkeeping for her father. "Maybe we can get a cup of coffee after your interview."

LaDonna followed Allysia into the large office. There was a beautiful view of New York outside the large window. The two women talked about the position and LaDonna's previous experience.

"I know I ain't got a lot of experience, but I'm a fast learner. And I really need this job, Ms. Donaldson," LaDonna pleaded. She felt at peace in Allysia's office. It was as if Ample Delights was where she belonged.

"Call me Allysia." She stood from her executive chair. "Now, let's go have that cup of coffee, so we can talk about when you start. Then we'll come back and fill out the paperwork."

LaDonna was so happy she jumped up from her chair and wrapped her arms around Allysia's neck. "Thank you, Ms. Donaldson, I mean, Allysia. Thank you!"

Again, she closed her eyes, thanking God above. He had a plan for her in New York City. She wasn't quite sure what that plan was, but she was ready to find out. She had a hunch that it had something to do with her new boss.

CHAPTER THREE

Allysia had just hired the sweetest sista she had ever met. *She's from some place in Georgia, Willahoochie or something like that. It sounds like the countriest place in the whole world, and poor LaDonna is the epitome of country!*

Allysia told her that she reminded her of Goldie from the *Flavor of Love* show and LaDonna said, "I didn't know that love came in different flavors." Then she asked Allysia why somebody would name a child Goldie! Allysia burst into laughter, and LaDonna couldn't for the life of her, understand what was so funny.

LaDonna had to have thought that Allysia wasn't going to give her the job after all, because all of a sudden she got the saddest look on her face.

Allysia noticed LaDonna's puppy-dog look, and told her, "Pick your chin up, because employees of mine have to walk with their heads held high." She seemed so excited.

I've never had someone who seemed so thrilled to be my personal assistant. The hug she thanked me with, just now made me realize that's I needed.

No, LaDonna wasn't the most qualified. However, I just couldn't send her back out on the street without a job; it was just something about her. Her simplicity and look of innocence was like a breath of fresh air. I knew I would really enjoy working with Ms. LaDonna Divine Jenkins. The first thing I had to do was transform her style. Actually, she needed a style to transform! She actually came in wearing a navy blue dress with that big ass white, sailor collar. That's not going to cut it at Ample Delights. My employees rock my designs and my designs are always fresh, Allysia thought.

Most of the thick celebs rock my designs. Those who can't do what they do best, and that's hate. They're just mad, because I won't make anything to fit their skinny asses. It's not my fault that they're not Thick Madames!

***

Allysia couldn't help but yawn as she reared backwards into her leather executive chair. She was weary as she ended yet another day of running her company. Ample Delights, was an exclusively full-figured, clothing design company. To be a well-known fashion designer, had been her dream since childhood. Now that she had accomplished her main goal, her life had turned into days of nothing but painful boredom. Not even thirty years old, she was already sick of the day to day operations. This wasn't how Allysia imagined her life would be; *I haven't even* reached my thirties.

Some days she even wondered why she left her ex-husband. If it was one thing he could do well, it was eat some kitty. Nevertheless, even with that said, he didn't do much else to make a sensible woman want to stay married to his ass. Their divorce was final six months ago. The bastard asked her to have an open marriage, with each partner sharing with others. Allysia Monique Donaldson was appalled! Sometimes when she was lonely and at her horniest, the idea doesn't seem half-bad, but she'd already said no, and that was her final answer.

She just needed to be touched and rubbed in places that the rest of her body had forgotten about. She drifted off into another one of her stimulating daydreams, smiling to herself while sitting behind her desk rubbing her wet pussy. She usually daydreamed of Davis, the deliveryman, with his tongue buried deep inside her love tunnel. Usually, when she got into the groove of it, someone would knock on her office door. Hoping that wouldn't be the case, she allowed her fingers to do the walking.

Like most women, Allysia loved thinking about having her juicy pussy licked and sucked. Nothing pleased her more. Some days she wondered why she hadn't gotten some dick or tongue action already. Six months was a long ass time to a woman like her, who was used to being sexed up nightly.

She didn't want another husband or a "baby daddy", but she damn sure needed a Splackavellie! While she didn't mind using her own digits to dial up her own orgasms, she was ready to enjoy somebody else's manual labor.

Sometimes the simplest of daydreams turned her on in such a powerful way, giving her such a rush! Her fantasies were what kept her going. In her mind, she didn't have time for love. Love would have to find her later in life when she didn't have shit else to do.

"Won't you join me?" I boldly offered. Without hesitation, Davis eagerly pulled me into his arms. Not knowing where to begin, he took one of my large, dark nipples into his warm, moist mouth. I squealed as I felt myself become hotter and wetter. I bit my bottom lip while Davis planted soft, wet kisses all over my bronze skin. His kisses started at my full lips, before his warm mouth traveled south. I reached out, grabbed Davis and gently forced his face into my hot

wet inferno. My body shivered when I felt the heat of his breath, blowing in the opening of Pandora's Box. I could hardly wait to feel his tongue inside of me. He eagerly licked cum from my pussy and then stuffed his hand inside of me. My pussy took to Davis' hand as if it was his dick. At that point, I began fucking his large hand, harder and faster. I continued until I built up the ultimate climax. Davis was holding me close, kissing me passionately. He had just made the most beautiful love to me. Davis then looked at me with his dreamy eyes and whispered the words, "I love you."

The 'L' word snapped her out of that daydream quick. As much as she wanted to feel that man's nature, she was not ready for love with anyone. Not even the beautiful, chocolate, Davis, even though she couldn't stop thinking about that sexy man!

If only Davis could have felt, what she felt. Davis Jackson was a widow and a single father. He had asked Allysia to join him for lunch, dinner, coffee, church, and everything else. He wasn't a man who would be satisfied with just fulfilling her sexual desires. Davis was looking for the one thing Allysia didn't really know how to give; he wanted love.

CHAPTER FOUR

Davis Jackson awoke with a seductive smile on his face as his heart raced and sweat poured from his brow. He had another dream about Allysia and as usual, right before he had the chance to make love to her, his alarm clock went off. He jumped up, took a long look at his wedding picture before kissing it, showered and got dressed in his uniform. He had to get his five-year-old to school in time for breakfast.

"I don't wanna go to school today, Daddy," the younger version of Davis whined. Five-year-old Tyshawn looked more like Davis with each passing day. "I wanna go on the deliveries with you!"

"Come on now, big man." Davis couldn't contain his smile. His son sat beside him with his arms folded across his chest with his bottom lip poked out. Tyshawn looked like Davis, but his actions reminded Davis of his mother's. How he missed that woman.

"You can ride with me on Saturday, the way you always do. But today, you have to go to school. Deal?" Davis offered his hand to Tyshawn for a shake that would seal the deal. "Deal!" Tyshawn chanted as he smiled, revealing his two missing front teeth.

After dropping Tyshawn off at school and giving him a big hug, Davis headed to a down-home diner not far from his office. He ordered his usual: scrambled eggs, cheese grits, turkey bacon, and a bowl of fresh fruit. A simple glass of milk would be enough to wash the meal down. He took his time enjoying his breakfast, while talking to some of the familiar faces.

Davis was in no hurry to get to the office. He knew once there, his aggressive co-workers would relentlessly hit on him. Of course, he was right.

The women in the office stared, mouths agape, as they watched the sexy, milk chocolate, man load boxes into the back of the delivery truck. Davis was sexy, simply because he didn't realize his own sex appeal. The man had lost his wife three years ago to cancer, and was raising Tyshawn as a single parent. Many of the women wanted to fill the void in his life, but Davis never showed any of them any interest. He was never rude, but he was obviously not interested in a relationship with any of them.

"If only I could run my fingers through that wavy hair," said Amanda, a petite brunette, as she chewed on her bottom lip, while watching his six-feet plus frame. Davis possessed an athletic build that would make a blind woman see!

Amanda tried seducing Davis on more than one occasion. Though he was polite, he still turned her down. Amanda couldn't believe that Davis wasn't interested in her. She was a young, beautiful woman in her mid-twenties. Her reputation preceded her; most of the guys in the office marveled about her oral skills. *Surely, Davis wanted to know firsthand what all the talk was about.*

"Tyson Beckford better watch out!" Selena, the bombshell Latino, whispered. She was another hot tamale, who tried to get next to Davis. She, too, had been rejected.

Davis could feel the eyes on him as he loaded his truck. The women in the office were gazing out the window at him as they always did. They were all beautiful women, especially Selena, but none of them was Allysia. None of them was as curvaceous or charismatic as Allysia was. If only Allysia looked at him, the way the women in his office looked at him. If only she wanted him the way that they wanted him.

Davis placed the last box inside the back of his delivery truck, and carefully secured the doors. The women were still watching, so he smiled and waved to them. He didn't want to lead them on in any way, but he wasn't going to be rude either.

Eager to get through another enjoyable day of work, Davis hopped in the cab of his truck. Working wasn't necessary for Davis; it was a choice. He had been born into wealth, but no one outside of his family knew of his financial worth. Davis wanted people to know and love him for who he was and not what he was worth.

He had a ton of deliveries to make and as always, his final stop would be at Ample Delights. His mother had always taught him to save the best for last, and Allysia was definitely the best! Davis couldn't contain his smile as he pulled out of the parking lot with naughty thoughts of Allysia racing through his mind. The things he wanted to do to and with that woman!

He couldn't deny his sexual attraction for Allysia Donaldson, but there was so much more to his feelings for her. He wanted to do more than just make love to her. Davis wanted to love the woman. He wanted to be able to let go of Carmen, his late wife. Three years after her demise to cancer, Davis still cried himself to sleep some nights, while clutching their wedding picture to his chest, knowing he'd never hold her again.

At times, he felt guilty about the way he felt towards Allysia. It was almost as if he was cheating on Carmen in some way; something he would have never done.

In his heart, he knew that Carmen would want him to move on with his life. She would want a woman in the home to help him raise Tyshawn, their only child, and he knew she would approve of Allysia

Davis asked her out on many occasions, but she always told him no. He didn't understand. The look in her eyes proved her attraction towards him. He noticed how her face lit up every single time he made deliveries. Maybe she just didn't think he, a deliveryman, was good enough for a professional woman like herself. If that was the case, she wasn't the woman that Davis had thought her to be.

After a long day of non-stop deliveries, Davis finally arrived at Ample Delights. He had not asked Allysia out since she turned him down a few weeks ago, so, he decided he would ask her one last time. If she said no, he would somehow put thoughts of him and her out of his mind.

CHAPTER FIVE

It was 7:30 in the morning, when LaDonna hurried into the office building. She was wearing a red dress similar to the navy blue sailor dress she had worn to her interview. Today she wore her red pumps, instead of the blue ones.

Walking with her head down, LaDonna almost walked right into Ronald, who was posted next to the elevators. "I'm sorry. I shoulda been watching where I was goin'."

"Well, good mornin', pretty girl." Ronald smiled, exposing his gold tooth. "I was waitin' for you." They stepped onto the elevator.

"Ooh, I'm so nervous," LaDonna told Ronald. "I ain't never liked first days, but Allysia seem so nice. Maybe it won't be so bad."

"Ms. Donaldson has always been nice to work for, and she gives nice gifts to ere'body at Christmas. I hope you'll like it here, LaDonna, 'cause I sho like you!"

No one so handsome had ever made her blush before. "Oh, Ronald, you makin' me blush, and Great-Granny Hattie May tol' me that blushin' equals lovin'." She giggled while checking the time on her wristwatch. "Uh-oh, I'm 'bout to be late! This here elevator takin' a mighty long time. In the South, if you weren't fifteen minutes early, you were five minutes late."

"Oh, don't you worry yo' pretty self 'bout that. Ms. Donaldson don't come in 'til round ten no way," Ronald reassured her with a huge grin. "You know," he continued, "you, sho is pretty!"

She smiled. "Oh Ronald! You jus' sayin' that!"

"Naw, LaDonna, I means it. I bet you done broke plenty of hearts 'round Georgia!"

"No, I ain't, Ronald!" LaDonna laughed. She thought that was the funniest thing she had ever heard. "I ain't never even had no real boyfriend befo'. I used to talk to boys on the porch and every once in a while, Momma would let me sneak and talk to them on the tel'phone. But that ain't no real boyfriend. I was still in high schoo'." LaDonna enjoyed talking to Ronald. She felt as if she had known him forever. She hoped that he liked her as much as he said he did, because she really liked him, too. "I'm sure you done left yo' share of broke hearts in Virginia, Ronald."

"No, ma'am. I ain't dated nobody since my ex-fiancée left me fo' some ball player. But, it don't matter, 'cause he left her a year later!"

"Well, that's what she get," LaDonna said, laughing. "You can't be mean and not get meanness back!"

"Ain't that the truth," Ronald agreed.

The elevator finally stopped on LaDonna's floor. Reluctant to end their friendly conversation, she said, "I guess this here's my stop."

"Okay, pretty girl. I'll stop by and see you later." Ronald tried his best to hide his sadness. He hated to see her go.

Allysia was even later coming in than Ronald had said she would be. So far, all LaDonna had done all morning was answer the phone and take messages. *This 'bout easy*, she thought.

"Hi, LaDonna! How are you today?" Allysia asked, as she emerged from the elevator. She looked so tired.

"I'm okay. How you doin'?"

Allysia responded with a weak smile and a shrug of her shoulders.

"If you don't mind me sayin'," LaDonna continued. "You look so tired." LaDonna truly was concerned. Her new boss wasn't wearing the other day's bold mask of confidence, when she finally came in to work.

"I'm fine, LaDonna. I just didn't get much sleep last night," Allysia answered. "Has the delivery man come in yet?"

"No, not yet. Here's your messages though."

"Thank you, LaDonna." Allysia accepted the sticky notes. She rushed into her office and shut the door.

LaDonna knew that more than fatigue was bothering her boss. She just didn't know what. LaDonna spent the next couple of hours answering phones and taking messages for Allysia, who did not want to be bothered unless it was urgent. When LaDonna went downstairs on her break, she never expected to see the handsome Ronald sitting there in the fancy coffee place called Starbucks as if he had been waiting for her.

"Hey Ronald!" LaDonna was smiling and waving as she hurried to his table.

"Hey there, LaDonna! Here I thought that you might be coming down for a coffee break and I got you one of those mucha lottos." Ronald was as country or even more country than LaDonna was, but you could never tell LaDonna that. In her eyes all Ronald was, was fine!

"Ooh, thank you, Ronald! I've always wanted to try one of those mocha luchas." She sat down across from him, but in her mind, she was sitting on his lap. She couldn't believe that she was already fantasizing about Ronald West. Nevertheless, she was and didn't really mind it at all. She was sitting in his lap, kissing his beautiful full lips, and licking his chocolate skin. Just tasting him, not caring who could see them... *What in the world had come over me!* She thought. Here she was lusting over a man she barely knew. She'd never done that with anyone before.

"LaDonna! LaDonna! Earth to LaDonna." Ronald laughed as LaDonna snapped back to reality. "I was askin' ya if ya wanted to go to one'a these here restaurants fo' lunch?"

"Ronald, I ain't used to all these different languages of food. We can jus' fetch something from McDonald's and watch the kids play in that playground over yonder." She didn't want no I-talian, French, or any of them other languages. That food didn't set right with LaDonna. It kept her up on the toilet all night!

"LaDonna, McDonalds is nice an' all, but I knows a soul food joint not far from here. It's called Mama Soul Food. They got collards, chitlins, neck bones, fatback, black eyed peas, and all kindsa good eatin'." Ronald could see her getting excited as he told her about the restaurant.

LaDonna licked her lips. It was nowhere near lunch, but her mouth was now watering. She closed her eyes and imagined the hog chitterlings sliding down her throat. "I hope it ain't too far aways. I don't wanna be late comin' back from lunch," LaDonna explained to Ronald. He assured her that he would have her back before the lunch hour ended. LaDonna could hardly wait until the clock struck twelve. Not only was she looking forward to the good food, but also she couldn't wait to be with Ronald again. "Thanks again for umm…uhhh, this here drink. That was very sweet of you, Ronald. I'll see you in 'bout a hour."

Shortly after twelve, LaDonna and Ronald were seated in his '79 Chevy pick-up headed towards Mama's Soul Food. The windows were down and LaDonna was able to take in all the beauty that Manhattan displayed. The buildings were so tall! However, nothing took her breath away more so than the smell from Mama's Soul Food. She could smell the aroma in the air as they pulled up.

The people had to be from down South. The food was awesome and the iced tea was cold and sweet. LaDonna and Ronald talked about their Southern upbringing as they enjoyed neck bones, rice, butter peas, macaroni and cheese, collard greens, and cornbread. LaDonna was so full that she had to get her dessert, sweet potato pie, to go.

"I sho would like to meet the cook. She put her foot in that food," LaDonna told Ronald as they headed back to the office. She was rubbing her full belly and trying not to let out a loud belch.

"She's a sweet lil lady from your neck of the woods. Her name Ms. Sadie. I thinks she's from some place called Cordele." Ronald was now pulling into the parking garage at their building. They spent ten minutes in the truck talking about any and everything. Even though they hadn't known each other long, LaDonna could she herself falling for him, and the feeling was mutual.

After returning from her wonderful lunch date with Ronald, LaDonna spent the next three hours trying to type up a one-paragraph letter for her boss to send off to twenty different people.

By the time she finished her one-finger typing, it was four-thirty, almost quitting time. After she gave Allysia the paper, LaDonna sat back at her desk to wait for the last minute calls to come into the office. She decided to pass the time with one of her favorite crossword puzzles.

"Hi there!" Startled, LaDonna looked up from her crossword puzzle. "You must be the new secretary. I'm Davis."

"Hey, Davis. I'm LaDonna. It's right nice to meet you." LaDonna couldn't help but notice his nicely packaged body. "Allysia was expecting you. I'll let her know that you're here, jus' as soon as I figga out this here system." LaDonna was now mumbling more to herself than talking to Davis. "Aww shucks! I'll jus' call her regular." Davis couldn't help but chuckle. "Allysia, the delivery man, Davis, is here with your package." LaDonna noticed a change in her boss' voice and attitude when she told her that Davis was there.

Allysia emerged from her office smiling from ear to ear. LaDonna immediately sensed an attraction between her beautiful boss and the sexy deliveryman. She pretended to be engrossed in her crossword puzzle.

"Hi, Allysia. You look beautiful today."

"Tha-thank you," Allysia stuttered. LaDonna couldn't help but smile. Allysia was acting like a nervous schoolgirl.

"Where do you want these fabric rolls?" Davis asked.

"Just bring them here into my office please," Allysia said, her eyes smiling at Davis as they disappeared into her office. LaDonna rolled her chair close to the open doorway.

"Allysia, I was wondering if you would go to dinner with me tomorrow night," Davis asked, hoping that for once her answer would be different. LaDonna was dying to hear her boss' response. *Say yes!* She almost screamed.

"No, Davis, I don't think that would be a good idea," Allysia heard herself say.

"Are you sure?" Davis asked, hoping that his smile and charm would change her mind. "I've got tickets to see *The Color Purple.*"

"I'm sure, sweetie. Thanks for bringing up the fabric." Allysia pretended to busy herself inspecting the fabric rolls.

LaDonna rolled her chair back to her desk while shaking her head. She couldn't believe that Allysia would pass up a date with Davis, especially when he had tickets to see *The Color Purple!*

Feeling defeated, Davis mumbled, "Have a good day." He bid LaDonna farewell and wished her a nice evening before boarding the elevator.

LaDonna knocked briefly before entering Allysia's office. "Allysia, I ain't tryna get in yo bizness or nuthin', but why you turn that fine man down? Chile, he 'bout as fine as a golden egg laid by a prized hen!"

Allysia smiled at her and said, "I know but he wants so much more than I do. I don't want a relationship right now. I just wanna get laid every now and then."

"Get what? What you talkin' get laid?" LaDonna was confused.

"It's just an expression. It means I'm not looking for a serious relationship. I just want someone who can..." Allysia didn't quite know how to put it. "I just need to release some stress sometimes. You know what I mean?"

"Hmm. Yeah. I know what ya mean, but life is 'bout mo' than just sex." Allysia didn't respond. LaDonna didn't understand city life. She couldn't. Things were a lot different down South. "It's 'bout time fo' me to go home fo' the evenin', but I just want to let you know that at the end of the day, your heart need a lot more than this company can give you. Think 'bout that." She gave Allysia a sisterly hug and left her with those strong words to ponder.

CHAPTER SIX

Allysia spent a full day at the office with no thoughts of work on her mind, absent-mindedly flipping through the fabric catalogues. The only thing on her mind was sex, and she needed to get laid in the worst way.

LaDonna's advice about Davis made sense, but Allysia still wasn't sure she was ready for dinner with him. She thought about having coffee with him, but he hadn't asked her out in weeks. *Sometimes when you snooze, you lose*, she thought. *With LaDonna and Ronald hitting it off so well, she has a better chance of getting laid than I do!*

She drove home with the top down, letting the wind massage her tense body. *If only I had a man to sit next to me in my ride. I want to be naked in the passenger seat, while my man drives me to a secluded area. I want my thick, ample thighs to feel the wind as he hits it again, and again, and again. That would be all good!*

Damn it! She had to come to a screeching halt to avoid hitting the car in front of her. *Get it together, Allysia.* If she kept thinking about sex, she'd be on the six o'clock news. *It's a damn shame that a grown ass woman ain't getting it on the regular!*

Once she got home, she parked her Mercedes Coupe in the garage and entered her big, empty house. Smelling her dinner for the evening, she wished there was someone to share it with. *Even the workers are gone for the day.* Allysia would've invited LaDonna over, but even she had a date. She and Ronald were really hitting it off. *I still owe that chick a makeover. I'm sick of the sailor dresses in every unimaginable color!*

Feeling the loneliness, she headed up the winding staircase. *If only Davis was up in my room waiting for me, the things I could do to that man. If only he would let me get my freak on without any strings attached.* Allysia didn't want to hurt him or get her heart broken while starring in a puppet show called, *Love.*

After a long, cold shower, she plopped down on her bed. With nothing else to do, she reached for the remote. Wouldn't you know the first channel that popped up was an HBO channel? There was a couple going at it! Frustrated, she quickly turned the channel. *Damn, cable TV wasn't much better!* Turning to *Animal Planet*, she hoped that just maybe the crocodiles wouldn't be mating. Wrong! A species of animals she had never seen before were fucking the hell out of each other. Everybody was getting some, except her. Completely pissed off, she turned off the TV and sent the remote sailing across the room.

Her body told her to call her ex, but her mind screamed *hell no!* After what seemed like an eternity, her throbbing center won the argument, and commanded her trembling hand to pick up the phone and dial D-I-C-K. He answered on the second ring. Her hungry pussy smiled at the sound of his voice. *We 'bout to get laid!* Her pussy even cheered by automatically flexing her muscles.

"So, to what do I owe the pleasure of this call?" he seductively asked. He already knew why in the hell Allysia was calling. She could imagine him stroking his dick while they talked, because she was definitely massaging her knob.

"I was wondering if you wanted to come over this evening. I have enough dinner for the both of us." Allysia nervously bit down on her bottom lip. "And I have all the dessert you can eat in my bedroom." She seriously missed his lethal tongue, and smiled at the very thought of feeling it again.

"We can be there in thirty minutes," he eagerly agreed. *We? We better be his ashy ass, his tongue, and his dick!* "Nina needs time to get showered."

"Are you fucking kidding me?" *Un-be-fucking-lievable!* His obsession with wanting her to see her fuck another woman had led to their divorce. *Damn, he still thinks he can get me in the bed with that fat, milky white, bitch of his! Hell no! I never should have told him about my experiences with women in college. That was college though. I chose between soft and hard and what I wanted was hard dick with no sides.*

"Come on, Allysia. It ain't like you never done it before. Why can't you do it for me? Let me see your big, sexy ass eat Nina out."

I know damn well he has lost his mind, Allysia thought. Her mouth wasn't going anywhere near that skank's rank ass! Besides, her pussy eating days were over and even when she did eat pussy, it was sweet chocolate, not buttermilk!

As horny as she was, she no longer wanted any from that clown. "Fuck you! You go eat that raggedy bitch's ass!" She hung the phone up and stared at it, daring him to call her back, but he didn't.

She really had no other options. The only way she was going to relieve any stress was with her damn vibrator. It wasn't the real thing, but it was as close as a couple hundred bucks could get. She pulled him out of her drawer and put in new batteries. She wanted a fully charged dick.

Allysia turned on her chocolate dick and watched the vibrations as it hummed seductively to her. That alone got her soaking wet as she inserted the full girth inside of her wet tunnel. *Damn! It sure has been a long time!*

With thoughts of Davis, she unleashed on her vibrator. In fact, she almost fucked the latex off of it! Just before she peaked, she pulled it out of her dripping wet pussy, brought it to her full, lucious lips, opened her mouth wide and took it in. Allysia eagerly licked and sucked her own juices from the shaft, all the while pretending it was Davis. *If only I could push a button that would shoot cum down my throat!*

She navigated her pretend dick back down South and called Davis' name as she peaked. "Davis! Aww-shit, Davis!"

Her body shook violently as the vibrator continued to hum and dance; she turned it off, turned out every light, and fell into a light slumber. However, her sleep didn't last long. She woke up just a few hours later, feigning for the real Davis and substituting for him would have to be "Davis the Dildo". Her pussy was already wet, but she still enjoyed touching herself, so she just had to reach down and massage her clit before inserting "Davis". Mmm…It felt so good that she wanted to taste herself again. Thinking about how good it would taste to Davis, she squeezed her vaginal muscles around her fingers and collected her sweet nectar, inhaling it before bringing to her full lips. *Damn, mmm…delicious as always!* She licked every drop of cum from her own fingers, as if each digit was Davis' dick.

Allysia put each one in slowly and pulled it out of her mouth the same way she longed to suck his massive dick. Then she plunged "Davis the Dildo" back into her, wet, love tunnel. She shoved it in and out of her pussy with a passion. Then propping it up on the hands-free stand, she climbed on top of the eleven and a half-inch dick, and went for broke. Spreading her legs farther and farther apart, taking all its girth into her wetness, saturating it with her love juices. Her intense love making session gave her repetitive, massive orgasms. After she came for what felt like the twentieth time, she climbed down from "Davis' Dick", she kissed it, licked her own cum off the head, before drifting off to sleep.

If only I could be in Davis' arms after making love to him. Maybe LaDonna was right. I need more than the satisfaction of running my company. I should stop running from love and embrace Davis. Allysia quickly decided that she would take the initiative of asking Davis out; maybe it wasn't too late.

Once she drifted off to sleep, she had one of the hottest and realest dreams about Davis ever:

She got out of her bed and stripped down to her bra and panties. She walked over to her dresser and grabbed the remote. Turning on her system, she scanned each of the disks in her five-CD changer until she got to the homemade romance mix. Allysia normally listened to the music when she cooked or cleaned.

Now she was hoping that the mood would be set for what the CD was intended for.

She made sure she had a tight grip on the remote and made a move for the bathroom. She wanted to catch Davis off guard. She loved the way she imagined that he looked naked and couldn't wait to see him that way.

A part of her was afraid of getting rejected. She knew she could pull any man she wanted and she wasn't afraid to go after what she wanted ultimately. Normally, she only wanted men who had money. She wasn't a gold digger, but her high expectations helped her weed out those who couldn't match her or her accomplishments.

The fast-paced, "Something For the People" song hyped her up and got her pumped. She knew her love was the shit. But Allysia couldn't go in the bathroom and just start sucking on his dick and riding him and getting wet. She needed to plan this right.

The guitar riffs and a slow melody in the background changed the mood. Allysia could still hear the shower running and she knew if she were to get Davis' dick tonight she'd have to make the first move. The first verse from Total's "Kissing You" spoke to her and as she sang along, she felt like the three women were pushing her, empowering her to go after her man.

Kissing him was all Allysia could think of and she wanted it to be good. She put some pep in her step, boldly gripped the doorknob and pushed the door forward. She put the remote on the counter and reached back to unsnap her bra. Once that was done, she took off her bra and tossed it backward, and slowly slid her panties down. She stepped to the side, leaving them on the floor as she pulled the shower curtain back. The sweetness of the liquid, black soap body wash reminded her of honey and mint. She always thought those scents smelled good on a man.

Davis turned around quickly and the only thing he was wearing was his wedding band. Fuck it, it was now or never. Allysia reached up and put her arms around his neck, and lifted up for the kiss. Davis didn't resist. Their tongues made love as the water continued to dance on their bodies and roll down their natural curves.

When their mouths broke away, Janet Jackson kept the pace going as she sang about needing someone to call her lover. For Allysia, that someone was Davis. He picked her up and pressed her back against the wall. She could feel the tip of his dick pressing against the opening of her love. She lowered herself slowly so she could receive it.

"Ahh," she gasped as she felt him bite her on the neck. Allysia arched her back, praying that Davis would get the hint and swing her body gently while applying that same pressure on her nipples. His tongue danced around her chocolate areolas and she could feel herself getting wetter. Her body trembled as she continued enjoying the dance he was having inside of her. She could feel his heart beat as his member pulsated between her legs.

Allysia hummed and danced as Davis continued to rock her silly. She lifted her right arm from around his neck and was happy that the shower curtain she grasped was sturdy. She put her other hand on the rail, noticing that one of the rings was in between her left middle and her ring finger.

Allysia loved the new pendulum shift their bodies were making. For her, it felt like every time she swung down, his dick went deeper and deeper, causing her to moan and tremble at the same time.

The orgasms she was experiencing compared to nothing she'd felt before, even from him.

She maneuvered her body as if she was doing pull ups. She didn't care that the heat was no longer coming from the water. They were starting their own fire.

The way he made love to her let her know that he had feelings for her.

As if on cue, she wrapped her arms back around his neck, and then hopped down. She stepped out of the shower and gently pulled his dick as if it was a leash and led him to the bed. Allysia felt her body being forced forward. As she landed face first on the bed, Davis stealthily got on top of her and entered her from behind, forcing her to grab the sheets. Her legs interlocked with his. Jeremih was bringing back those early R. Kelly vibes as he sang about birthday sex.

Allysia tried to think as to when his birthday was, but the orgasm she was currently having made her lose focus. She turned her head to kiss him again. Davis' strokes were coming deeper and faster. She could feel his breathing increase and his dick seemed to grow another inch inside her.

She loved the way he came inside her. His strokes would get short, deeper and had more power in them. It was almost as if she could feel him releasing his soul inside hers.

That's what she loved about Davis; he was one of the very few men to have been inside of her, and she loved it.

R. Kelly started singing about the best sex he'd ever had and for Allysia, she felt that this was it. She wanted to rest up a minute and go another round with him. Instead, she felt him breathing at a steady rhythm. His body rose up and down slowly and a small, light snoring could heard; he hadn't moved from on top of her.

Normally, she detested any man staying on top of her once he busted his nut, but for some reason, she didn't want Davis to move. He was still hard inside of her, which was even more amazing. Before R. Kelly could sing his nursery rhyme-like harmony, Allysia found herself falling fast asleep, right along with him.

Hours later, Allysia woke up looking for Davis, with her pussy still throbbing as if she'd really just made the best love of her life.

CHAPTER SEVEN

The fine and sexy Davis was sleeping soundly in the king-sized bed that he once shared with Carmen, his departed wife. God, how he missed that beautiful woman! At the same time, he longed for Allysia. Had Carmen been alive, he wouldn't see Allysia as anything more than a friend. As sexy as that woman was; his devotion to his wife was dear to his heart, but Carmen wasn't alive. Cancer had taken her away from him and now, his attraction to Allysia was very real.

Davis had dreamt of Carmen; and she had given him her approval of Allysia. No sooner than he took Carmen into his arms, she disappeared into the same thin air from where she appeared. This time he wasn't sad though; he actually felt at peace. Moreover, when a very thick, sexy, and sassy Allysia appeared, he felt horny as hell.

"Oh Allysia, I love that pussy, ride me harder!"

"Oh shit, Davis, I'm cummin'! Mmm…oh yeah! Oh yeah! Yes! Yes! Oooh yes!" Allysia plunged him deeper into her hot, wet, huge inferno. She then exploded all over his huge manhood. "Oh Davis, that was so amazing, baby!"

"My queen it isn't over yet," he told her as he turned her around and penetrated her wet pussy with his thick, long tongue. "Allysia, girl, you taste so damn good!" He stuck his tongue deeper and harder into Allysia and the more she moaned, the harder his manhood got. Davis didn't even know that it was possible for his dick to swell any more than it already was. "Baby girl, I'm cummin'! I'm cummin'!"

"Get off of me, Davis! I wanna swallow every drop," Allysia instructed him, her voice filled with passion. He loved her take-charge attitude. Just before he released his love juices in Allysia's

mouth, Carmen appeared in the doorway with tears rolling down her face, but before he could run to her and grab her, she disappeared.

Davis awoke in a cold sweat, with tears running down his face. He looked over at his alarm clock; it was just ten minutes before time to get up and get Tyshawn ready for school. He got up and went to the bathroom to wash his face. The last thing he wanted was for Tyshawn to see him crying. He then went back into his bedroom, turned off the alarm clock, and headed down the hallway to wake his son.

"Good morning, Daddy!" Tyshawn exclaimed, as happy as he always seemed. *If only I could know Ty's happiness.* "Good morning, son. And how are you today?" Davis asked his bright-eyed son.

"I feel good, Daddy. Today we gonna plant our garden at school and the teacher said it's gonna be big!" Tyshawn exclaimed, extending his little arms as wide as possible.

"That's nice, son," Davis said, trying his best to hide his sadness from his son. He pasted on a smile and said, "Come on, let's get your bath."

"Aww, do I have to, Daddy?" Tyshawn whined and laughed at the same time.

"Ty, now you know the importance of being clean," Davis said in a stern voice. The active child had been so tired the night before that he had fallen asleep without taking his nightly bath.

As Davis was helping Tyshawn out of the bathtub, the child looked up at Davis with curious eyes and asked, "Daddy, what's the matter?"

"I miss Mommy," Davis explained. He was trying so hard to blink back tears.

"Daddy, was Mommy pretty?"

"Ty, your mommy was the most beautiful woman in the world," Davis told his son proudly.

"Daddy, can I stay with you today, please?" Tyshawn asked, just as he did every school morning.

"No, son; you know that you can't go with me on the weekdays. But, Daddy's off on Saturday and we are going to the park. Just you, me and Poopy."

Davis' thoughts ran to Poopy, the dog. There was a funny story behind how he got his name. Tyshawn was two when Davis' mother bought him the puppy. Tyshawn could not say puppy, so he was calling the dog Poopy and the name stuck. Davis laughed to himself, remembering the happy moment. Then he remembered that Poopy came into their lives, right before Carmen passed away. He tried so hard to get Tyshawn to name the puppy something else. However, Carmen reminded him that Tyshawn was only two, and that if he wanted to name the dog Poopy, then that's what the dog's name should be.

"Ty, are you dressed?" Davis asked, as he was cleaning all of the water off the bathroom floor. Sometimes Davis did not know who left more water on the floor, Tyshawn or Poopy.

"Yes, Daddy, I'm ready."

Davis was hoping and praying that Tyshawn did not have that same Batman shirt on. Davis had been trying to throw that shirt away for a year. Every time, Tyshawn would take it right back out of the trash and put it in the washing machine.

Just as Davis feared, Tyshawn had on the Batman shirt. He didn't even say anything about the shirt; he just didn't have the fight in him today.

"Come on, son. Let's get your breakfast and get you to school."

After Davis dropped Tyshawn at school, he went to the diner to eat his usual: scrambled eggs, cheese grits, turkey bacon, and a bowl of fresh fruit with a glass of milk. Davis even talked to the other diner customers that he usually talked to whenever he was at the diner. As usual, he hated having to go into the office; he just did not want to be hit on by those relentless women he worked with today.

Davis could not get over that dream of him and Allysia, where Carmen, showed up crying. He had recently dreamed of her giving him her approval of his feelings for Allysia. *Why did she come back sad and crying?* It just did not register with Davis.

Davis made his deliveries, with his beloved Carmen on his mind. He had to slam on the brakes several times that day, due to not paying attention to the cars in front of him. Finally, after a long day of boring deliveries, he finally arrived at Ample Delights.

Davis stopped in the coffee shop before heading up to Allysia's office. There he saw LaDonna and Ronald. The two were sharing a Grande Mocha Latte with chocolate sprinkles. They seemed so in love and he envied what Ronald had; a living woman who wasn't afraid to love him.

"Hi, Ronald. Hi, LaDonna." He pasted on a smile when they looked up at him.

"Hey there, Davis!" both LaDonna and Ronald exclaimed at the same time.

"Davis, Allysia is upstairs. She's been expectin' you directly," LaDonna told him in her adorable country drawl.

"Thanks, LaDonna." Davis grabbed his black coffee and headed upstairs. The ride up the elevator seemed too short. Davis needed time to figure out what to say to Allysia. If he did not try to get her to go out with him, then she would notice that something was wrong. However, if he did ask Allysia out again, he felt like he would be disrespecting Carmen.

As soon as he walked into Ample Delights, Allysia's beautiful face was the first one he saw. It was as if she had been waiting on him all her life.

"Hi, Davis! How are you doing today?" Allysia sang, her thousand-watt smile beaming at Davis.

"I'm good, Allysia. How are you?" Davis smiled at her with his sexy ass eyes. "You look beautiful as always." She did; she was wearing a pantsuit that hugged her hips snugly. She looked professional, yet sexy.

"I'm good, Davis." He couldn't help but to notice that she was wringing her hands as if she was nervous. "Listen. I was wondering if we could go out for coffee and dessert this Sunday evening." Allysia's eyes were filled with hope and joy.

"I'll have to make arrangements for my son. Can I call you in the morning and let you know?" Davis asked, shocked that Allysia asked him out.

"Sure thing. My number is 917-555-2354. Call me." She kissed his cheek, handed him her business card, and took the small box of fabric samples. She disappeared into her office, switching her shapely hips as if she had no doubt that Davis was standing there staring at her every movement, which he was.

Wow! Davis was shocked, surprised and mesmerized as he entered the elevators. He wanted to go out with Allysia. He wanted to go out with her for months, but now that he had his chance, he didn't know what to do.

When the elevator descended to the lobby, LaDonna was waiting as the doors opened. "What's wrong?" she asked Davis. "You look like you just seen a ghost."

Davis felt that way. He didn't know LaDonna well, but she looked like someone he could talk to. "Allysia asked me out."

"So why the long face? Thought you liked her."

"I do, LaDonna. I…I just…I had a bad dream about my late wife. I feel like I'm disrespecting her by going out with Allysia. I know it sounds crazy, but I loved Carmen so much. I feel like I'm cheating on her," he admitted sadly.

"Ain't nothin' wrong with a man lovin' a woman. But, you're still a young man wit' yo' whole life 'head of you. You got to figure out a way to let yo' late wife go." She took his hand in hers and patted it as if he were a child. "'Cause no matter how much you love her, she ain't comin' back." LaDonna took her leave by way of the elevator.

I know why Carmen came back! Because, my heart still belongs to her, I haven't let her go!

LaDonna was right and Davis now knew it. He just had to figure out a way to let Carmen go so that he could freely give his heart to Allysia.

☐

CHAPTER EIGHT

As promised, Davis got up early Saturday morning and took Tyshawn and Poopy to the park. His plan was to spend the entire day with just the two of them playing, and trying to forget about his worries. Then Sunday he would spend his day with Allysia. *Finally.*

He looked up from running around with Tyshawn and Poopy to see his co-worker, Amanda. She immediately noticed him and ran over.

"Hi, Davis! Who is this cutie?" the office whore asked, while pretending to be interested his son.

"Amanda, this is my five-year-old son, Tyshawn." Davis turned to his son and said, "Tyshawn, tell Ms. Amanda hi."

"Hi, Ms. Amanda! This is my dog, Poopy!" Tyshawn grinned, baring the space where his missing two front teeth should be. He was so adorable. "Come on Poopy, let's go play!" Off they went. Poopy was fast on Tyshawn's heels.

"Don't go too far, Ty," Davis called after his son. Turning to Amanda, he asked, "What brings you here so early on a Saturday morning?" He had never seen her there before.

"Oh, just trying to get in a lil' exercise. I wanna keep my body sexy and tight." The whore attempted to bat her fake eyelashes at Davis, while pushing up her fake boobs.

"Is there something wrong with your eyes?" Davis asked her, with a puzzled look on his face.

Feeling embarrassed, she replied, "No. My eyes are fine." She couldn't help but to roll her eyes at Davis. He was fine, but he had to be slow if he didn't know she wanted to take him home and fuck his brains out.

Just then, Tyshawn ran up to them. Amanda bent down and kissed him on the forehead. Quickly, Tyshawn wiped the kiss off. When she noticed Davis checking out a nicely dressed, fat woman, she reached up to hug his neck, pressing her firm body into his. He gently nudged her away. Her behavior was very inappropriate in front of his son and the other people in the park. Davis finally pushed her away. It was then that he noticed that Allysia had seen the whole scene. If the look she returned to him could kill, Davis would have died right there. Without saying so much as a hello, Allysia stormed off.

Davis turned to Tyshawn and told him, "You and Poopy sit right here and wait for Daddy. Understand?"

"Yes, Daddy." Tyshawn stroked Poopy's silky coat.

"May I stay here and keep him company?" Amanda asked. She was quite satisfied with herself when she saw that heifer run off. Why would Davis want someone that huge when he could have her, a perfect size six?

"Sure." Davis wanted her gone to be honest. It was best not leave his son in the busy park alone. "Thanks."

"Allysia! Allysia! Please wait!" She turned around with a look of pure disappointment on her face. He saw the tears in her eyes, even though she was trying to hide them.

What do you want, Davis?" The once sexy tone of voice was replaced with one of anger. "Don't you have to get back to your young, skinny, white wife?" Before he could even offer an explanation, she said, "Don't bother calling me, Davis." With that said, she turned and walked away.

***

LaDonna and Allysia sat in Allysia's office, having one of their heart-to-heart conversations. It was almost lunchtime. Their girl talks had become the norm when it was slow in the office. LaDonna and Allysia had become fast friends. Allysia was so thankful that she had hired LaDonna, despite her lack of experience.

"LaDonna, I took your advice and asked Davis out. I was very excited over our upcoming date."

"So what went wrong? Why you sound so sad if y'all going out?" LaDonna didn't understand why the two of them couldn't get it together. Davis liked her and she knew Allysia liked him. They were just making the situation a lot harder than it had to be. They should have just stopped beating around the bush like LaDonna and Ronald had done from day one. When you like somebody, you don't play games because life is way too short.

"We're not going." Allysia was so very disappointed. "I saw him with his wife and kid at the park. He was trying to play me."

His wife?" LaDonna was confused. Davis had told her his wife was dead. There had to be some kind of mistake.

"Wife, girlfriend, it's all the same. I saw him with another woman in the park. And of course, she just had to be a skinny, white woman!" Allysia was so frustrated. It was so hard to find a good, black man, especially if you weren't a skinny model type with dead brain cells. She wasn't prejudiced, but seeing Davis with that white woman made her so mad. On second thought, maybe it wasn't because the woman was white. Maybe it was because Allysia had mustered the courage to ask him out, only to have her heart broken no sooner than she let her down guard.

"Maybe you need to talk to Davis and find out just what's goin' on, Allysia. Thangs ain't always what they seem," La Donna advised.

"I'm still not ready to speak to him. I don't even want to talk about him anymore." Allysia could be stubborn sometimes. "Anyway, tell me what's been up with you and Ronald?" Allysia asked, trying to change the subject.

"Well, we've been seein' each other ere'day since my first day here." LaDonna beamed. At just the mention of Ronald, she got a certain glow about her.

She seems so happy. Allysia was happy for her, but she wanted her own happiness as well. Truth be told, she still had feelings for Davis. That's why it hurt so much to think that he could be just another married low-life, pursuing her.

"Ms. LaDonna, you can take a longer lunch today. I've got a long business luncheon to attend," Allysia told LaDonna after she listened to her funny stories about her and Ronald's lunch dates. The two of them were perfect for each other.

"Okay, Allysia. And ere'thang'll work out soon," LaDonna encouraged her before leaving Allysia's office.

Allysia left for her meeting, hoping and praying that LaDonna was right.

LaDonna called Ronald on his cellular phone and told him that she was able to take a long lunch.

"Baby, I's packed us a lunch basket. How 'bout we have a lil picnic right at your desk?" Ronald was so in love and wasn't afraid to show it.

"I'd really likes that, boo. I's see you in a few minutes." She then hung up the phone, smiling as wide as the sun was bright that day.

Just then, Davis walked in. He knew that Allysia took her lunch around this time and he thought that it would be better to deliver the package while she was not there.

"Hi, LaDonna." Davis tried to paste on his best smile. LaDonna noticed that he wasn't his usual self; he was just as miserable as Allysia. They were going to drive LaDonna crazy if they didn't get their act together soon.

"Hi there, Davis! How you doin'? You seem real sad. What's a matta?" LaDonna asked.

"Allysia saw me and my son at the park Saturday. One of my co-workers had just joined us. I had no idea that she would be there. Allysia saw us together and assumed that she was my wife because Amanda, my co-worker, unexpectedly hugged me. I tried explaining myself to Allysia, but she wouldn't listen to me," Davis said, with a look of despair on his face.

"So, the woman Allysia saw you wit' wasn't your wife or girlfriend'?"

"When I told you my wife was dead, I wasn't kidding. That girl, Amanda, is far from my type. I don't mean to disrespect women, but she's the office whore. I would never jeopardize my life or my son's life like that. I'm sure that she likes me, but I'm only interested in Allysia. I even wrote her a poem." He reached inside his shirt pocket and removed a piece of folded paper. "I was wondering if you would please put it on her desk." Davis thought the poem might be his last hope of winning Allysia over.

"Sure! And don't you worry none. I's talk to Allysia fo' you." *I been doing a lot of reassuring today.*

"Have a good day, LaDonna. And thank you so much."

"You too, Davis." LaDonna bid him good day. She then sat the box of fabric samples in Allysia's office and placed the poem on her desk. She was in such a hurry to get ready for her lunch date with Ronald that she completely forgot to leave a sticky note, saying that the poem was from Davis.

Ronald was always so prompt and she didn't want to be late. She ran into the private restroom that Allysia had reserved for her and freshened up. She finished off with a reapplication of her lip-gloss. She thought about buying lipstick, but had no idea what color would go good with her skin. In Willacoochee, everybody just wore fire hydrant red lipstick, if they wore any at all. LaDonna opted to be natural and just wear lip-gloss or wrap her Vaseline in aluminum foil so she could stick it in her purse.

She heard Ronald outside in the office calling for her. "LaDonna, baby!"

"I'm in here, baby." She blushed at their affection for each other. "I's be out in a minute." *I gotta look good fo' my baby.*

Ronald had gone from being Ronald, to *her baby*, and she wouldn't have it any other way. Her heart did a flip-flop. She was in love and it felt so good!

CHAPTER NINE

Allysia was sitting at her desk reading a poem that she thought LaDonna had left for her. She really didn't know how to tell LaDonna in a nice way that she was strictly dickly. However, she knew that she had to tell LaDonna something, and fast! The poem was about making love. That was not going to happen between them! It had been awhile, but not so long that Allysia would settle for a clit, instead of a dick.

To Make Love

To make love to my mind is to

make love to my soul. to make

love to my soul is the equivalent

to making the most beautiful love to my body.

So, you see, to make love to me is to make love to all three.

To make love to all three is to truly love me.

After reading and re-reading it, she finally called LaDonna into her office.

"LaDonna, can I see you in here for a moment please?"

"Sure Allysia, jus' a minute." LaDonna always responded so quickly. Professionally, she had come a long way in a short time.

She walked into Allysia's office, looking wide-eyed with curiosity. "Did I forget to type something or copy something fo' you?"

"No, LaDonna, that's not it. Have a seat." She took the seat across from Allysia. "I found this poem on my desk, and I was wondering if it was you who left it for me." LaDonna opened her mouth to explain, but she was on a roll.

"Because if it was you, then sweetheart, friends we will always be, but that's all we will ever be. I don't mess with women." *Anymore. LaDonna was cute and sexy in a country, Bama way, but she doesn't have that hard dick my body was craving.*

LaDonna could not stop laughing.

"LaDonna what is so funny?" This chick was now standing in front of Allysia, slapping her thighs, laughing as if she were a clown at a circus.

"Even though I ain't had no man, don't mean I want the same thang I got!" LaDonna exclaimed adamantly. Tears were rolling down her face from all the laughing.

"Oh, LaDonna, I apologize. Please forgive me?" Allysia felt so stupid and hoped like hell that she hadn't offended her. She had been a wonderful friend.

"Don't worry 'bout it none. I guess I fo'got to say it was from Davis."

"From Davis?" Allysia balled it up and prepared to throw it in the garbage.

"Wait, don't do that!" LaDonna exclaimed. "Davis ain't married, and he ain't got no girlfrien' either. Davis' wife died few years back with cancer. That woman you saw with them in the park was a co-worker. Davis said she really get 'round the town, if you know what I mean. She want him, but he don't want nobody but you." LaDonna had to pause long enough to take a break. The laughing and now the long speech had no doubt left her feeling winded. She pointed her finger at Allysia. "And quit ackin' like you don't want him. You know you want dat fine man, jus' as much as he want you."

"The child is his son, right?" she asked nervously. She'd always been nervous about family life. Allysia longed for a family but knew that she wouldn't have the amount of time needed to dedicate to a child. "I'm not ready for kids, LaDonna. Sure, I'm sick of being lonely, but I'm still not ready for any kids."

"Allysia, I love you, but quit making excuses. Get to know Davis and his son. Let yo'self be happy! Let God be yo' guide." For LaDonna to be so young, she was so wise. "Allysia, please think 'bout what I done said. I'm goin' on a coffee break. Can I get you anythang befo' I go?"

"No, I'm fine. Thanks, LaDonna. For everything."

LaDonna left her with a whole lot of thinking to do. It shouldn't have mattered that Davis had a son. He obviously took very good care of him and made an effort to spend time with his son. *LaDonna was right; I needed to pray about the situation. It had been awhile since I prayed sincerely about anything. It was high time I started,* Allysia thought.

"Dear Lord, if this is the man for me, please let me know. I'm not asking for a huge sign or nothing. Just a knowing or feeling in my heart. I also want to thank you for all of your blessings. In Jesus' name, Amen."

Allysia felt so much better after praying. She went into her private bathroom and took a long, hot, luxurious bubble bath. That was one of the benefits of being the boss. Everything was at her disposal. Afterwards, she felt so relaxed and rejuvenated. She had made up in her mind and God had set it in her heart that Davis was her blessing and she was finally ready to accept it.

"LaDonna, whenever Davis comes in with today's last delivery, please be sure and let him know that I want to see him in my office."

LaDonna answered affirmatively as Allysia pictured her friend grinning.

"Thank you. You can go ahead and take the rest of the day off when Davis comes." Allysia smiled to herself as she turned off the intercom.

She retreated to her chaise lounge and waited for Davis' arrival. Naughty thoughts entertained her as time ticked on.

Finally, after what seemed like an eternity, she heard Davis' sexy ass voice outside. "Are you sure, LaDonna?"

"I'm sho'. She gave me direct orders to tell you to come into her office when you got here."

Allysia overheard LaDonna bid Davis a good evening as she got on the elevator. Then she heard a knock at the door.

"Come in," Allysia said, seductively as possible.

As he entered, she opened her arms and beckoned him to come to her. *No more playing hard to get. No more doubts. I'm ready to truly relax, relate, and release!*

Davis looked confused. "Hi, Allysia. I'm surprised that you wanted to even see me, much less hold me."

"Davis, I'm tired of beating around the bush. I want to hold you, learn to love you, and make love to you." She eased her legs open, ready to open them and her heart to Davis and there was no turning back now.

Davis finally walked over to her and kissed her more passionately than she could have ever fantasized. Grabbing him, she kissed him back with the same passion. Then she took his hand and gently pushed him down on the lounge. Standing over him, she whispered, "Take off your shirt." He did. *His dark chest was so wide and beautiful,* she thought, as she reached to rub it before removing his pants. His dick was even bigger than she had imagined. Allysia had to stop and stare for a moment at that beautifully huge manhood, standing straight up out of his boxers. His dick looked so good and she couldn't wait to taste it.

Davis reached up and opened Allysia's silk robe, only to see that there was absolutely nothing on underneath. "Baby, were you really waiting for me?"

"Yes, Davis. I was waiting to give myself to you, if you want me." She looked at him with pure desire in her eyes.

"*If* I want you?" Davis looked at Allysia as if she had lost her mind. "Woman, there is nothing I want more."

He took her large breast into his hands and eased his mouth around her pert nipples. The more he sucked, the more she felt like silk. She eased herself down onto his lap and watched him devour her hard flesh as if it was the best meal he had ever tasted. *If you like that, baby, just wait 'til you taste this wet pussy.* She eased off him and began kissing his shoulders and his chest. *Mmm…he tastes so good, so clean and his cologne smells so erotic.*

Then she pushed his boxers off with one hand and grabbed his long, erect dick with the other, before taking his swollen manhood into her mouth. Davis' moan of pleasure was all the ammunition Allysia needed to suck him feverishly, as if it would be the last time she would ever be able to taste him. She stroked and massaged his nut sack with her pinky finger, while making passionate love to him with her mouth until he shook uncontrollably, releasing all of his love juices. Allysia happily swallowed every drop. He got up, came up behind her, spreading her legs and pussy lips farther apart, penetrating her with his tongue. It was then that Allysia knew that their love had just begun.

CHAPTER TEN

Tonight's my big date with Ronald, and he said it's gonna be real special-like. LaDonna got ready for work, fussing to herself. "I don't have nothin' special to wear. Ronald done seen all my clothes." LaDonna put on what even she hoped would be her last sailor dress. "Allysia will know how to help me!"

LaDonna was so excited about asking for Allysia's help that she only took the time to kiss Ronald good morning, before dashing onto the elevator. "I's see you when I takes my coffee break, baby." She waved to him as the elevator doors closed.

"Allysia! I needs help!" LaDonna screamed; thanking God that Allysia had come in early that morning. *Lord always knows what you need and when you need it!*

"LaDonna, what in the world is the matter?" The way LaDonna was screaming, Allysia would have thought that someone was after her. She was waiting for someone to step off the elevator any moment, shooting up the place.

"Tonight's my big special date wit' Ronald and I's sick of wearing these dag-gone sailor dresses. I ain't got nothin' special like to wear. Help me please."

Allysia looked down at LaDonna's outfit and smiled. She thanked God that LaDonna had finally seen the light and come to her for help. She had wanted to approach her, but didn't want to offend her.

"LaDonna, I'll tell you what. Why don't we go to the spa today? I don't have any meetings scheduled. We can shut the office down and spend the entire day at the spa."

"The spa? I's always wanted to go to the spa." LaDonna's bright eyes grew wide and a huge smile formed across her lips.

"Yes girl, but first, let's go down to the warehouse and get you some clothes!" Allysia knew just what would flatter LaDonna's face and frame. "And let me call Davis. Instead of having lunch together, we can have dinner."

LaDonna couldn't help but smile. She was so glad those two had finally gotten together. She would never tell Allysia that she had come back to retrieve her purse that day, when she sent her home early. LaDonna didn't want her boss to know that she heard the two of them getting busy. It sounded like they were making twins!

"What about the packages?" LaDonna asked. Davis was there every afternoon with a delivery.

"Thanks, LaDonna," Allysia said, before turning her attention back to the phone. "And Davis, will you please leave today's delivery with the lobby secretary? Thanks. Can't wait to see you either. Sure. I don't mind if Tyshawn joins us. Okay. Bye for now."

LaDonna knew it was rude to listen in on other people's conversation, but she couldn't help it. "I's so glad that you finally lettin' yo'self be happy, Allysia."

"So am I." They boarded the elevator. "So am I."

Allysia took LaDonna down to the ground floor of the building to Ample Delights' clothing warehouse. There were beautiful dresses, pantsuits, and lingerie everywhere! LaDonna felt like a kid at a toy store! "I like this one!" she said, pointing to a gown with real shiny beads on it. It was beautiful.

"Yeah, LaDonna, this is a special occasion gown, but you aren't going to a formal event," Allysia explained to a very confused LaDonna.

"So, this too promy-like?"

"Yes." Allysia shook her head. She knew she had her hands full with LaDonna's makeover.

"What about this one?" LaDonna held up a cute denim jacket dress.

"That's a cute piece, but not for tonight." Allysia took the dress off its padded hanger and handed it to LaDonna. "But it will be good to wear to work tomorrow. Go ahead and get it. I designed it so it could also be worn as a jacket."

LaDonna hesitated. She couldn't pay for more than one dress.

"It's on the house, LaDonna."

Allysia was getting a kick out of seeing LaDonna getting so excited over the stylish clothes. Allysia spotted the perfect dress for that night's date. "Lady," as Allysia often times called LaDonna, "this is the dress for you for tonight." She held up a sleek black satin knee length, form-fitting dress with a little flare at the hem. When she held up the dress, she knew LaDonna loved it.

"I ain't never seen nothing like that except on the television set," LaDonna marveled.

"Well, tonight, you can feel like the star you are. This one's a fourteen. Go and try it on."

The dress fit LaDonna to a tee! Allysia could hardly believe that her beautiful secretary was transforming into a sexy diva. She couldn't wait until they arrived at the spa!

LaDonna looked in the mirror. She couldn't believe her body had been hiding under those dang-blasted sailor dresses. "Maybe I shouldn't. I likes it, but maybe it showing too much." LaDonna turned from side to side, admiring her own shapely hips.

"Baby, if you got it, flaunt it! And just because you're advertising, doesn't mean you're selling!" Both women laughed. "You look beautiful and you deserve nothing less, LaDonna."

LaDonna's large eyes expanded like a balloon when she walked into the spa. "Allysia," she whispered as she nudged her boss. "Why is these women half naked?" Almost every woman she saw had a towel wrapped around her body. A towel and nothing else is all that covered their private areas. LaDonna immediately covered her eyes with her hands.

Allysia laughed. LaDonna's innocence and inexperience was too cute. She pulled LaDonna's hand from her eyes. Still, LaDonna squeezed her eyes tight. "It's okay, LaDonna! Women come here to relax. That's why they only have on towels. Besides, we have to get the works. So, we don't need any clothes in the way as we get in the sauna, get massages, facials, and all that good stuff."

"Massages?" LaDonna's eyes popped open. She had always wanted a massage, but couldn't find anybody to do that in Willacoochee. "I always wanted me a massage and a facial. But what we gon' do 'bout this thick hair of mine? Lawd knows I's tired of that hot comb every mornin'!"

LaDonna had beautiful hair. She just didn't know how to style it. Luckily, Allysia had everything under control. She gave LaDonna a sisterly hug and said, "Relax! I got this."

She didn't lie; LaDonna felt so relaxed after sitting in the sauna and getting her massage. Allysia sure knew how to pamper herself. LaDonna left the spa, looking and feeling like a new person. Her long hair was now layered and feathered. Her beautiful skin tingled. She got her first ever manicure and pedicure and she felt like a true diva. No one would look at her and guess that she was from a small town called Willacoochee.

"You look beautiful!" Allysia had gone back to LaDonna's apartment to help her dress for her date.

"How can I ever repay you, Allysia? I know all this wasn't free." LaDonna couldn't help smiling at her own reflection. She really did look and feel beautiful.

"You don't owe me anything, Lady. If anything, I owe you even more for bringing Davis and I together."

They hugged again until the doorbell rang. It was Ronald.

When LaDonna opened the door, Ronald's jaw fell to the floor. "Girl, I'd drink your bathwater!" he said to LaDonna and followed up the statement with a long whistle. "You sho' look even mo' beautiful than usual."

"Thank you." She blushed. "I owe it all to Allysia."

"No. You owe it all to your mother," Allysia said. LaDonna gave her a confused look. "I didn't give you that beautiful smile and that junk you got in your trunk!"

"Stop it!" LaDonna playfully slapped Allysia on the arm. "And get on out of here, so you won't be late for yo' date with Davis."

"I sho' is glad you got all prettied up. This gon' be a special night," Ronald told LaDonna as they walked downstairs. "We taking a cab tonight."

LaDonna didn't know what Ronald had up his sleeve, but she felt like Cinderella.

CHAPTER ELEVEN

Allysia was so nervous. She was about to meet her boo's son for the very first time. Yes, Davis had gone from being just Davis to her boo. She had seen pictures of Tyshawn and he was absolutely adorable. She could only hope that she would have a kid just as cute and smart one day, but first things first. She had to meet the kid Davis already had first.

As she was stepping out of the shower, her phone rang. Allysia was reluctant to answer the phone, but she did anyway, without checking her caller ID. "Hello?"

"Hey, sexy gal," Fred sang. You could tell he was grinning through the phone. "Can I come see you?"

He had some damn nerve! The last time she actually wanted some from him, he tried to bring his white bitch with him. *I know damn well he doesn't think for one hot minute that I'm going to let him crawl up between my thick thighs tonight, or any other damn night.* "Hell no, Fred! I don't need or want to see you anymore. Goodbye." With that said, Allysia slammed down the phone; he had his chance, and he'd blown it.

She had to sit down on the window seat and take a deep breath to calm down after she hung up the phone. Fred was the one person who could alter her mood without saying much of anything. As much as he had upset her, she found myself smiling. It felt good to let him know that she was doing just fine without him. After a minute or two, she was fine. She just had to relax, relate and release.

She got herself together, walked into her closet and tried to decide what to wear. Allysia wanted to look nice for Davis, but didn't want to overdress for the occasion. After all, they were taking Tyshawn to Uno's for pizza and then to the aquarium. She needed something simple and conservative, yet slightly sexy, hugging her body. In the end, she selected a pair of jeans, a black shirt, and black boots.

Allysia had told Davis that she would pick them up around seven. Not wanting to be late, she applied her favorite scented lotion all over her body. The pear fragrance tickled her nose and brought a smile to her face. Instead of makeup, she decided on lip-gloss and just a touch of mascara. After slipping into her outfit, Allysia grabbed her purse and keys and rushed to the car.

"Say hi Ms. Allysia," Davis instructed the handsome little boy, who stood shyly at his father's side. They lived in a beautiful building. Their apartment was nice too. Simple bachelor taste, but nice.

"Hi, Ms. Allysia!" Tyshawn ran up and gave her a big hug. It surprised Allysia, but it was a nice surprise.

"Hey, gorgeous." Davis looked at her and she was ready to melt. It was going to be hard to keep it together, but she knew that they had to, being that they were not alone.

"Hey, yourself." The minute she'd said it, he started laughing at her. *Did he know what I was thinking?* They stood there for a long time, just staring at each other, before his son brought them back to reality.

"Daddy, I'm hungry…" Tyshawn whined. He tugged at his daddy's shirtsleeve.

"Of course. Let's go." Allysia took Tyshawn's hand. It was nice holding a little hand. She looked at his handsome father and asked, "Ready?"

"Yeah, baby, just let me just grab my jacket." Then out the door they went.

"Ms. Allysia, I can count to fortry!" Tyshawn announced. He was so cute.

"You mean forty, son," Davis corrected, obviously trying his best not to laugh.

"Yes, Daddy, that too." Tyshawn was a hoot. Flashing his toothy grin at Allysia, Tyshawn asked her, "The way I say it sound better, don't it, Ms. Allysia?"

"Well, Tyshawn," Allysia was trying not to laugh too, "the way your father told you is the right way. Don't you want to grow up to be just as smart as your daddy?"

"I guess. I just don't like saying stuff perfect all the time," Tyshawn rationalized, more to himself than anyone.

"Did you enjoy your pizza, Tyshawn?" Davis asked his son. Allysia loved watching the two of them interact with each other, and could picture herself being a part of their world for the rest of her life.

"Yes, Daddy. Can we go see the fish now?" Tyshawn asked, with wide eyes and a huge smile.

"We have to let Ms. Allysia finish her pizza." The two of them had finished their meals and there she sat, so wrapped up in their interaction that she had barely touched her food.

"Actually, guys, if you're ready, I can take this to go. It's really not a problem," she reassured them, which made Tyshawn a very happy little boy. He was lovable, bright, respectful, upfront, and friendly. All the decent qualities that he would need to make it in the real world as an adult.

Tyshawn was telling Allysia all about the different things he liked to do in school before they were rudely interrupted by a familiar face. The same skinny ho—that was pushing all up on Davis the last time she'd seen him at the park—ran right up to him and kissed him on his cheek. *The nerve of her!* She acted as if Allysia's big ass was not even there.

"How are you, Papí?" she asked Allysia's man. *I have her Papí all right,* Allysia thought, but before she could say anything, Davis let her have it.

"Amanda, first off, I have no interest in you whatsoever. Second of all, this kind of behavior is not appropriate in front of my son. And last, but most definitely not least, this is my girlfriend and you have no right to disrespect her like that." Davis had a look of fury on his face that not even that slut could mistake for any other emotion.

Davis took Tyshawn by the hand and slipped his other arm around Allysia's waist. Amanda was left standing with an ugly scowl on her face, as the three of them walked away.

***

"Davis, I had a beautiful time tonight." They had just tucked Tyshawn into bed; watching him drift off to sleep as Davis read to him, made Allysia's heart do flip-flops.

"Baby, I loved having the two most important people in my life finally meet." Davis looked into her eyes and she knew he was serious. Her heart began beating fast. It was as if she knew that she wanted Davis and Tyshawn to be a part of her life and that her once lonely days were over.

CHAPTER TWELVE

Ronald and LaDonna had just been seated at their table. Ronald had made reservations at Olive Garden. LaDonna was so impressed. She had never been to a restaurant where the wait staff got all dressed up. Ronald even asked for a bucket of ice. The server looked at him strangely, but she obliged the confident Ronald. Once the server returned, Ronald reached into his pocket and said, "Here you go. Thank you." He had given her a dollar.

"Umm...thank you, sir." The server couldn't help, but chuckle to herself as she turned and walked away.

Ronald pulled out a bottle of Pink Champale from his pocket. He placed it in the bucket of ice while smiling at his lovely date. He had a night full of surprises for LaDonna.

"Oh Ronnie!" LaDonna squealed, while batting her eyelids flirtatiously. She felt so special in her beautiful dress. All eyes were on her and she couldn't thank Allysia enough for the makeover.

"Baby, I done tol' ya how special you is to me." It was as if he could read her thoughts. "And you just so fine tonight, LaDonna." He winked his approval, causing her to blush.

A little later on in the dinner he asked her, "You likes teddy bears don't ya?" When she nodded yes, he handed her a bear with a box in its hand. "Open dat there box, baby."

She was expecting it to be a pretty locket or something, but never did she think her eyes would see what they saw. It was a beautiful three-quarter carat diamond engagement ring.

"Oh Ronnie! Oh Ronnie! Oh my…Ronald…" she gasped. It was beautiful. "I's ain't never had nothin' this pretty befo'. This what I's thank it is, Ronnie?"

"It ain't no cubic 'conia. It's the real thang!" Ronald boasted. He was proud of himself. He had saved up enough money to buy her that ring from Walmart. It had even been special ordered.

"That ain't what I's meant, Ronald West." LaDonna wanted to make sure it was an engagement ring before she overreacted.

He began to laugh. "Yes, baby." He got out of his chair and down on one knee. "LaDonna Divine Jenkins, I love you with all my heart. Will you marry me?"

"You serious?" LaDonna asked, obviously in shock.

"Yes, baby, I'm ser'ous. Please say sumthin'," Ronald begged, praying that she wouldn't say no.

"I, uh, oh Ronnie...yes!" LaDonna screamed, with joy in her eyes and in her heart. She started running around to every table, showing off her brand new engagement ring, screaming, "I's gettin' marr'ed now!" The people all nodded and smiled at her. They finally gave her a round of applause as joyful laughter filled the dining room.

Ronald was happy that she was happy, but he wished that she would rejoin him at their table so that he could kiss his fiancée. Finally, he stood up and said, "Baby, com'ere." His new bride-to-be rushed to his side, happy as could be.

"Yes, my love." She felt warm all over. She looked at him with seductive eyes and he grabbed her and gave her the most passionate kiss ever. After she finally came up for air, LaDonna beckoned the server. "Check please, ma'am." Then she whispered to her soon-to-be husband, "I've always wanted to say that," and giggled.

LaDonna could hardly wait to return to Willacoochee and exchange vows with Ronald. Her family would be tickled pink when they saw her diamond ring!

☐

CHAPTER THIRTEEN

After several months of steady dating, Davis and Allysia seemed quite happy. Allysia and Tyshawn got along well, and had become the best of friends. However, Davis knew that something still wasn't right.

Davis prayed that God would send Carmen's spirit to him just once more. He had to let his late wife go. He wanted to give his heart fully to Allysia. However, he first had to release Carmen. She would always be his first love, but Davis was ready to build a life with Allysia in Carmen's absence.

Carmen finally came to him while he was napping. "Hello, my love," she whispered in his ear.

Davis shot upright in bed when he heard Carmen's voice. "Carmen?" Tears filled his eyes as he took in her beauty. She stood before him as if she had never left him.

"I felt you, Davis." Carmen explained as she clutched her hand over her chest. "I could hear you calling out to me. What's wrong?"

Davis didn't know just how to put his thoughts into words. "Carmen, I met someone. And I like her a lot. She's great with Tyshawn. No one will ever take your place, but—"

Before he could finish she responded, "You need someone who can love you in a way that I can no longer love you, Davis. I had God to send her to you. Allysia will be good for you and for Tyshawn. You have my blessing. Make her yours and love her completely."

Davis reached out to hug Carmen, but she blew him a kiss and faded away before he could embrace her. In the midst of his tears, his lips drew upwards into a smile. Finally, his heart felt free. He could finally give Allysia his all.

Davis knew that meant only one thing. He was ready to propose to Allysia and ask her to be his wife. Nevertheless, before he could ask Allysia for her hand in marriage, Davis wanted to talk to his son.

The next morning, Davis called Tyshawn out of his room. "Come here, son."

"Am I in trouble?" Tyshawn asked. Davis assumed that his son thought something was wrong by the serious tone in his voice. "Daddy, I didn't mean to roll off all of the toilet paper. I just wanted some and the smell good roll gave me all of it."

Davis couldn't help but burst out laughing. "Tyshawn, I wish you had told me, instead of letting me find clean toilet paper all over the floor. But that's not why I called you. I want to talk to you about something else."

Tyshawn breathed a huge sigh of relief. Of course, mimicking what he had seen adults do, he over exaggerated this act by wiping his brow, and then putting his hand to his chest and saying, "Whew, that was so... close." Tyshawn was such a ham.

"Ty, how do you feel about Ms. Allysia?" Davis asked his comedic son, who couldn't seem to stand still to save his life.

"I love Ms. Allysia. She's pretty like Mommy and she's really nice to me," Tyshawn told his father as he jumped up and down for no apparent reason.

Davis tried to explain why he was asking Tyshawn about Allysia, as clearly as possible. "Ty, son, the reason I'm asking you this is because...I would like to make Ms. Allysia a part of our family."

"You mean she would be my new mommy? Now, I'll have a mommy here with me and my angel mommy?" Davis nodded affirmatively. "Yeah...I'm gonna have a mommy here with me!" Tyshawn screamed.

He was relieved to see that Tyshawn seemed happy with the thought of Allysia being a part of their family. Now Davis really prayed that she wouldn't turn him down. He prayed that she would say yes.

***

"Allysia, does this fit right on me?" an excited LaDonna asked as she tried on her wedding undergarments. She was putting the garter around her neck. Allysia couldn't help but laugh at her friend.

"Yes, Lady, except that garter goes on your thigh, instead of around your neck." LaDonna was so very funny, so innocent; most people loved that about her.

Her wedding was just two months away and Allysia couldn't be happier for her; she had even begun thinking about weddings and marriage herself. She could easily see herself being Davis' wife and a mother to Tyshawn.

"These some awful big er'rangs." Allysia had to turn around to see what LaDonna was talking about. When she looked and saw that she was talking about the charms that are supposed to go on her shoes, Allysia laughed so hard that she almost fell out of the chair.

"LaDonna, those are shoe adornments." Allysia shook my head. "Don't worry about those. They just came with the set. You don't need them on your shoes."

"Oh okay. 'Cause I was thankin' them some mighty big er'bobs."

"LaDonna, what the hell are er'bobs?" *Surely, she couldn't be talking about earrings,* she thought.

"You know...er'rangs."

Laughing, Allysia said, "Come on and change so we can go to lunch."

When they got back from lunch and were sitting in her office, Davis knocked on the door. When LaDonna opened the door, he was dressed in a tuxedo and was holding a bouquet of red roses and a small black box.

"Davis..." Allysia immediately lost her voice to shock and surprise.

"Come here, sweetheart." He asked her to sit down near where he was standing. As she kissed him, he handed her the beautiful roses. "Allysia Monique Donaldson, you have impacted my life in ways that I will never be able to express with words, but, I would like to show you my gratitude and my love for the rest of my days." He dropped down to one knee. "Will you be my wife?" He opened the black box revealing a beautiful, three-carat, heart-shaped solitaire diamond, set in a platinum band.

For the first time in her life, Allysia was speechless, and LaDonna started screaming, "Say yes! Say yes!"

"Davis, I can't think of anything I'd rather be doing with my life than spending it with you! Yes, I will marry you!" She was so very happy. He slipped the beautiful ring on her finger. When they kissed, Allysia knew without a doubt that they would be together forever.

LaDonna ran up to them, looked at her friend and said, "We's gone both be marr'ed ladies now!"

☐

CHAPTER FOURTEEN

A few months later, LaDonna and Ronald were loving their lives as newlyweds.

He moved the blue and white roses and bottle of Grey Goose to his left arm as he reaches into his right pocket and pulls out a set of keys to their blue and white themed apartment. As far as the eyes could see was an assortment of blue and white items, including blue shade pictures of jazz musicians, and Dallas Cowboys banner. It was well known that blue and white were some of her favorite colors.

LaDonna is sitting on the couch in a royal blue, Ample Delights negligee as she looked at her nails. They were crisp and looked natural. She had her cell phone on speaker, talking to someone.

"Girl, let me call you back. My hubby is home." Without waiting for a response, she hung up the phone.

"Ooh for me! These are my favorite colors."

"I know."

LaDonna puts the phone on the table and she takes the roses and the Grey Goose from Ronald. She smelled the roses, puts the roses in the empty vase on the table, and then places the Grey Goose next to it. Ronald sat down on the couch.

"And you giving me the headache I like." Ronald said, while rubbing his manhood through his pants. "Got some Aleve?"

"All day strong. All day long." LaDonna flashed her million dollar smile. She walked to where Ronald was sitting and straddled him on the couch. She wrapped her arms around him and gave him a kiss. She slowly began to slow wine in his lap.

"Ohh...Yeah. Don't stop, girl."

LaDonna and Ronald continued to kiss as he lifted her up, putting her on the table. He continued to kiss her neck, as she eagerly reached down to unbuckle his pants. The pants fall and she nearly tore his underwear as she tugged and pushed his boxer briefs down. Ronald began kissing and sucking on her breast through her negligee.

"That tickles, baby."

He moved his fingers to her sides and tickled her as he continues to bite and suck on her neck and breasts.

"Ooh Ronnie..."

"What's my name?"

Before LaDonna could respond, a neighbor in the hallway replied, "Ronald, your name is Ronald."

Ronald and LaDonna stop as they look at the neighbor in the hallway, watch them through the door, before continuing on their way.

Chuckling, Ronald said, "I guess the neighbors know my name."

LaDonna pushed Ronald off her, "Whatever Trey Songz, go close the do'." She sashayed off to their bedroom.

Ronald quickly reached down to pull his boxer briefs and his pants up, rushing to close and lock the door.

Once he reached the bedroom, he went in the nightstand and pulled out a Fire & Ice TROJAN condom. LaDonna takes the condom, as she leads Ronald to the bed.

"You don't need this tonight, baby."

Ronald stopped with a confused look on his face, "What you mean, baby?"

"I mean, I think I'm ready to make love to my husband, uncovered."

☐

CHAPTER FIFTEEN

Davis and Allysia had a whirlwind engagement. They hired Manhattan's most fierce wedding planner, Allysia's high school friend, Sunshine Royal. She chose gold, ivory, and burgundy as her wedding colors. She not only designed her own gown, but the gowns for her bridal party. Their wedding was October twenty-fifth, Allysia's mother'sbirthday. Their day was so special; it had been touched by God.

What made their beautiful moment in time complete was when she and Davis made love for the first time as husband and wife. Their lovemaking was amazing before they got married, but it was nothing compared to after exchanging vows.

That night as Allysia emerged from the bathroom of their honeymoon suite; Davis looked at her with pure desire in his eyes and said, "You have never looked more beautiful than you look right now. Come to me my Caramel Vixen."

"Mui necesito papi pene!" she told her new husband excitedly. Allysia wasn't sure if Davis even knew what it meant either, but the fact that she was speaking Spanish turned him on anyway. She whispered in his ear, "I need Daddy Dick."

Davis took her into his arms and said, "Lyssi, I love the way you look, the way you feel, the way your curl hangs slightly over your eye. You just look and feel so sexy."

Her husband took her hand and placed it on his thick, long, and massive, pulsating manhood. The move she made next, not only surprised Davis, she surprised herself as well. She boldly pushed Davis on the edge of the heart-shaped bed and ripped his black silk boxers off his body. Then she dropped to her knees and took her husband's full length into her warm and eager mouth. Davis' carnal moan of pleasure only excited her and egged her to go further. She stroked and licked him until pre-cum oozed from his shaft. Allysia had been using a tiny clitoral stimulator while sucking on him; she was already wet and eager for her new husband to penetrate her throbbing pussy. Discretely, she removed the stimulator and mounted Davis with her thick and luscious thighs. She placed his strong hands on her ample and curvy hips, leaned forward and kissed him with the wonderful taste of him still on her lips.

Allysia opened her legs wider and invited his alluring dick inside her awaiting pussy. She grinded her hips in rotation with his, and they made their connection as man and wife.

A girl can have it all. She has her company and love. In addition, it surely didn't hurt to learn that her husband, the delivery guy, was born into wealth. Above all, she had a family to come home to.

☐

CHAPTER SIXTEEN

"Baby, I got a letter from LaDonna today." Allysia smiled at Davis as he sipped his morning coffee. He looked so sexy even this early in the morning.

"Oh cool, babe. What does it say?" The four of them were best friends.

Dear Allysia and Davis,

How ya'll doin'? I hope y'all and my lil Ty-ty are alright. I miss y'all! Y'all gon' have to come visit soon. I bet Ty-ty growin' like a bunch of weeds. Please send us a picture of him.

Guess what? Me and Ronnie havin' a baby! I'm three months with child and Ronnie done already named the baby John-John. Mama and Daddy are thrilled. Daddy has already gotten to work building the baby a crib and all.

We wanted to ask y'all to please be the baby's godparents.

I love y'all and I miss y'all. Call me soon.

With Love,

LaDonna or, as you say, Lady

"It was so nice hearing from her, baby. You know I would love for us to be the godparents to little John-John. I just hope that they will be the godparents to our little one."

With a confused look on his face, Davis said, "Baby, what you talking about? LaDonna and Ronald are already Tyshawn's godparents."

"I know, Davis." Allysia looked at him and rubbed her belly, hoping he would catch on.

Davis suddenly got this wide-eyed look on his face as if he finally caught on to what she was trying to say. Then he asked, "Are you saying what I think you're saying? We're having a baby?"

"Well, I would rather it be you, but I guess I'll do you the honors." Allysia couldn't stop smiling and laughing as Davis wrapped his arms around her. "Yes baby, I'm having your baby." She looked at her husband and fell in love all over again. She loved him so much and now, she was blessed with the ability to give him the ultimate gift of love, a baby.

They laughed and cried tears of joy, knowing that the new baby would be just as special and just as loved as their precious Tyshawn.

☐

CHAPTER SEVENTEEN

One year later…

"Davis baby, I can't believe I'm actually excited to be going to LaDonna's family reunion."

"Boo, maybe you're just excited about seeing our friends again, and seeing our godson, just as much as you know LaDonna and Ronald are pumped up to see our little baby girl."

"True, daddy, I am. I can't even front." Allysia said, grinning from ear to ear.

"Mommy, Daddy!" Tyshawn was standing outside their bedroom screaming at the top of his lungs. "Can I come get in bed with y'all?"

"Come on son," Davis replied. Allysia wouldn't have it any other way. Her life was complete. She had the best husband on the planet and two beautiful children who she absolutely adored.

"Lady!" Allysia screamed as she laid eyes on her best friend.

"Lyssi!" LaDonna screeched back at her as they ran into an embrace. "I so happy to see you!"

"Girl, you know I'm happy as hell to see you." Allysia grinned. "Look at you, Ms. Devine Diva."

"Ronnie, bring the baby here!" LaDonna screamed, not even realizing that her husband was right behind her.

"Davis, baby, come here, bring the kids with you." Taking the baby from Davis' arms, Allysia proudly announced, "LaDonna, Ronald, this is your goddaughter, LaDonna Monique Jackson."

"She is absolutely precious," LaDonna cooed as she took the baby girl from Allysia's arms. "And this y'all godson, Jonathan Ronald Davis West."

"Well, hello handsome…" Allysia immediately fell in love with her godson, as LaDonna did with her goddaughter.

"Daddy, Uncle Ronnie, what are Mommy and Auntie LaDonna so happy about?" Tyshawn had a puzzled look on his face. "Babies don't do anything but, eat, burp, sleep and cry."

Roaring with laughter, they scooped Tyshawn up and filed into the house.

CHAPTER EIGHTEEN

TWO YEARS LATER

"…When I look around

And I think things over

All of my good days

Outweigh my bad days

I won't complain…"

After the soloist had finished the last line of the beautiful song, Bishop Paul McCoy stood and said the closing prayer, and then asked everyone but the family of the deceased to remain seated. He came down and shook Davis, Allysia, and little Tyshawn's hands and kissed a sound asleep little LaDonna. Tears silently slid down Davis' cheek, but he was trying his best to remain strong for his family. Since he was the only child, he had to be the rock of the family, since both of his parents were now gone. With his mother, the first woman he ever loved being taken to her final resting place, Davis felt as if a piece of his heart had been taken from him all over again.

Allysia was grateful for the fact that she and her mother in-law had gotten the chance to know one another and had formed a friendship. While the elder Mrs. Jackson didn't agree with the fact that her daughter in-law didn't like to cook, she had come to accept her for who she was, and Allysia Donaldson-Jackson appreciated that. As the casket passed by the family, Davis broke down and Allysia passed the baby to her mother and went to comfort her husband, who was shaking and crying uncontrollably. "It's okay baby, its okay. I'm here. I love you."

Allysia really didn't know what to say to comfort her husband, but she was doing the best she could. The casket finally passed and the family slowly followed it out of the sanctuary; though the sun was shining bright, it felt as if a dark cloud had hovered over the Jackson family as the heart of the family had been called home to glory.

***

Later that night in their home in upper Manhattan, Allysia and Davis sat in their living room, just holding each other, neither speaking to the other. Davis was simply seeking the comfort of listening to his loving wife's heartbeat when their son, Tyshawn walked in.

"Mommy, Daddy, I wanna go to church so I can go to heaven and see Granny again." Davis immediately felt guilty, because he hadn't taken Tyshawn to church the way he had been taken to church every Sunday morning. Without waiting for a response from his parents, Tyshawn turned and walked out of the room. That was the one thing that Davis' mother had begged him to do for years, was to take his son to church. Davis hadn't set foot back into a church since his first wife Carmen passed, when Tyshawn was just a baby. He had sworn that he didn't want to go to church anymore, because it reminded him of Carmen dying in his arms at a Wednesday night prayer service with Tyshawn at their side, but if his son really wanted to go, he was committed to going, as a family.

"Lyssi, I think he's serious. I think it's high time that we go to church as a family."

"I guess so, Davis."

☐

CHAPTER NINETEEN

"Allysia, you ready?"

"Nah, I really don't feel like going. You and Tyshawn go ahead. Me and the baby going to just chill."

"What do you mean you and Donna are gonna just chill? I thought we were all going to church together as a family?"

"We were Davis, but I don't feel like it anymore."

"But, why baby?" Davis tried to keep a brave face, but she could tell he was hurt. He looked at her trying to read her emotions, but Allysia was stone faced.

"Because I just don't want to do it. Damn, stop asking me." She stormed out of the room and slammed the door.

"Allysia! Allysia!" Davis couldn't figure out for the life of him why she was so angry. "I know you hear me calling you! Come here, woman!" He ran out the door after his wife. Her behavior puzzled him, because she had never spoken to him in that tone and it hurt his feelings. He looked and saw the front door open and her purse and keys missing; he knew that wherever his wife had gone, she wanted to go alone.

"Ma-ma, Maaaa-ma!" Davis turned his head to see his baby girl toddle her way into the room, and of course, she was looking for her mother.

"Com'ere baby." Davis held his arms open to his daughter.

"No, Ma-ma." LaDonna walked around, looking for her mother, peeking her head into every room. "Ma-maaaa!" Davis knew that his daughter would be in tears soon, and he was not looking forward to handling that situation. He went and scooped up the baby and took her into the kitchen to feed her. Next thing he knew, Tyshawn was coming out of his room dressed and ready for church.

"Dad, where's Mama?" Nine-year-old Tyshawn, looked around in confusion. He knew that something was wrong, but was too young to pinpoint what it was.

"Me want Ma-ma!" LaDonna began to cry.

"Donna, shut up!" Tyshawn spat at his little sister.

"Tyshawn, that is not nice, apologize to your sister. Now!" Davis gave his son a look that let him know that he was asking for a spanking.

"Sorry, crybaby." Tyshawn started laughing, but it didn't last long. Davis promptly started spanking Tyshawn on his bottom. "Okay, okay, I'm sorry." Tyshawn went over and sat down on the sofa, and turned on cartoons. "Daddy, I thought we were going to church?"

"I thought we were going too, son. I thought we were going to church too. Lil bit, go sit with your brother and watch TV." He took LaDonna off the counter and sat her on the floor. "What do you guys want for breakfast?"

"Pancakes please." Tyshawn grinned, showing off his pearly whites.

"Taushase." LaDonna was asking for sausage, but like most two year olds, couldn't pronounce most words clearly.

"How do you ask, LaDonna?"

"Pweese…"

"Alright. Pancakes and sausage it is. Oh Ty, go change and put on some play clothes, then watch TV and play nicely, okay?"

"Okay Daddy." For the most part, Tyshawn was a well-mannered and obedient child and his parents really appreciated that. Davis was confused and slightly angry, but was determined not to let his kids see his current emotions.

Allysia didn't return until a couple of hours after both kids had been put to bed. "Hey Davis."

"Hey. Where you been Lyssi? I've been worried about you."

"I can't tell; you only called me twice." Allysia said dryly.

"Don't be dramatic. Your children and I waited here all day for you to come back home. Why didn't you answer your phone?" Davis' voice got higher as his frustration shone through his words.

"I didn't want to go to church or hear you gripe about us not going, so I left."

"Gripe?" Davis looked at his wife in disbelief.

"Yes, gripe. Complain, fuss, whine." Allysia rolled her eyes at her husband and turned towards the closet to hang up her coat and purse.

Davis walked towards her and turned her around to face him. "Just tell me one thing."

"What?" She stared him square in the eye and pushed him off her. "What the hell do you want?"

Davis pushed her back as his anger grew. "You don't have to tell me, because I'm starting to wonder on my own, if you even believe in God! I rarely hear you acknowledge Him for His goodness. I don't think you believe in Him at all!"

Shocked and hurt, Allysia slapped Davis and then broke down crying. After what seemed like an eternity, she screamed; "Yes, I believe in God! I just don't believe in church. Bad things happen in church!" She started shaking like a child in fear of the boogieman.

Davis asked, "Bad things like what, baby? I'm sorry, I'm sorry, tell me what bad things." Uncontrollably sobbing she contemplated opening up to her husband about her deep dark secret, but decided against it. *If I tell Davis, what happened, he won't want me.*

Allysia took off her clothes and walked into the shower, and turned the water on full blast. She grabbed her loofa sponge and began to scrub as if she can wash her painful past away. *Ugh, I hate my body.* She thought as she stood there feeling violated all over again. She cried silently as she remembered the day that her living nightmare started. She stepped out the shower, dried off, slipped into her nightshirt, climbed into bed, turned over and went to sleep, without saying a word. Davis was hurt, Allysia had never gotten into bed without saying goodnight and saying, she loved him.

Allysia slept, but it was far from peaceful. She tossed and turned all night long. In her sleep, she fought her attacker as hard as she could, but nothing seemed to deter him from his mission of having her.

***

"Lyssi, baby. I don't wanna fight anymore. I don't like the silent treatment. Please just tell me what's wrong. Why don't you like church?"

"Davis, please honey. I really don't wanna talk about it. Okay?" Allysia turned away from her husband's warm embrace. She hated herself for acting that way, but she didn't want to deal with the demons of her past. Remembering Deacon Sauls' violating hands on her, made her feel disgusted and disgusting. As if she was undeserving of her own husband's loving arms holding her.

Her phone rang, and grateful for the distraction, she reached into her jeans and answered it, walking off from Davis, and avoiding her painful past, at least for now.

She walked back into the room, "Davis, I'm going to my mom's for a few days. I just need to regroup." She grabbed her bag and started throwing clothes and toiletries in a hurry.

It's as if she can't wait to get away from me, Davis thought.

Allysia kissed her husband on the cheek and was out the door.

After twenty-four hours of not having heard from his wife at all, he was determined that he was going to go get his woman and bring her home where she belonged.

***

"Oh Davis," Allysia exclaimed, completely surprised to see him at her mom's door. She silently thanked God that her mom wasn't home. She was a sweetheart, but nosey.

Before she could ask him what he was doing there; he grabbed her and kissed her with more passion than he had in a long time. His kisses always left her wanting more, but rarely left her completely breathless.

"Allysia, I have missed you so much," he whispered in her ear as he caressed her body. Davis traced every arousal point on his wife's body as he followed the map of her body that his fingers had drawn out, with his deliciously full lips. He lifted her with his beautifully defined muscular arms and carried her into my mother's loft, closing the door with his foot. He sat Allysia down gently on the dining room table, taking her thick hair out of its ponytail. He softly pulled it down to frame her face.

"Davis, I love you," Allysia proudly proclaimed. "I always have and I always will."

The look in his eyes as she told him the words Davis had needed to hear her say, said everything that she needed to know at that very moment. He began to undo the buttons on her dress, kissing her as he revealed more and more of her soft, caramel skin.

"Stay right there, Lyssi," he said excitedly as he ran to the living room. He quickly returned with a pillow. He laid it on the other end of the table and instructed her to lay back on it. She was really liking his take-charge attitude. It was a side of him that Allysia hasn't seen for a long, long time, a side of him that she had forgotten had existed. He kissed her thighs, and naming one of them Grace and the other Mercy and then he spread them and calling her sugar walls, Heaven. Heaven is what he wanted, and that is exactly what he got.

"Baby, is there any chocolate sauce?" He asked, bearing that devilish grin that always turned Allysia on. She was shocked to hear him ask her that. She had gotten him to use it a few times, but he had never asked for dessert toppings before.

"Umm…yeah baby, brand new bottle in the pantry." Allysia knew she was going to have to replace it before her mother noticed it missing, but she really didn't care. She was ready to lay back and just enjoy having her boo partake of her body as if she was his last supper.

It wasn't long before Allysia was eager to taste and feel her lover, confidant and best friend, so she pulled his six foot five frame closer to her. Pulling his throbbing dick to her lips, she began kissing the head as if she was French kissing his lips, all the while massaging the shaft. "Mmm…oh my Allysia, yeah my queen, oh shit, oh!" She had never made him cum within the first five minutes of oral pleasure before. "Lyssi, lay on your back, I'm hungry again." She complied. She was more than happy to do anything that meant that she was about to get more of the pleasure and stimulation that her body desired.

She wasn't even paying attention; she just assumed that he was preparing to penetrate her with that delicious dick of his, while stimulating her breasts with his sweet mouth. However, what he did next was pure and instant pleasure for her. He poured warm chocolate sauce on her pussy lips and then took to devouring her as if she would be the last meal he ever had.

He penetrated her with his tongue, swirling it around and around her clitoris, causing her to cum repeatedly until she couldn't take it anymore and began begging him to fuck her.

"Davis, fuck me, please!"

"Is that what you want? Say you want it." Davis was being demanding sexually and she loved it.

"Yeah, Davis, that's what I want."

"Say that shit louder then, girl. Let everybody know that you want it."

"I want it, Davis!" she screamed.

"Then bend over so I can give it to you, since that's what you really want."

He feverishly drilled his manhood into Allysia's thickness, not even slowing down to fully release his juices in her. He somehow flipped her big, juicy ass over without breaking the connection his huge dick had with her warm, wet pussy. A few short minutes later, she'd spun around on her husband's manhood, milking him as she worked her body on top of him.

"Mmm…Davis, take your hose and put my fire out, baby." She swooned and crooned as she slid up and down his pole, her thick thighs wrapped tightly around his waist, her head bent backward, and her heavy breast bouncing up and down as she rode her man to ecstasy.

"Allysia, baby, I need you!" The sexy man said breathlessly as he suckled her breast and pumped his soul into her. "Tell me you're mine!" he demanded. With each thrust, he took away her ability to even speak, so she simply nodded. "No, tell me!"

After several minutes of trying to catch her breath, enough to speak, she finally said, "I'm yours," kissed his lips and released all of her inhibitions, as well as her nectar unto his manhood.

All of a sudden, the door was opened and in the doorway stood Allysia's mother with her jaw dropped. Allysia Donaldson-Jackson knew it'd be a long time, before she could look her prim and proper mother in the eye again.

☐

CHAPTER TWENTY

"Mama, Daddy! I'm home!" Tyshawn had to make this announcement every weekday when he came home from school.

"Sshhh... Mama's on a business call, son. How was your day?"

"It was good, Daddy." Tyshawn reaches up and hugs his father, grateful to be able to do so without his younger sister, LaDonna grabbing at him too. "My friend, Bobby was telling us all about the fun that he has at Sunday School and Children's Church. I want to go too!"

Davis wanted to immediately tell his son yes, but he wanted to be sensitive to his wife's feelings and discuss it as a family. He only wished that he knew why Allysia felt so strongly against going to church.

"We'll talk about it at dinner with Mama, okay son? Now why don't you go change out of your school uniform and go play for an hour. Then you have to start your homework."

"Okay Daddy."

Tyshawn ran off to play, but Davis' heart felt so heavy. He felt as if he had turned his back on his commitment to God and to his late mother. Just as he sat down on the sofa and picked up the Bible that hadn't been touched since before his mother passed, Allysia walked into the room.

Allysia had been in a bad mood ever since she came back home and her wildly passionate husband had returned to being the loving, but boring husband he had become, before their exotic tryst on her mother's dining room table.

"Hey baby, did I hear Tyshawn come in?"

"Yeah, he's home. He's in his room playing for an hour, and then he's been told to start his homework."

Davis stood up and said, "I'm stepping out for a while, I'll be back. Love you." He kissed his wife on the cheek and walked out the door, clutching his Bible. He wasn't sure of where he was going, but he knew that he needed to go, at least for a little while.

Allysia stood there, staring after him, curious as to why he had such a need to leave, and then she thought that maybe she shouldn't have worked from home that day. *Sooner or later, I'll have to tell him about why I don't like church and who made me that way.* Just the thought of it made her sick to her stomach and she rushed into the bathroom before she got sick all over herself.

***

A few hours later, Allysia had finally pulled herself together, and gotten dinner started. She was upset, but refused to let her children see her so angry. It was getting late and Davis still hadn't gotten home, so she decided to feed her babies and get them ready for bed herself. Usually, that was something that she and Davis always did together. It hurt her that he didn't want to be there to share that special moment, but she wasn't going to ruin it for them.

"Ty! Donna! Dinner's ready. Go wash your hands. Tyshawn, help your sister, please, so that she doesn't make a mess."

"Yes, Mama. Where's Daddy?"

"I don't know, Tyshawn, but go do what I said." She didn't mean to snap at her son, but she was dreading that question and as if on cue, he had asked it.

No sooner than she had sent the children into the bathroom to wash their hands, did she hear LaDonna hollering, "I do myself! I do it!"

Then she heard Tyshawn hollering right back, "Mama said for me to help you, stupid!" Normally, she would have gone in there and popped Tyshawn for calling his sister names, but she was too tired and emotionally drained to do anything except what she was doing. Going through the motions of setting the table, was all she could do.

"Mama! Ma-ama!"

"Mama, Donna won't let me help her!" Where was her husband when she needed him?

"Are her hands at least clean, Ty?"

"Yeah, I guess."

"Well, wash your hands and come on. I don't have time for all of that arguing today." Little LaDonna comes out of the bathroom with soaking wet hands, and tugs on her mother's sweatshirt.

"Mama... Daddy at?"

"I don't know baby, sit down so we can eat."

"Mama, can I say grace?" Tyshawn asked with a small grin on his face. Allysia was happy that Tyshawn had a genuine interest in God, but was so afraid that he or LaDonna would be hurt just as she had been, if she allowed them to go to church.

"Yes Ty, you may say grace."

"Bow your head… God is good, God is great. Lord we thank you for our food, by His hands we shall be fed, give us Lord our daily bread, amen."

"Mayyyy-men!" A little LaDonna was grinning from ear to ear, and Allysia couldn't help but smile at her babies. "Ma…ma! Salad."

"How do you ask, LaDonna?"

"Pweese?"

"All right." She shook her head at her little girl. LaDonna was just as spunky and funny as she was told she was at her age.

Allysia hated that Davis was missing these small but special moments…

***

Three hours later, Allysia walked in on Davis rocking a sleeping LaDonna, singing "Jesus Loves Me" it warmed her heart. She couldn't even stay mad at him anymore. She knew that she wanted her babies to have a close relationship with Christ. In her heart of hearts, she knew that she'd have to overcome her issues. Not just for her, but for her family. Allysia decided to go to counseling to try to work through her past, so that she and her family can have a relationship together with God.

***

Allysia attended her first counseling session and felt that it wasn't helpful at all. Afterwards she called LaDonna and asked her to pray for her. LaDonna prayed right there on the phone and assured Allysia that everything will be all right. The next day, she got an invitation in the mail from LaDonna and Ronald, inviting them down for little Ronnie's christening. Allysia was apprehensive about going to a church again, but she was determined not to miss her godson's christening.

One week later, they were in Georgia for their godson's christening and Allysia felt a strange sense of peace. Davis leaned over and told

Allysia how happy it made him that she decided to stay for the church service after the ceremony. Later that night in their hotel room, Allysia told Davis how she was feeling; he felt the emotional closeness he once shared with his bride, and they made sweet, slow love.

The next day, after having breakfast with their friends, LaDonna took Allysia into her personal prayer closet and had an extensive prayer session with her friend, before they leave for their flight home. It was just what Allysia needed to give her the courage to do what she needed to do.

CHAPTER TWENTY-ONE

A few days after they returned from Georgia, Davis decided to take the kids to Wednesday night prayer service without Allysia's knowledge. However, he didn't count on Tyshawn coming directly home, telling his mother all about it, and inviting her to come along next time. He thought that Allysia would be angry but she wasn't. He was relieved but curious as to why she was all of a sudden cool with it.

It was time for her to come clean with her husband about the work she had been doing with her therapist. Allysia really appreciated Davis patiently listening to what she had to say without interrupting, so she invited her husband to join her for her next session, which was the next day. They chose to make a day of it. They went to an early morning matinee, had lunch at Sylvia's Restaurant, and then went to her therapy appointment, walking hand in hand.

Allysia's therapist gave her the assignment of going to either Wednesday night prayer service or to a full Sunday morning service with her family. He also wanted her to document how attending made her feel that day. Allysia seriously considered not doing the assignment and not going back to the therapist.

Davis tried to persuade her to keep with the progress she had been making, but Tyshawn, begging her to join them for Wednesday night prayer service convinced her to do the assignment, and to work through the process with God, her family, and Dr. Jeffery August. The following Sunday, they all went to church as a family. A surprised Allysia realized that it wasn't anything as she thought it would be and actually enjoyed herself. It wasn't long before she'd immersed herself into different activities with the church. No one there pressured her about joining and she didn't feel rushed. She just enjoyed fellowship with God and other believers.

Allysia became especially active in the food pantry ministry, which was spearheaded by the senior pastor's wife, Patricia SaulsHarding. It wasn't long at all before the two women were friends. She hadn't met him yet, because he was out of the country on a mission trip.

The fifth anniversary of the senior pastor and his wife being of service to Hillman Missionary Baptist Church was quickly approaching and Patricia commissioned Allysia to design a ball gown for the Pastoral Anniversary Banquet. When she went to collect the check, Allysia finally met the senior pastor of the church. She realized that he was the son of the man who'd sexually molested her at church when she was a little girl. She grabbed the check and ran out of the church office and to her car, vowing never to set foot in any church again, ever.

☐

CHAPTER TWENTY-TWO

After nights of crying herself to sleep, she finally opened up to Davis and admitted her secret of being molested as a little girl by Deacon Sauls. Davis is in shock and feeling helpless, knowing that eventually Allysia will have to work this out for herself, and all he can do is love her through it.

***

"Donna, I'm not mad at him, I'm mad at me for taking this out on him. What do I do?"

LaDonna says, "Girl, you have a very good man and you need to be thanking God that he's trying to love you past your pain, instead of fighting him."

"I don't wanna fight Donna, I just don't know how else to react to him trying to make me fix it." Allysia began to cry.

"Lysia, he's not trying to make you fix it, he's trying to make things better for the woman he loves so much. Just pray on it, boo, and I'm praying for you. I love you."

"I love you too."

After talking things out with her best friend LaDonna, Allysia called Dr. August and scheduled an appointment for the next day. The doctor tells Allysia that to move on, she'll have to confront her past. Allysia voices her fear. Dr. August reminds her that she's a grown woman and that this man can't hurt her anymore. He handed her the phone and looked up the number for Pastor Sauls. The doctor encourages Allysia to explain to him who she is, and ask about the whereabouts of his father. Pastor Sauls reveals that his father's dead, but agrees that she still should confront him, so Pastor Sauls and his wife agree to meet Allysia and Davis at his father's gravesite.

The confrontation at Deacon Gregory Sauls Sr.'s gravesite was so therapeutic. She thanked his son, Pastor Sauls for being so understanding and was shocked when he revealed thathis own father molested him too. After that emotion filled afternoon, they all went to dinner. Still discussing the powerful visit to the gravesite and agree to remain in touch. Allysia popped the trunk to their SUV and handed Patricia her dress as well as an envelope containing her check back.

"Allysia, why are you giving me this back?"

"Because I want you to put it into the food pantry ministry."

***

It took several months, a whole lot of patience and understanding, but not only did Allysia join the church and start a ministry of her own, a local branch of Dress For Success, specializing in providing necessities for the plus sized clients that they assisted in rebuilding their lives. But the greatest blessing that came from her giving her life to back to God was that he blessed her and Davis with another son, Davis Jerome Jackson, Jr.

Turned Out Widow

Nea

I was so distraught when the love of my life, my soul mate, was taken from me; I did not think it would be possible to move on. I remember receiving the unexpected telephone call like it was yesterday. I was sitting at my desk about to have my leftover seafood lasagna for lunch, when the phone rang.

"Hello?"

A woman's voice said, "May I speak to Karrine Warrington?"

"This is she. May I ask whose calling?"

"Yes, ma'am. My name is Lynn Baxter and I'm calling from John Hopkins Hospital. There has been an accident and we need to you to come down as soon as possible."

"Why? What happened? Is it my husband, Carlton?"

"Ma'am, I'm sorry; I cannot release that information over the phone. Please come to the emergency room and ask for the head nurse."

I shouted, "I don't understand, why won't you tell me what's going on?"

I noticed my co-worker, Veronica, standing next to me. She reached for the receiver. I reluctantly gave it to her and watched as she spoke to the female stranger on the line. She nodded, while telling her we were on the way.

"What's going on, Veronica? What is it about Carlton? Why do I need to go to the hospital?"

"I need you to try and relax, Karrine. We have to go to the hospital now, okay," she said, reaching for my hand.

The thirty-minute drive to the hospital was in silence, because I didn't know what to say. I attempted to pass the time by browsing Facebook, but none of the posts kept my interest. My thoughts were racing and I remember looking out the window, but never really focusing on anything in particular. I didn't know what to expect, despite the fact my heart already told me something bad happened to my husband.

When we reached the triage desk, Veronica requested the head nurse. I looked around the waiting area of all the sick, injured people and I trembled. I felt Veronica's arms around me.

Another minute passed before Ms. Baxter walked up to us. I watched as Veronica spoke with her. I saw their mouths moving. I didn't understand everything they said, but I remember Ms. Baxter saying there had been a real bad accident at the construction site where my husband worked.

Then she guided us to an elevator that went to a lower level of the hospital. I overheard her say something about the roof collapsed and he didn't have a chance. My hands suddenly became clammy and my heart began to race, and I felt dizzy.

When we exited the elevator, coldness enveloped us. I entered the bare walls of the morgue and immediately the smell of metal and antiseptics assaulted my senses. I watched as the medical examiner walked over to the metal table and slowly pulled the white sheet from the body.

"Oh my God! Carlton! No, not my Carl! No!" I heard myself scream.

I grabbed the sides of the table as I looked down at Carlton's expressionless, bruised face. It looked as if he were sleeping. I leaned forward, kissing his cold lips. I wanted him to open his eyes.

Veronica wrapped her arms around me and I began sobbing uncontrollably. "Please wake up, Carlton. Please."

After what seemed like an hour of letting the tears fall, I finally said my goodbyes. We left the hospital, the last thing I remember was Veronica tucking me into bed after giving me two Xanax, and telling me that she would handle everything.

The days following and leading up to his funeral went by in a blur. I don't recall much, but I knew I wasn't ready to see my husband's face for the last time, but the day had come.

Since we weren't members of a church, his home going service was held at a small funeral home. One of the members of the staff agreed to preside over the funeral and preach the eulogy. As his sister, Carla, began to read the obituary, I looked around the room and noticed that the majority of the mourners were women. They were women I'd never seen before, except for one.

I caught a glimpse of his ex-girlfriend, Connie, sitting near the second row. Once his sister finished, she asked if anyone wanted to share any thoughts. A woman walked up to the podium and started to speak. After giving her praises to God, she boasted about how a wonderful man my husband was. I listened attentively, trying to remember if I'd ever met her.

After she left the podium, another woman spoke, followed by another. Each of them gave the same wonderful man speech when referring to my husband. I didn't know who these women were, but I refused to let them have the last word. Those bitches knew him a little bit too well for me not to have met any of them before.

I approached the podium and spoke into the microphone. "Hello. As I'm sure you all know my name is Karrine Warrington."

I began to speak about how lovely our marriage was and how much I was going to miss him, but then something came over me that made me stop mid-sentence. I looked directly into the eyes of two women that had spoken to me.

"May I ask you a question?"

There was no response from the women. They sat motionless, looking dumbfounded. I didn't wait for them to answer and continued, "How do you know my husband and why are you here?"

I heard his sister gasp and my sister Diana started to get up but I gave her a look that made her stay in her seat. After a minute of silence, the woman who gave her respects last stood up and spoke.

She cleared her throat before beginning. "My name is Tiffany. I don't think it matters how any of us know your husband. I think I can speak for everyone that we are simply here to pay our last respects."

I shook my head and stepped down from the podium.

"I'm going to ask you again. How do you know my husband?"

Out the corner of my eye, I could see my sister making her way across the room. At the same time, I heard Tiffany whisper something.

"I'm sorry what did you just say?"

"I said, Carl and I were having an aff—"

I didn't give her a chance to finish. My right hand connected with her cheek with such force, she stumbled back. I went for her throat, but my sister and a couple Carlton's friends grabbed me.

His sister stood in front of me pleading, "Not here, Karrine. Oh my God, not here."

I spat, "I hope my husband has a wonderful time in hell." I broke free from their hold and briefly looked into his casket, before using all of my strength to knock it over.

As everyone stared in total shock, I walked down the aisle and out of the funeral home without looking back. Tears were streaming down my cheeks, mascara running down my face; they mixed with the concealer and I could feel the vomit rising in my throat. I swallowed hard.

My sister was calling my name from behind me, but I kept walking. I had no idea where I was going, but I knew I just needed to be away from there.

A few blocks away, I spotted a taxi and got the driver to take me home. I arrived at my house and sat in the living room for several minutes, replaying everything that happened. It hurt like hell, but I couldn't cry anymore and Carlton didn't deserve another tear from me.

I went upstairs and when I walked into our bedroom, I wanted to vomit again. I went through the room, knocking all of the pictures on the nightstand and armoire to the floor. I felt the tears threatening to spill from my eyes, but I wouldn't give him that.

I continued to move aimlessly throughout our bedroom, before deciding to take a shower. I'd just removed my stockings when I heard the doorbell ring. I sighed and continued undressing and proceeded to take a shower.

The bell rang again. It had to be my sister; she should've known not to bother me. A few minutes passed and it rang again. Whoever it was would go away when I didn't answer. A minute passed and the bell rang again. I grabbed my robe from the bed and headed downstairs.

I looked through the peephole and rolled my eyes when I saw it was Connie.

What the fuck does this bitch want?

I watched as she shifted her weight from one foot to the other. She pressed the bell again. Annoyed that her dumb ass wasn't getting the picture, I swung the door open.

"What the fuck do you want, you thot ass homewrecker?" I spat.

Connie flinched taking a step back. "Okay. I deserve that," she whispered.

"Yes, you do. Now I'm going to ask you again, what the fuck do you want? There's no one here that wants you. The man you used to fuck doesn't live here anymore. Remember you just buried him."

"How could you be so cold?"

I stepped towards her. "Excuse me? How can I be so cold? Uhh, let's see. I just found out that my husband of ten years has had countless mistresses."

"I'm sorry, I didn't—"

I cut her off. "And don't worry about how I can be so cold. Of all people, how dare you bring your ass here? I'm sure you were still fucking him too, weren't you, Connie? You and the rest of those bitches were at my husband's funeral. I have every right to be cold and you must be stuck on stupid to have the audacity to come to my door without expecting to get your ass whipped."

"Please," she said holding up her hands. "I'm here because I want to apologize."

"Go ahead, say just how sorry are. I'm listening."

She shuffled her feet. "Uhh, it's not just that. I also have some things I need to tell you. Please allow me to get this off my chest."

There was sincerity in her voice but I wasn't buying what she was selling.

"Nah bitch, you can't get that."

"Please, Karrine. I know you don't believe me, but I really want to put this behind us."

I closed my eyes to thin slits as I spoke through gritted teeth. "I'm not sure what you have to say, Connie, but make it quick, because I'm two seconds from fucking you up."

"Can we at least go inside, Karrine? I hope you realize that you are standing out here in your robe."

I wasn't about to let this chick in my house, but then I realized she probably had been inside plenty of times before so it didn't matter anymore at this point.

"I'm definitely selling this shit," I mumbled.

Then I took a step back and opened the door for her to enter. As we walked into the living room toward my maple brown sofa, I could've sworn I felt her fondle my ass. I turned my head to see that she was closing the door.

We sat down and for a moment, she stared at me. I was getting uncomfortable and was about to speak on it, but then she began.

"First of all, I didn't come for an argument. Like I said, I just want to speak my peace."

"Go on. I'm listening."

"I apologize for any additional pain I may have caused, but you are right. We were still hooking up from time to time. Matter of fact, we were together earlier this week."

Was this bitch crazy? Did she just admit that she was fucking my husband up until his death?

I felt a crease in my forehead forming and my ears were beginning to burn. I remained motionless, because I felt a slap coming and I wasn't about to tell her. Copping the shit out of her without warning would give me the satisfaction I needed, since I couldn't get that whore, Tiffany, as I wanted to. I nodded for her to continue.

"I told him that as your husband, he should share this with you, but he felt you wouldn't understand or agree."

"Hold up. What are you—"

"Wait, let me finish. You need to know that he loved you more than any of those women at that funeral, but this was a lifestyle he had for a long time, before you came into the picture."

I started to get up because I wasn't so sure anymore that I wanted to hear what she had to say. I felt her grabbing my wrist. I glared at her and she let go.

Then she blurted out, "Look, Carl and I were in a swingers' circle. Most of the women there were from that circle."

I felt like I had choked on a chicken bone. "What?"

"Carlton—"

"I heard you," I retorted. I stood up shaking my head. "I don't believe this shit. It doesn't get any better than this."

"Come on, Kay; we are both adults here."

I picked up on the way she made a little nickname for me, as if we were girlfriends.

She continued, "You had to know something was up with all those crazy hours he kept. He wasn't at some new construction site or working overtime, that's for sure."

She was right. Even though I wanted to show her the door, something made me inquire about his swinger's lifestyle. I sat down.

"So how and when did this happen?"

"Well, it was back when we were together. I've always been into girls and when I told him about it, he wanted the fantasy lived out. Once I gave that to him, he was hooked."

I sat expressionless as she revealed years of them going to parties, hooking up with other couples, and switching parties or joining in orgies. It never dawned on me that Carl was even into that kind of stuff. I thought I was freaky enough for him with the type of sex we had. Anything he ever wanted, I did, but he never shared this with me. I wanted to know why.

Suddenly, I felt Connie touch my thigh. I snapped out of my thoughts and cut my eyes at her. I moved away from her and tightened the belt on my robe.

"Hold up! I don't get down like that. I know you might feel relieved to share your indiscretions with me, but I'm not into the carpet munching."

She sat back with a smirk on her face.

"What?" I asked, cocking my head towards her.

"I guess this is what Carl was talking about. You *are* a prude."

"Excuse me? He said I was a prude? Please, I gave that man everything he asked for. He never shared this with me."

"Why would he? I mean, you just said you not into carpet munching."

"I'm not."

"So you're a prude. Get with the times, boo. Everybody's getting down and freaky."

I raised my eyebrow.

She chuckled, "No, don't worry about that. Carl never fucked with the guys. He wasn't into that. Switching partners and girl-on-girl, he was definitely down for."

I shook my head again. "I can't believe this shit. All this time and I never had a clue."

The next thing I knew, she was sliding towards me. I stood up and she stood up.

"I think you should leave now, Connie. I've heard enough."

"I'm not finished, though. I promised Carl something and intend on following through with it."

"What's that?"

She walked up to me, grabbed a handful of my hair and pulled my face towards hers. Since we matched in height, it was easy for her to lean forward and press her lips against mine. I tried to pull away, but she tightened the grip on my hair, yanking me closer.

I couldn't lie that her lips weren't soft. When her tongue slid between my lips, I felt my body responding. I shoved her away.

"What the fuck do you think you're doing? I'm not a lesbo!" I yelled.

She ignored me and grabbed me around the waist, pulling me closer to her body. She passionately kissed me again and this time, I couldn't resist the way she felt. Her soft curves against mine made the temperature between my legs rise. I couldn't really gather my thoughts appropriately, because my clit was beginning to throb.

Then she slid her hand inside of my robe and began massaging my right nipple, before she moved her head down. Her mouth and wet tongue were sucking on it. I found myself caressing the back of her neck, as she continued the suck fest on my breasts.

Within the next few minutes, my robe was off and Connie was working her way down to my belly button. I still couldn't figure out why I was allowing her to do this. *She knows I'm not into this and I'd never had any interest in being with a woman.* I tried to push her away again, but she came back at me with full force. I lost my footing and sat down on the couch.

She slid my robe off effortlessly and then she removed my thongs. I opened my eyes to see Connie and her hot body naked before me, including a chocolate strap-on that she's sporting. I'm nervous, yet curious at the same time. She kisses me deeply and her mouth makes its way down my body, stopping at my nipples, my thighs, and then she found her pot of gold as she begins to encircle my clit.

Her expert rhythm was beginning to lift me to cloud nine, and creating rasping moans that escaped my mouth. She then enters me slowly at first; I let out a deep gasp, and then she proceeded to enter me more deeply. Boldly, I start to push my hips up to meet her thrusts. We are on rhythm and on point; my wet pussy matched each thrust, and the belt holding this strap in place is rubbing my clit with each thrust too. I come hard multiple times, but I did not want to be a selfish lover, even though it was my first time. I then casually rolled over so that the length of my body is parallel to hers. I reach over and rub my hand over my clit. I place my fingers into my mouth, lubricating them and continue to play with her pussy, but paying close attention to her clit. I wanted to taste her and made my way down to her thighs, so that I could finish the job. Connie began to remove the strap in between moans. My tongue slid inside her hot walls. Then I removed my tongue and replaced it with my three fingers. My tongue continued to flick back and forth on her clit while I finger fucked her pussy real good. I felt her legs trembling as an orgasm unlike any other went through her body.

"Oh God! Yes!"

Then she sat up, proceeded to attach the strap back on and instructed me to get on top; I began riding her hard. I grabbed her breasts, squeezing hard as I went up and down. My nectar spilled onto her lap as I repeatedly came.

Finally, I fell forward, completely worn out. I'd given her everything my body had. She nudged me so that I would face her. She kissed me lightly and squeezed hard.

Her eyes met mine and she whispered, "Thank you for letting me keep my promise."

I nodded, knowing exactly what she meant. We both knew it would not be the last time we embarked on this roller coaster ride of pleasure. I didn't know whether to call myself a lesbian or bi-sexual, but one thing was for sure. My pussy, oops, I mean, I am definitely looking forward to our next escapade together

Kenni York

Website: www.kennienterprises.com
Facebook: Author Kenni York
Twitter: Kenni York
Instagram: Kenyetta York

BBW Author MìChaune

facebook.com/bbwauthormichaune
twitter.com/Author_MiChaune
instagram.com/bbwauthormichaune

bbwauthormichaune.weebly.com